Broken

John Paul

First edition, December 2025

ISBN 979-8-9934818-0-7 (paperback)
ISBN 979-8-9934818-1-4 (ebook)

This book contains mature content, including graphic sexual situations, brutal violence, sexual violence, drug use, foul language, and gay-themed material.

www.iamjohnpaul.com

Prologue

I am broken.

From unloving parents and uncaring nuns to a plethora of artificial affection from an assortment of part-time families, the last couple of decades have been challenging for me. Some might even say lonely. I am not sure I would agree with the loneliness part, but the years have certainly been tumultuous — chaotic even, and I have no idea how much freedom I have left before I am finally caged. I am confident that someone is watching me, so I must tell this story before it is too late.

You need to hear this story — *my* story. Anything anyone else tells you about me will undoubtedly portray me as a bad person — an isolated, sadistic killer incapable of love, and that is not entirely true.

I want you to understand — no, I *need* you to understand that under all my layers of darkness, violence, and hatred, there is — or was love. At least, I believe it was love. It looked like the love you see in the movies and sounded like the love professed in greeting cards — at least, it did to me. Maybe I was looking at it all through rose-colored glasses. Either way, it never lasted.

Perhaps I wanted to be loved so desperately that I never stopped to think about what it meant to be loved or what it should look or feel like. My parents were not around to teach me about the birds and the bees, and they certainly were not around to show me any love, let alone teach me about love. They left me alone —

abandoned me when I was six years old—when I really needed them the most.

My parents left me vulnerable and exposed—unprepared for the real world. Some people make the right choice at the proverbial fork in the road; others are not so lucky. *'It's the devil's work,'* the nuns would tell me when I was younger and did something wrong, which was often. Some would argue that I constantly took the wrong path and struggled at every fork. But my path was for me: it was not for anyone else to experience—to get lost on or to paint morbidly red.

My path was challenging, exciting, and usually deadly for those who crossed it. Along the way, though, I found love—I felt loved. The problem is that it never lasted, and too often, it ended in a blood bath.

I am broken.

Hopefully, my story will help you understand how broken I have always been—maybe even how I came to be broken. I am not looking for your forgiveness or apologizing for my actions. If your loved ones died at my hands, well, that is too bad. I don't regret anything. My life has played out as it should—not as I thought it might or hoped, but as best it could. That is what happens when you are broken.

I am sharing my story with you now because I want you to know that there are other broken people in the world—I am not alone, and I am not making excuses.

Think of my story as an alarm bell—a warning of the wrath still to come, and not just from me. For all the parents and caregivers, love your children unconditionally and listen to their screams for help, however silent they may seem. If you are not careful, your child could end up broken, just like me.

For everyone else, please keep an open mind as you hear my story. While I have been known to sensationalize some of the facts, the truth remains clear: I am a killer, and I am broken.

01

Country music quietly echoed through the pub. You had to listen carefully to comprehend the song playing; otherwise, it was just white noise—loud enough to know the DJ was doing her job, but not loud enough that you could sing along.

It was still early. Happy Hour had barely begun, yet some patrons were already slung over the bar, passed out—remnants of the lunchtime crowd, no doubt. In one of the booths directly across from the bar, too many girls were crammed into the small space, all drinking white wine spritzers. One was wearing a veil; her bachelorette party was in motion. Their cheers and excited screams drowned the music out even more.

The Drunken Unicorn is not a large pub—not by American standards—but was significant by London standards. Inside, a single bar runs along one wall while the other is lined with booths. There were many high-top tables down the middle for Happy Hour, but they get put away as the night goes on, and the late-night, younger crowd moves in to take over. At the back of the pub is a large dance floor, accompanied by smaller booths. Near the entrance, on either side, is a set of spiral stairs that lead to a catwalk that wraps the entire pub. It is more private up top—standing room only—and an excellent place for someone to make out in a dark corner or scope out their next target. It was my favorite pub.

I've been in many pubs all over London, and I have been in my share of dive bars in Boston and around Burlington, and they all have one thing in common, aside from being filled with drunk idiots, I mean. They are all filled with easy prey. It is scary—sad even, when you think about how pathetic people are, especially the ones you find in a bar. I find myself creating ways to challenge myself and even challenge my victims—almost giving them an unspoken warning. The smart ones would heed that warning and write me off as some asshole in the bar. But the weak or vain ones get so wrapped up in my words—my good looks, and before they know it, well, they... don't ever make it to another bar.

The challenge for me, sometimes, is deciding which idiot to lure in. This night was one of the easier nights. The pub was already a happening spot. It usually was on a Wednesday night, which always seemed odd. How is the middle of the week the one night when everyone decides to go out, stay out late, and get pissed? They have to work the next day and the day after, but that does not stop them. Even back in Boston, it didn't matter what night of the week it was—the bars were always packed.

This particular night, I thought of finally talking to the cute bartender. We've been playing that game—the one where I stare at him, he looks up at me, and I turn away, then we switch roles, and it goes back and forth like that for hours—for days. For us, it has been months. I am supposed to be the strong one—in control, but there is something about him, this bartender, that makes me weak in the knees.

I watched him move back and forth behind the bar like a relay swimmer—smooth and in control. He had a rhythm. It was mesmerizing. I finally decided to go up to the bar—this was going to be my moment, but as I approached, he got called to the other end of the bar. I was left standing, waiting.

Then I found myself almost humping the bar as my two new *'friends'* sat like bookends, holding me captive while they sat captivated by my story, another monologue about my youth. The bartender heard many of my stories over the last few weeks—some more than once. This night was a new one, I think. I finally had the bartender's attention, but I was stuck—no, stuck is not the right word. Stuck would imply that I was trapped and could not get out of the situation. I could tell you that I lost my courage to talk with him, but the reality was that as I approached the bar, I found someone weak—someone looking to be attended to in a way that would turn out badly for them, and I felt compelled to feed my inner urge, to try and fix what was broken.

*   *   *   *   *

I recall one specific day vividly. I was playing in our backyard, or at least what my parents called a backyard. I was not doing anything special. I was keeping myself occupied while my parents fought inside. I did not know at the time, but looking back, I now understand that the violence I witnessed that day triggered something in my brain – it woke me up and pushed me down a path I still struggle to walk today.

"That is so fascinating," the boy said, not listening to me as much as he was enjoying the movement of my lips.

Our neighborhood was a collection of mobile homes – I think you call them caravans here – with no private backyards. Everyone shared the open space of dirt and weeds between each of the dilapidated structures we called home. As that 4-year-old child, I believed there were hundreds of mobile homes in the area, but as an adult, I learned there were a dozen or so, all in disarray. Almost none exist there today – at least not in a liveable state. Regardless, the place I called home at the time did not provide the best living conditions for me. It is safe to say that my life was destined for trouble from the very beginning.

"Oh, you poor thing," the girl chimed in. "That can't be true. Look at you now, a handsome stud." She gripped my bulging bicep—holding tightly, almost as if trying to hurt me and turn me on at the same time. I am pretty sure she found me quite dreamy—a lollipop she wanted to lick all day. She was one of those girls who you know is always watching the door—always looking for something better—someone better to walk in and take her away from whatever man she was with at any given moment—as if no man was ever good enough, complete enough for her.

She noticed me when I first walked in—a 10 in a room full of sixes, thinking they were nines. I was much more handsome than the guy she was with, but she was not about to say that out loud. I knew she wanted to take me home and get me into bed as quickly as possible before losing her courage.

I smiled and nodded, silently accepting her drunken compliment as I continued my story. I was a little surprised that neither of them asked about the violent incident I referenced—a clear sign that neither of them was actually listening, but I knew my audience. I knew that people in the pub were not there to listen. They wanted the music to drown out the talking so they could navigate their way through the night, looking, touching, and feeling their way in hopes of getting lucky.

We lived in an impoverished part of Vermont where everyone struggled to make it through each day. As much as everyone suffered through their pathetic existence, they all found time for unprotected sex: condoms are a product for the privileged.

The boy and the girl laughed out loud, almost spilling their drinks on themselves. The bartender smirked, too, as he half-listened to the monologue. I was slightly annoyed that my new *'friends'* continued interrupting my story, as if my telling it was a critical part of our conversation. It wasn't, but it still irritated me when people interrupted me—interrupted anyone. I spent years being talked over by my parents, by the nuns at the orphanage, by almost everyone everywhere, until I decided that was reason enough to take a person's life. It was one of my triggers—one of the checklist items that helped me justify killing someone, not that I really need to explain or justify my thirst.

*   *   *   *   *

Oh, sorry. I just blurted that out, didn't I? Well, this is my story—the story of how I came to be who I am, how I grew up to be someone who kills people. I am not going to label it—label myself by saying I am a serial killer. I don't think serial killers do that—say that they are serial killers, I mean. It wouldn't serve their purpose—my purpose, would it? Most serial killers want attention. I've heard that psychiatrists say serial killers just want to be heard—seen and ultimately want to be caught, which is pretty messed up if you ask me. I don't kill because I want someone's attention. I kill because I like it. I like the sight of blood—I love the taste of it. I love making people suffer, but we can discuss that more later.

*   *   *   *   *

If these two had not been so infatuated with me, they would have heard the tone of my voice change—they might have even seen the red flag that silently indicated that I am a hot mess and not the one they should take home. But they did not see any sign. They saw a strikingly handsome young man fully engaged with them, telling a story while making them feel like they were the prettiest in the room. Damn, I am good.

Too many young people wandered around our trailer park—kids, many close to my age then. We were left to roam, often barefoot. Some wore nothing more than a saggy diaper—a nappy, and many of us were filthy a lot. It was the life we lived. It was the only life we had ever known.

"That sounds pretty messed up," said the girl. "Did... did you... hear that... darling?"

"I am right here, darling," the boy responded with less of a slur as he leaned on the bar so she could see him on the other side of me. "I can hear everything just fine." He really couldn't.

"I'm sorry," I said to them both. "I am sure you find this story extremely boring. We should discuss something more lighthearted—something upbeat. Maybe we can talk about how you want to use me—use my body tonight."

I knew they didn't—wouldn't find my story boring. It did not matter what words came out of my mouth—everyone loved my stories. They had a lot of drama, suspense, and excitement. I knew these two idiots were desperate for my attention—any attention from someone new.

"No, not at all," the girl replied. "I am Poppy, by the way, and that drunk knob next to you is Nigel."

"Nice to meet you both," I said in a thick New England accent, which neither picked up on. "I am Adam."

It is funny to think that we three had been sitting there against that bar, drinking and talking the night away as if we were old buddies, and yet it took us so long—them so long to introduce themselves. If I am being honest, their names could have been anything. Those details did not matter to me. I knew that neither of them would see another sunrise.

"Nice to meet you, too," Nigel replied, putting his hand on my right knee while Poppy caressed my left calf with her stocking-wrapped foot. Her shoe had fallen off, or she had kicked it off, lost in the sea of feet piling up at the bar. The happy hour crowd was multiplying quickly, and these two drunks were getting frisky.

"Stop interrupting him, darling," Nigel continued, unsure if she was interrupting me. It was clear that the alcohol in his system was beginning to blur his judgment, which was a good thing. The more numb he got now, the less pain he would feel later. "Let the handsome man finish his story."

I turned towards Poppy and then Nigel, smiling at each before looking straight ahead to smile at the cute bartender and wink at him. He was adorable and not a mess like many of the bartenders at this pub. While I was staring at the bartender, the two drunks leaned in and kissed me at the same time. The bartender bashfully smiled back at me as he voyeuristically watched the two lovers sloppily crash into my cheeks.

*   *   *   *   *

We met an hour earlier—Poppy, Nigel, and me. Poppy and Nigel had been sitting at the bar, privately discussing their desire to bring a third person into their bed. Listening to them babble on and on about this one simple thing had me convinced that this was a topic these two had frequently discussed. You know those kinds of people — they talk the talk but never walk the walk. I've known many of those kinds of idiots in my short lifetime. I've screwed a number of them and even killed a few. Those people annoy me. You know what I mean? They say they want to do something, to go somewhere, or meet someone, but they never do. Instead, they talk about it repeatedly to anyone who will listen — anyone stupid enough to listen and not point out that they should do it already. Damn, people irritate me.

Anyway, it was Wednesday night. I was on the prowl and was unlucky enough to have to listen to Poppy and Nigel ramble on. They vented about their bosses through their first pint, and by the second pint, they were back to talking about expanding their sexual circle. I stood next to the girl, to Poppy, waiting for the cute bartender to take my drink order, not that I should have had to give it to him. I had been coming to this pub for a long time, and I ordered the same thing each time — two fingers of whiskey with one ice cube. He took that order a hundred times, but every time, he would ask what I wanted to drink — maybe he thought I would mix it up one day. I didn't — mix it up. Not with my drink. I liked what I liked.

Finally, I had to say something to the girl — to Poppy. She and Nigel were debating a menage a trois. They needed closure, and I needed blood, so I interrupted them. They were both startled. I thought she was going to hit me at first, but once she got a good look at me and heard my proposition, she smiled and started whispering to her boyfriend.

I was almost done with my drink when the two came out of their huddle and proclaimed that I could go home with them as if their decision needed to be proclaimed. They said it like they were doing me a favor. I mean, they were, just not for the reasons they thought.

So there you go. There I was, squished between two horny drunks telling another story about my past, not that either of them really listened. I think that once we had all agreed on what would happen later that night, the two of them tuned out of listening to me completely, really hearing the words coming out of my mouth. I am sure all either of them could think about was getting me naked. All I could think about was killing them so I could get the craving out of my system. I had bigger plans that night—ones that included the cute bartender, and, believe it or not, they did not involve killing him.

02

One of my earliest memories is of me sitting on a picnic table outside our trailer, shooting stones at Chester with my slingshot. Chester was a big dog. I was too young to know his breed, but I remember he was a large dog. He was loud and always sounded angry. He belonged to Mr. Picklebury, and Chester did not like anyone. He constantly barked, growled, and showed his teeth as if trying to challenge you to a fight. I was not a good shot, but then I was only four.

While shooting pebbles at Chester that day, I watched a mother and daughter step out of the trailer next to Mr. Picklebury's. I had only seen them a few times, and I recall thinking that the mother looked much younger than my mom, who was only 19 years old. I assumed the daughter was learning to walk—she moved around quite awkwardly. I never saw a man go in or out of their trailer, but that was typical of our trailer park, probably in all trailer parks. A lot of the kids in our trailer park had teenage mothers and invisible fathers. Dads were a rarity, which made me special since I had both, at least for a while.

As the little girl walked with her mother, trying to comprehend balance, her sporadic movement agitated Chester much more than my feeble attempts to stone him to death. He was barking and lunging toward the girl with all his might, completely ignoring my game. He always ignored my games. Chester was a strong dog: all muscle. I watched him move around methodically, loosening the clothesline pole he was tethered to so he could lunge at the little girl—as if he knew exactly what he was doing. He did. The entire clothesline shimmied and shook when he got excited. I want to think that my hitting him with pebbles only worsened the situation, but I cannot recall them even getting close to him. I am surprised that the clothesline stood for as long as it did.

I remember hearing a loud noise, and when I looked up, Chester was dragging part of the clothesline across the yard, running towards the little girl with the speed of a marathon runner approaching the finish line. The few clothes hanging to dry were dragged through the dirt, chasing Chester as if to stop him—or help. Before the mother could react, Chester tackled the little girl and tore into her arm, chewing on it as if it were his favorite bone. The girl let out a high-pitched, hurt-your-ears kind of scream. I remember chuckling as I watched Chester naw on her arm. The mother yelled at Chester, but he ignored her, almost oblivious to her presence. She picked up an old metal baseball bat from the ground and began hitting him with it. Chester was unfazed. He held on to that little girl's arm and refused to let go. I was impressed, but more so, I was excited.

It was mesmerizing to watch how the bat hit Chester. I relished the sound as the metal met Chester's head—a heavy bonk as two hard surfaces collided. With each blow, Chester bled more, but he did not lose his focus—he did not let go of the little girl. Before that day, I had never seen an animal beaten, nor had I seen one tear into a human. Watching it happen right in front of me was so exhilarating. I get aroused just thinking about it today.

By the time Chester finally let go of the little girl, he was covered in blood, both hers and his own. He wobbled around, clearly trying to shake off the pain he felt from the baseball bat as he hobbled around the yard, still dragging the clothesline with him. The mother threw the bat at Chester as he walked away. She was exhausted but relieved that Chester was no longer tearing into her only daughter. By then, a crowd had formed—neighbors who were not passed out from drugs or alcohol had emerged from their nasty trailers to assess the commotion. They were addicted to the drama as much as they were addicted to their drugs.

The little girl's arm dangled from her body, and blood spewed out of her like water from a firehose. I had never seen that much blood before. It fascinated me. I wanted to bathe in it, to drink it. I did not know then that the human body was so flimsy, so weak. I was not sure why the sight of the blood excited me, but at that moment, I only wanted to see more blood—to taste blood. And I am not talking about blood from a small cut. I wanted a lot of blood.

When the police finally arrived, Chester, with a new sense of energy, ran straight toward the officers as they exited their cars. The clothesline tore through the dirt, weeds, and spots of grass; nothing held Chester back. He was still hungry for flesh and blood. I watched Chester run right past me, still dragging the clothesline. As I turned to watch him lunge at the police, the two officers pulled out their guns and fired multiple shots. The large dog fell to the ground next to the table where I sat. Chester's blood went everywhere—like a water balloon exploding. Thankfully, the officers had surprisingly good aim—they could have easily missed Chester and put a few bullets in me.

A lot of Chester's blood sprayed towards me, painting one of my legs and part of the table where I sat. It was tantalizing to feel the warm red substance erupt all over my leg. Instinctively, I dragged my finger through the blood and was about to taste it when one of the police officers yelled at me to stop. It was many years later before I finally got my first authentic taste of someone else's blood, and it was as wonderful as I had imagined as that little boy.

Eventually, one of the police officers called for an ambulance and animal control, but it was too late. The little girl was already dead. She bled out in her mother's arms. The mother held her daughter tightly, rocking and crying, screaming as loud as she could. The two were covered in blood, but the mother did not care. I remember wishing in that moment that I could have been that mother covered in all that blood.

As an adult now, I often wonder if the loved ones of my victims are as distraught and lost as that mother had been when they discover the body of their son or daughter, boyfriend or girlfriend, mother or father, lying in a puddle of their blood. I am never around to see that pain and suffering. I don't care about those secondary characters. They are irrelevant to me—unimportant in my mission to kill—my quest for blood.

As one officer talked with the mother, a second officer covered the little girl's body with a dirty bedsheet that had been hanging on the clothesline that Chester dragged around the yard, contaminating the crime scene. A third officer, the one who kept me from tasting Chester's blood, asked me if I knew which trailer belonged to Chester. I pointed to Mr. Picklebury's trailer as I tried to touch the blood on my leg again. The officer saw what I was trying to do and wiped my leg and the table clean before walking towards Mr. Picklebury's trailer. I remember thinking that I wished Chester had killed that officer, too.

Mrs. Rattleson, the older woman who lived next to us, eventually came out of her trailer and sat beside me on the table. She was wearing a tiny silk house robe. I remember it so well because her boobs were bursting out of it. They burst out of everything she wore. It would be years before I learned that Mrs. Rattleson was the owner and headliner of Rattle Tails, the strip club on the far end of town.

No one answered when the officer knocked on the door to Mr. Picklebury's trailer. I often watched kids knock on that door, and Mr. Picklebury was always quick to answer. I could have shared that information with the officers, but I didn't. Instead, I sat next to Mrs. Rattleson with my head resting on her boobs, and we watched the police try to make sense of what just happened. Eventually, the police officer stopped knocking and stuck a note on the door handle.

When the last police car finally drove away, Mrs. Rattleson looked down at me and asked if I wanted to join her for lunch. We leapt off the table and walked to her trailer, hand in hand. Her hand was soft and comforting. In those moments, Mrs. Rattleson was more of a mother to me than Lori ever was.

03

"Stop interrupting," Nigel yelled. "We haven't got all night."

"Sure, we do," I told them both, chuckling.

"You can do that?" Poppy asked. I never clarified if she thought I was a rent boy or not, but the look on her face when she asked the question screamed, 'You're a prostitute!' She did not know I disliked labels. I could have told her, but there was no point in doing so. She would be dead before she would have the chance to make that mistake again.

"I can do anything I want," I said as I kissed her cheek while simultaneously grabbing Nigel's crotch. He was pretty excited. I thought he would explode as he let out a squeal of excitement.

"It's time to go!" Nigel yelped as he called the bartender over to close out his tab. Poppy and Nigel were busy arguing about which one should pay the tab, which I found odd. Perhaps they enjoyed arguing about everything. I took advantage of the moment, grabbed the bartender's arm, and pulled him close.

"I'll be back for you later tonight, so don't go anywhere."

The bartender blushed.

Poppy and Nigel finally paid the tab, and within minutes, the three of us were in the back of a black cab heading towards Fulham.

"We've never done anything like this before," Poppy said as she started counting the little papers in her purse. "But I think you already knew that."

I did not hear her. I was busy raping Nigel's mouth with my tongue. I like it a little rough at times. I bit his tongue and lip, drawing blood, and as much as I knew it hurt him, Nigel played along, excited to be kissing a boy and still afraid that he might explode at any moment. I was not an idiot. I knew which one of the two needed to be seduced if I wanted the night to go as I had hoped.

Poppy wanted in on the action, too, and before I knew it, the three of us were making out in the back of the cab. I looked up to see the driver looking back at us a few times with a disgusted expression. He was older and probably Muslim, so even though he was living and working in a modern city, his faith—his God—had him believe that the three of us were sinners and, if he had his way, we would have been thrown to the lions.

Twenty minutes later, the three of us climbed the stairs toward a one-bedroom flat on the third floor of the walk-up that Poppy and Nigel rented from Nigel's older brother. I only knew this because when the two of them weren't trying to suck up to me, they rambled on and on with uninteresting and unnecessary details about their lives, as if I were moving in.

Their flat was not a fancy place and was much more depressing than I had expected. For some reason, I had it in my head that their flat would be something like a post-university, minimalist, mismatched set-up, but instead, it looked more like a flat remodeled with dumpster dive treasures occupied by sewer rats. Poppy and Nigel were slobs, and trust me, I have been in enough flats in London to know the varying degrees of mess. Their mess was off the charts, and of course, they justified it all with more diarrhea of words.

Poppy was the real slob. She even admitted it. Early in their relationship, Nigel tried to clean up behind Poppy, as she left a wake of messes wherever she went, in the kitchen and bathroom; it didn't matter. Cups, plates, clothes—anything would be placed anywhere. After a while, Nigel said he gave up, and that is when everything got worse—they both gave up cleaning, washing, and dusting. As neat as they both appeared at the pub, their home was a disaster.

Once inside, Nigel pulled some bottles from the fridge, and the three of us sat on a stained, beige settee that had to be cleared of piles of clothes—a mixture of clean and dirty, and once again, I was squeezed between Poppy and Nigel, all three of us holding a bottle of beer. The cushions were worn, and the stuffing had long since lost its fluff. There was a sour odor to the whole place. I was astonished at the filth. I scanned the room and noticed the stacks of books and clothing, as well as the spread of dirty dishes, empty bottles, and cans. I wanted to ask if they had a party the night before, but I could tell this was not a new mess. This was how the two of them lived.

The three of us sat sunken and silent like teenagers on a first date, unsure of what to do next—what to say next. Of course, I was purposely quiet. I wanted my hosts to feel in control, even though they were not. I wanted to see if they would strike up a conversation. They did not. At that moment, I realized how boring —how dull a life Poppy and Nigel had together. I could tell that the two had stopped loving each other, and I hoped that that night would bring them closer together, as if a third person was the answer. It is as stupid as two adults in a rocky relationship who decide to have a baby because they believe the baby will solve all their problems. Wake up, people. More people in the mix do not solve the core problem, but I was not about to lecture them on relationship matters. I would be back at the bar within the hour if I had my way. I continued the story from the bar as if someone had hit the 'play' button.

I remember sitting on a broken picnic table behind our trailer. I often sat at that table and listened to my parents fighting. They fought about almost everything and almost every day. The whole neighborhood could hear them fighting, thanks to the cheap construction of mobile homes back then.

The words and punches that my parents threw at each other made me cry a few times when I was younger, but I quickly became numb to their violence towards each other.

"That is so sad," Poppy chimed in. "I am so sorry you had to live through that at such a young age, but this story is not helping set the mood here."

"Stop interrupting him," Nigel pleaded, almost yelling, as he slowly moved his free hand toward my crotch while taking a swig of his beer.

I ignored them both.

Even when I heard them yell about how much they did not want me and how I was the mistake they regretted most, I remained steadfast. There was no point in crying over and over. It would not have made them love me; it would have only irritated them more.

Poppy wanted to say something, but she looked over and saw Nigel giving her an evil stare as if to say, 'Don't do it.'

"Thankfully, I was a resilient child," I said, sounding more upbeat, "I learned to take care of myself from a very young age, and the one lesson I took away from my parents is that if you do not watch out for yourself, you will be forgotten—lost. And if you ignore the space around you, you could find yourself in a precarious situation."

"Oh, you poor thing," Poppy interrupted yet again, ignoring my foreshadowed warning.

"Will you stop?" Nigel asked. "He is never going to sleep with us at this rate." Nigel sounded defeated and frustrated. He had been waiting to have a threesome—to be with a man, for such a long time. I am sure he could feel the blood rushing away from his groin. For Nigel, it was Poppy who made the whole situation soft, not me with my dark story.

"Oh, don't you worry," I said as I turned to Nigel, kissed his chapped, raw lips, and grabbed his crotch. "Clothes will be coming off soon."

Nigel blushed at the attention, and Poppy, momentarily jealous, put her beer on the table and leaned in to unbutton my shirt.

"Before we get too far along, though," I said as I pulled back from Nigel and pushed Poppy's clammy hands away. "We need to talk about my payment and any safe words." I did not care about either of those things, but this was all part of my cover story. I needed them to believe I needed those things to make this night successful.

Without saying another word, Nigel jumped from the settee and ran to the bedroom, adjusting the new excitement in his pants. A few minutes later, he returned and dropped ten pieces of paper on the table.

"500 for the night, right?" Nigel asked.

"Not for a sleepover, but yes, 500 will certainly be enough for what is about to happen," I replied, removing my shirt to reveal my pale, lean, toned body. Poppy leaned back towards me and

24

excitedly rubbed her hands across my washboard. Her hands were so cold and clammy. I wanted to push her away, but I didn't.

"Platypus," Nigel sang, almost too excitedly, looking down at Poppy and me on the couch, afraid to return to his seat.

"Sorry?" I asked.

"That is our safe word," Poppy chimed in as she continued to rub her hands over my muscular abdomen. "Platypus."

"Good to know," I replied as I stood up, leaving Poppy sitting alone. "Now, who has been naughty?" I asked, letting out a deep, evil laugh that seemed to echo throughout the flat. Then, without warning, I pushed the coffee table out of the way with my foot and kicked Nigel in the balls. Then, without hesitation, I turned back towards the couch, swung my right arm around, and punched Poppy in the face.

"What the fuck?" Nigel yelled as he fell to the floor, hitting his head on the coffee table. While Nigel was on the floor, I turned back around, stood over him, and kicked him in the stomach twice.

"I think you broke my nose," Poppy yelled, trying to hold the blood from swimming through her knuckles as she cupped her nose. "What the hell was that for?"

I turned and looked at Poppy again. She was getting blood everywhere. Poppy was a big bleeder—something I had not expected but was thoroughly enjoying. I leaned over to get close to Poppy, licking her hand and tasting the warm fluid rushing down it.

"I thought you liked it rough," I whispered in her ear, sounding joyful and innocent. I had grown bored of them faster than anticipated and decided I had had enough foreplay. I wanted to see Poppy and Nigel suffer—to die. After all, I had a bartender to get back to.

I pulled away from Poppy, grabbed her beer bottle from the table, and hit it against the wooden surface, breaking the base off and spewing liquid all over the tabletop. Then, without hesitation, I jammed the broken bottle into the side of Poppy's neck. Blood gushed over her, the settee, and me. She never had a chance to scream.

I basked in the red geyser, watching Poppy take her final breath. Her lifeless, sky-blue eyes stared back at me as if to ask, 'Why?' while Nigel was still curled up on the floor holding his balls and stomach, moaning like a child, completely unaware that I had just murdered his girlfriend.

04

"Why are you doing this to us?" Nigel finally asked, choking on his words as tears ran down his face. "Babe, are you okay?"

Poppy did not respond.

"Why not?" I asked, still basking in the volcanic explosion of blood that had poured out of Poppy's neck. I put my hands around her neck, filling them with the warm red liquid. I bathed in it all, rubbing Poppy's blood all over my chest, and then I licked my fingers as if I had just eaten a basket of saucy chicken wings.

Nigel tried to stand up. I noticed him moving, so I turned around and kicked him in the stomach again, keeping him lying on the floor. He annoyed me, and I was upset with myself for killing Poppy so quickly. That was not my plan at all. I got wrapped up in the moment, and like a teenage boy masturbating for the first time, I went too fast; I got too excited too soon and lost control. It had been so long since my last kill, and I missed that sensational feeling. I had planned to torture Poppy and Nigel slowly, but I got caught up in all the excitement, and then I became mad and disappointed in myself. I knew then that the only thing I could do was take my anger out on Nigel and make him suffer—make the whole evening worth the trouble of even going home with these two idiots.

As I stood between Nigel and the settee, I looked around the room, studying the mess—their mess, not mine—for ideas on how to torture Nigel. I noticed Nigel watched the blood drip down the fabric of the settee. He yelped, so I kicked him again, but harder this time.

"Somebody please help!" Nigel whispered, unable to yell. I am confident that I broke a few of his ribs from all my kicking, but I did not care. "Please… help… us."

"Stand up, you little prick," I remember yelling at him, and I knew he could hear the anger in my voice. "No one can hear you, and no one is coming for you, so stop whimpering. The more noise you make, the more painful this will be for you." I know I probably sounded much meaner than I was showing with my actions, but I wanted him to shut up. I needed to think about what I wanted to do with him — how I was going to torture him.

*   *   *   *   *

For the first time that night, Nigel heard Adam's American accent. He had been too drunk or infatuated with Adam's good looks to have heard it earlier, not that Adam had been hiding it. But now that he feared Adam — feared for his own life, he heard Adam very clearly.

Since university, Nigel had thought about hooking up with a man, but he had never done so. He had been attracted to girls but found himself wondering more and more about the male body. It was not until he and Poppy started the conversation about bringing a third into the bedroom that Nigel started getting aroused at the idea of being with a man. He had always considered himself to be straight — maybe even bi-curious. Poppy never questioned why Nigel was so willing for their third person to be a guy. She was sure he would want a second girl in their bed when she introduced the idea. She was pleasantly surprised that he quickly agreed with her idea of their shared person being a man.

Nigel, who was uncircumcised, had only ever seen uncircumcised dicks up close—mainly in the showers after a rugby match when he was still a student. They were all ugly—shriveled sausages that looked more like Tardigrades. He didn't even like looking at his own. As time passed and he became more intrigued with the male body, Nigel hoped to one day see a circumcised penis in the flesh. They looked so beautiful in the gay porn magazines he secretly yanked into.

*   *   *   *   *

"You're American!" Nigel said with surprise in his tone.

"I said to stand… the… fuck… up! Are you fucking deaf?" I know he was scared, and I could tell that he was conflicted. I am sure he was wondering what more I was going to do to him and if I was going to kill him, too. I had already smashed his balls enough times, so I knew he was in pain. I liked watching him suffer, but at the same time, I was growing impatient with his deliberate procrastination and his defiance in giving me what I wanted when I wanted it.

Of course, once he stood up and turned towards Poppy and me and saw the full scope of my destruction—Poppy dead and covered in blood with the beer bottle still stuck in her neck, still spitting up red liquid, Nigel turned back around. He vomited all over the coffee table and himself, then started crying.

"Please don't kill me," Nigel begged as he wiped his mouth with his shirt sleeve. "Platypus. Platypus."

29

I could not help but laugh then. I thought it funny that Nigel thought some 'safe word' would save him.

"Take your filthy clothes off," I yelled. "You stink. Get completely naked and throw your clothes over there, away from me. I cannot stand that fucking smell."

It was true. For all the violence that I can cause, vomit was my kryptonite. If potent enough, the smell of someone's vomit could force me to puke, too. That happened once in Boston, before I met Charles. I was torturing a young college girl. I had her tied up in her basement—her hands zip-tied behind her back and her legs zip-tied to the legs of the chair. I had been enjoying a slow torture—we were hours into the fun, and I was just watching her naked, dirty body try to wiggle free. I took a knife and sliced open her left thigh, enjoying the slow flood of blood covering the girl. She instantly hurled on me, causing me to throw up. Furious, I took my knife and slit her throat, then walked away. There was so much more I wanted to do to her—to skin her alive, but she ruined it for me. Vomit always ruins it for me.

I was surprised to see the growing bulge in Nigel's trousers. For all that I had put him through that evening, he continued to amaze me with his on-again-off-again boner. I mean, I get it—this stuff gives me a hard-on, too, but I have never seen one of my victims so aroused by my techniques. I was impressed. For a brief moment, I thought about sparing his life and enjoying a night of wild sex, but then the idiot decided to try to seduce me.

Nigel wiped the tears from his eyes and started to remove his shirt. He unbuttoned it slowly, seductively, hoping to buy time to let his Tardigrade settle down, I am sure. His erotic striptease appeared well-rehearsed. Poppy must have loved it when Nigel performed for her in their bedroom—her own private Chippendale, but Nigel was not getting the same response from me, not as long as he stunk.

"Hurry the fuck up!" I yelled as I grabbed Nigel by his belt and pulled him close. I smeared Poppy's blood on Nigel's exposed abdomen. The two of us were so close that he could taste my breath. I know that he wanted to kiss me, to take in my American flavor, but standing so close to death and feeling the warmth of Poppy's blood on his skin freaked Nigel out even more. I pushed Nigel away, sickened by his breath: his stench of vomit, and as soon as I did, Nigel turned away and threw up again.

"Sorry!" Nigel whispered as he wiped his mouth again. Then, he quickly kicked off his shoes, frantically removed his trousers and boxers, and stood a foot in front of me in nothing but his argyle socks, a big toe with a broken nail sticking out of the left one.

"Those, too!" I said to him, pointing down at his socks. I wanted to see his feet because I am a foot guy. Yes, I appreciate good-looking feet; unfortunately, not many people have attractive feet. The number of times I have been seducing someone—guy or girl—who was quite beautiful—you know, the type with the great smile, perfect figure, and all, well, I get all excited until they take off their socks and they have stubby little feet or funky toes. It is a total buzz kill. It will not stop me from killing them, of course, but it will undoubtedly turn me off from seducing them or having sex with them. I know I am not the only person in this world with a foot fetish, but I might be the only one to kill over it.

Afraid to look away from me, Nigel lifted one leg at a time to pull each sock off. He let them fall to the floor, landing in his vomit. It was like he was purposely trying to piss me off more and more with every action he took.

Completely naked, finally, Nigel cupped his crotch—hiding his small Tardigrade. I am sure he was happy that it had shriveled up again—easier to hide, although I am not entirely sure what he thought I would do with it. I was not there for sex. I was there for blood. His entire body shook as he whimpered, trying not to cry out loud, so I grabbed him by both arms and smeared more of Poppy's blood on him. Nigel flinched and stepped backward into the wet, chunky vomit as it squished between his toes. I am sure he wanted to throw up again. I know I almost did, but instead, I lifted him by both arms, swung him around, and tossed him onto the settee next to Poppy's limp body. He was much lighter than I expected.

Sitting naked on the settee, he begged me not to kill him. For someone so afraid of dying, his sex drive was relatively high. I watch his crotch salute again, almost as a last-ditch effort to save himself. But nothing he could do would help him. I was not there for anything but my enjoyment, which would climax when they were both dead.

I grabbed a beer bottle from the table and kicked the coffee table further out of the way to stand directly above Nigel, almost straddling his legs.

"Open your mouth!" I said.

Nigel looked up at me, more frightened and aroused than he had been that night. I could tell that he was afraid to open his mouth—fearful that the bottle in my hand would end up in his neck.

"I am not going to say it twice," I said, smacking him across the face. He reluctantly opened his mouth a little.

"Wider!"

Giving in, Nigel stretched his mouth open as if he were in the dentist's chair, ready for a good cleaning. I could tell he was scared shitless. He had no idea what I was about to do, and sitting next to his dead girlfriend did not ease his mind at all. Without warning, I whipped out my penis with my free hand and pissed into Nigel's mouth and all over his chest—waving my water gun around as if I were writing in the snow. My warm yellow liquid blended with the red of Poppy all over Nigel. It was a little erotic, I am not going to lie.

I am sure Nigel felt like he was being waterboarded, and yet the blood continued to rush to his penis. I finished peeing, took one last swing of the beer, and then swung the bottle towards Nigel so hard that I knocked him unconscious. I stepped back to look at the work of art on the settee. My two victims sat motionless, bleeding out, and I was feeling happy, pretty pleased with the evening so far, but I was not done. I was not about to leave without finishing off Nigel.

I found a butcher's knife and a fire extinguisher in the kitchen, and with Nigel still unconscious, I stuck the nozzle of the fire extinguisher into Nigel's mouth. I pulled the trigger, filling Nigel with nitrogen, potassium bicarbonate, liquid water, and bromochlorodifluoromethane. Immediately, he began choking as foam oozed out of his mouth—temporarily revived. I laughed so hard my stomach hurt, and then I jammed the butcher's knife into Nigel's stomach. I pushed the knife in, then pulled it out quickly. Nigel screamed as best he could with a mouth full of chemicals. I held the knife close to Nigel's face and wiped part of it on his cheek, feeling Nigel's warmth, and then I licked blood off the knife before stabbing Nigel's thigh. Nigel screamed again, more clearly now.

"Please stop!" Nigel begged and cried, spitting up foam.

"Okay," I replied sarcastically as I pulled the knife out of Nigel's thigh. Then, as a final act, I jammed the blade into Nigel's chest, penetrating his heart. Once again, I was basking in a blood shower while Nigel choked up blood.

I stepped back and admired my work only to have Nigel vomit one last time, spewing beer, nuts, foam, and blood down his chest—letting out his final few breaths. He tried to speak, but I could not make out any words. I was across the room, trying to avoid throwing up by ransacking their flat.

Back in the living room with jewelry and some cash, I once again stood before my new friends, admiring my latest work of art. Nigel was no longer begging to live—he was no longer breathing. The bloody vision before me was what I needed to get excited—to get off. I touched myself and exploded all over Poppy and Nigel before heading to their bathroom to shower.

Ten minutes later, clean and refreshed, I squeezed into some of Nigel's clothes that I found in their bedroom. Even in some slightly ill-fitting clothes, I looked handsome and wondered if the bartender would notice that I had changed. I looked at one of Nigel's watches, now perfectly wrapped around my wrist, and realized that I needed to get moving if I was going to make it back to the bar in time to keep my promise.

With almost two thousand pounds in cash stuffed into my pocket, I listened to Big Ben chime in the distance—it was 11 o'clock. I ran out of their flat, and once on the street, I hailed a cab and headed back to the pub.

05

Chester's owner, Mr. Picklebury, lived in a dilapidated trailer. The siding was peeling off, and the skirt was gone, exposing the rusted steel trailer frame and flat tires. Weeds crept up around the trailer's edges, making it look like Mother Nature was trying to swallow Mr. Picklebury's trailer — to save the world from another eyesore. Ours did not look any better.

A couple of windows had cracks in the glass, and inside, all the windows wore dark curtains to keep the light out. I cannot recall seeing Mr. Picklebury step outside, but I would see him at his front door, either welcoming guests or letting Chester out. In those rare moments, I would see a haggard man who might have been fit in his youth but had grown into an out-of-shape, older man with thinning hair and a fuzzy chest.

He always opened the door wearing boxers or nothing at all — he did not seem to care who saw him. I never got close enough to understand the colored patterns that completely wrapped around his left shoulder and arm down to his wrist, but from what I could see, they matched the swirled collection that started at his upper thigh and wrapped his left leg down to his ankle. His entire left side was a canvas of color — possibly the story of his life in graphic form. Mr. Picklebury never seemed to be a people person, nor did he appear to care about his appearance or what others thought. However, for a single, older man, he had a lot of young visitors —

too many teenagers for a man with no children. Clyde and Morris were the two who visited him the most.

I couldn't say or assume what they did, certainly not back then—I was four. But now, looking back and knowing what I know, I can make some pretty good assumptions about what the teens and pedophile Picklebury were doing, especially after what James Pearson told me about Mr. Picklebury.

*   *   *   *   *

"What are you reading?" Adam asked James, sitting on a bench in the manicured courtyard of the orphanage, in the shadow of a large cross that was the centerpiece of the nun's hard labor. James was slim in stature and not that attractive, but not ugly. He kept to himself, almost afraid of other people.

"Nothing," James replied, looking up at the young kid before him. James had not been at the orphanage for long and did his best to stay away from the other kids, so he was taken aback when Adam walked up and started talking.

"You must be new here," Adam said, looking at the disheveled hardcover book James had tried to conceal. "My name is Adam. What's yours?"

"James," he reluctantly replied, trying to hide the book behind his back. The book was the last one James' mother read to him at bedtime. She read it to him every night until he was in middle school. It was his favorite book, if for no other reason than it reminded him of her.

"When did you get here?" Adam fired back, determined to have a conversation. "I have been here for years, on and off. I've just returned from my third foster family. Man, they all suck."

"I have been here for a few weeks," James replied, giving in to Adam's pressure to spark a conversation.

"That's cool," Adam said as he sat beside James. "Where'd you come from?"

After a long pause, James began to tell his story to Adam. He was not forthcoming; instead, he offered tidbits of information, almost forcing Adam to keep asking more questions, which he did. Adam was surprised to learn that James grew up in a trailer park not that far from the one Adam once lived in, and was even more astonished that James' father had lived in the same trailer park as Adam, but on the other end of the property.

"That is where I lived," Adam said with some excitement.

"Then you must have known Mr. Picklebury," James blurted out.

"You knew Mr. Picklebury?" Adam asked. "He lived next door to me, but he is dead—has been for many years."

"Good!" James yelled. "He deserves to be dead."

*   *   *   *   *

I liked James. He was quiet and never brought any attention to himself. I wish we could have become better friends, but not long after he told me some bullshit story of why he was at the orphanage, James was adopted. The prick did not even go through the foster process—some family from who knows where just showed up one day and took him home. The nuns put us kids on display like zoo animals waiting to be petted, but the family never made it far enough down the line to meet me. They looked at James, heard his backstory, and decided he was the son they had been desperately seeking.

James was one of the lucky ones. He was in and out of that shit hole in a matter of months. We promised to write to each other, but I lied as the words came out. I was not one to invest in someone like James—someone I'd never see again. James wrote to me a few times, but mostly because his therapist made him write out his feelings—share some secrets, all part of his healing process, or some shit like that. James was not ready to share those secrets with his new family, so I was his audience.

In his final letter, James explained why he was glad Mr. Picklebury had died. He also confessed to lying about why he was sent to the orphanage and wanted me to know the truth—all part of his healing process.

James told me that he had been raped multiple times by his older stepbrother, Kenny. His letter went into graphic detail about what his stepbrother did to him, how he beat James into submission, and then violated his little boy's body in what the nuns would call "unspeakable ways."

I was a teenager when I read those letters. Sure, I had done some bad things by then, but I had not done anything as bad as Kenny. I would remember my days in the trailer park, trying to visualize Kenny, but he was older than my parents when I was born. Hell, even James was much older than me. As I grew older, James' story stuck with me. Kenny had some issues—he was fighting some demons, much like me, and I sometimes wonder if I will end up like Kenny.

In his letter, James told me that Kenny bragged to James about having violent sex with Mr. Picklebury — bondage shit that James did not quite understand. Kenny would be as violent with James as James imagined Mr. Picklebury must have been with Kenny. It was the only way James could justify why Kenny would do what he did to him.

In the end, James told me that Kenny was caught violating him — James' mother walked in on the abuse. The way James tells the story, Kenny freaked out and jumped out of James' bedroom window, half-naked. James never saw Kenny again, but that was because Kenny ran to his dad's trailer and deep-throated one of his father's pistols, shooting his brain all over the living room wall. Eventually, he was found, his body covered in blood and filth.

James said his mother was so mad that she went to Kenny's mother's trailer and started beating the shit out of her. James and Kenny's dad showed up and started hitting James' mother. Neighbors saw the three drug addicts fighting and called the police. His parents were put in jail, and James was sent to the orphanage. That is a pretty fucked up way to live. It almost makes my story pale in comparison.

I often think about James and Kenny. I wonder if Kenny was broken like me and if he broke James. I wonder if all people are broken in some way — by someone or something. Of course, I never knew Kenny to ask him, and at that time, I didn't care enough to reach out to ask James. As I got older, I thought about trying to find James and ask him how his life turned out — to learn if he had improved or was broken, too.

*   *   *   *   *

Adam never did reach out to James, and if he had, he would have learned that James had taken his own life. That last letter he wrote to Adam—the one where he shared all his secrets-was the last letter he wrote to anyone. After walking to put that letter in the mailbox, James stepped off the sidewalk and into the road. The oncoming traffic never had a chance to slow down. James' body bounced between two cars before being clipped by a bus and dragged thirty feet to his death.

06

"Back so soon?"

"I told you I'd be back," I said, winking at the youthful-looking, shirtless man cleaning a martini glass.

"You say many things here," he said, chuckling bashfully. "What can I get you?"

"I will start with a gimlet and hope to finish with you. What time do you get off?"

The bartender and I continued our flirtatious game for the next several hours. While he tended to other patrons, I sat silently, watching his expressions as he interacted with the strangers. I observed how the drunken people disrespected him; they were loud and obnoxious. Granted, the pub was buzzing with activity by now: dozens of boys and girls were on the dance floor gyrating to the hottest new club tunes. The quiet bustle of the happy hour pub crowd had transformed into a younger, louder, and more intoxicated dance club crowd. The air was thick, the bodies were wet, and the alcohol was flowing. And yet, the bartender maintained his composure through it all — he always did. He would look back at me occasionally to smile or wink, probably wanting to be sure I was still watching him. I was.

"Do you want one more before I end my shift?" he asked, pointing to the empty glass before me. I declined. I was tired and ready to escape the noise. Killing people can be exhausting. The bartender disappeared behind a closed door, returning with his shirt and coat on moments later. He grabbed me by the arm as he walked past, leading me through the crowd and out the front door.

Once outside, we stood silently for a moment, almost awkwardly. We could finally talk for the first time without yelling over the music.

"I'm Murray," he finally said, almost whispering, extending his hand to me. For a moment, I thought it odd that we had gone the whole night, months even, without exchanging names, as if we both liked the anonymity of our cat-and-mouse game.

"Adam," I replied, bashfully confident as I grabbed Murray's hand, enjoying the firm handshake of soft skin that almost engulfed my hand.

"So, would you like to grab a coffee?" Murray asked, still locked in my grip.

"Only if it's being served at your place," I replied with a smile, grabbing his hand more tightly.

Murray blushed and hailed a cab.

*   *   *   *   *

If it had been any other night or any other person, I would have killed again that evening. Instead, I went home with Murry, and the two of us formed a friendship, a bond unlike any I had experienced up to that point in my life. Murray was quiet, calm, and kind. I was reckless, murderous, and devious, yet I found solace in the Ying and Yang of our lives. I hoped that Murray would never learn about the devious side of my life, but unlike my victims, Murray learned more about me, my past, and my struggles growing up. I always stopped short of letting Murray see my darker side. I shielded Murray because I liked him, and as best I could, I tried to protect him from ever knowing the real me, or at least that darker side of me—the broken me.

You see, I liked Murray a lot, and our friendship grew over the months, giving me a sense of stability and consistency—something I had not had in a long time. And, while we bonded quickly, I did not move in with him. I spent many nights sharing Murray's bed each week, but I let him believe that I lived on the other side of town—not some place he ever needed to visit. Murray could have questioned the strange quirks of our relationship, but instead, he reveled in the joy I provided. At least that is how I perceived our relationship.

*   *   *   *   *

Murray lived alone in a refurbished carriage house in Camden Town—a graduation present from his parents when he left University. His parents had hoped Murray would use his degree in criminal justice for something good, perhaps even joining his father's law firm, but instead, Murray spent his days sleeping and his nights pouring drinks for strangers, and he loved it. He loved the simplicity of his job. Sure, as a bartender, Murray had to put up with a lot of shit from customers, especially the overly obnoxious, drunk ones, but he still liked that he could walk away from it all at the end of his shift. Unlike many of his friends in suits, Murray never brought work home with him—unless the guy was cute, and even then, it was just for one night.

Murray did not date—not anymore. While at University, he focused on his studies. He hooked up a few times, but as much as he enjoyed what happened under the darkness of the sheets, he would be gone by morning light—slipping out silently and unapologetically. After graduation, and without a book to hide behind, Murray felt the pressure to socialize—to get out and meet people. Some of that pressure was his own, but much of it came from his parents. They knew their son was gay, so the pressure was not to get married and give his parents grandchildren. No, it was about making sure that their only child was happy—fulfilled.

One lousy date followed the next, and Murray found himself repeating his bad behavior—sneaking out before his trick woke. Eventually, Murray woke in a bed where he felt comfortable —snuggling with a man he believed he could spend the rest of his life sleeping beside. That relationship lasted for one week, and that was a year ago.

After that, Murray swore off men and dating. He was done playing 'the game.' Instead, he would flirt with patrons at the pub and occasionally get frisky with some in the bathroom. He stopped taking men home, and he stopped looking for love. He was happy, or so he thought. He believed nothing was missing—no one was missing from his life—until he watched Adam walk through the pub door for the first time.

*   *   *   *   *

The pub where Murray worked, The Drunken Unicorn, attracted a large gay clientele even though it was not a gay bar. It was one of the older pubs in the city with a reputation for welcoming anyone looking for a good drink, good music, and a no-questions-asked good time. It did not always have this reputation.

At the turn of the century, the pub was quite elitist—no women, no immigrants, no people of color; in fact, you had to be of the highest caliber to get in—secret codes and all. In a way, it has always been a sought-after pub—just these days, there are no secret codes.

It was the first pub Charles introduced Adam to when they arrived in London—two Americans looking to frolic in a foreign land. Charles had traveled to London often over the last few decades, and the Drunken Unicorn was his favorite watering hole. Truth be told, Charles frequented the pub often enough, and his reputation was known well enough that desperate twinks would flock to him like piranha when he walked into the pub—each hoping to be his next boy toy. Charles did not mind. He loved the attention, especially at his old age.

Charles was the only child of parents who were also only children. He grew up living a privileged but lonely life. He was raised by nannies more than by his parents—both of whom were always too busy with work or some philanthropic endeavor, neither of which ever included Charles. While Charles was in college, both of his parents drowned in the middle of the Atlantic Ocean when their yacht collided with a cargo ship. Just as his parents never experienced Charles' childhood, they never had the opportunity to see him grow into a man, get married, and have a child of his own. They never got to experience his divorce or his coming out, either.

Charles's work, not his sexuality, was the root cause of his divorce. Like his parents, Charles was more interested in success than in the people around him. It was long after his divorce, when he came out and slowed down working so much, that Charles realized that he had treated his only child the same way that his parents had treated him. He missed dinners, school plays, his son's hockey games—everything because of work. He was convinced that this horrible behavior went back generations, so when he came out, Charles was committed to changing how he behaved. Unfortunately, he was too late for his son, who had no interest in his father. Charles sold his family business and took more time for himself. He spent more time traveling and exploring his sexuality. He filled the void in his life with young boys who, for the right price, would treat Charles as if he were the love of their life. This false way of living was enough for Charles.

Charles behaved the same way in Boston. He would frequent bars looking for temporary love, and some of the boys he met would stick around for weeks and months, but Charles never considered bringing any of them with him when he traveled abroad. Finding new, local boys for entertainment was more straightforward and a greater treat.

So after several weeks together in Boston, when Charles told Adam about an upcoming trip to London, Adam convinced Charles to bring him along. Unlike every other boy that Charles kept, Adam was not territorial, and he often encouraged Charles to invite one or two others home when they were at a bar or club. Adam had always used Charles far more than Charles thought he was using Adam. If Charles had been close to his son, he might have seen how dangerous Adam was to him.

*   *   *   *   *

Murray noticed Adam the first night he walked into the pub, looking lost and overwhelmed, even though his arm was wrapped around a much older man, but he did not judge. Murray was gay, living in a world where it was not always good to be gay. He recognized Charles, though. For an American not living in London, Charles was a regular at the Drunken Unicorn. When Charles entered the pub alone, all the single guys gushed for his attention. Murray would laugh at how pathetic he thought all those guys looked trying to catch themselves a sugar daddy. Many would go home with Charles, but none got more than a night of fun; none had what Charles was looking for. Adam did.

Murray watched for Adam and Charles every night since that first night. He watched them, served drinks to them, and talked with Charles as he always had, but Murray did not speak to Adam or engage in small talk. Murray had sworn off dating, but not flirting; yet, for some reason, he was embarrassed and intimidated by the idea of flirting with Adam. Unlike every other boy who surrounded Charles, Adam appeared aloof and confident, as if he were in control. The others all stank of desperation. Adam's confidence intrigued and intimidated Murray, so instead, he quietly watched Adam.

Adam watched Murray, too. He watched the cute bartender look back, always trying to catch a glance. The two would see each other staring in each other's direction, and instinctively, Adam would smile and often wink. Murray would blush and return to mixing drinks, pretending he had not been staring. Their game lasted for months.

After a few months of the same routine night after night, Murray noticed Adam coming to the pub without Charles. He wanted to ask where the old man had gone, but Murray knew people who sucked on the nipple of the 'kept-boy' lifestyle, and he knew none of those relationships lasted, so he let it go. It wasn't Charles he was interested in anyway.

Without Charles by his side, Adam went to the pub less frequently. He had an entire city to explore — to kill, and he needed to take advantage of his time with Charles' money before people noticed that Charles was missing. Adam did not set out to kill Charles while in London, but some of his best, most memorable kills were spontaneous.

*　　*　　*　　*　　*

I spent the last few months living on the streets or crashing at the homes of the people I seduced and then killed. With Charles dead, I no longer had the comfort of that warm bed to retire to each evening, so I had to get creative.

As I stood on the sidewalk, waiting for a cab with Murray, letting my hand rest in the warm comfort of his, I felt confident that I would be sleeping in a bed I didn't have to kill to enjoy. I could have stayed at Poppy and Nigel's flat that night. I could have enjoyed the pleasures of their tiny palace, but I took a chance — a leap of faith that if I returned to the pub, then I could go home with the cute bartender I had admired from afar for too long.

07

Neither Clyde nor Morris lived in our neighborhood, but they spent a lot of time hanging around, selling drugs to anyone with cash or the willingness to have sex with one or both of the awkward underage boys. Clyde was the taller of the two boys. He had long, dark, and somewhat greasy hair that sometimes hung in a ponytail. Thinking back now, he was not very handsome. Clyde was skinnier than Morris. I always saw him wearing an off-white, tight-fitting wife-beater and cargo shorts—it was his uniform. The dozens of tattoos painted sporadically from shoulder to wrist complemented his long, slender arms. It was as if someone threw paint in the air, and Clyde put his arms out under the falling colors —no rhyme or reason for the chaos.

He had an awkward smile; Clyde did—no good way to describe it. It was not quite a grin nor a smirk. It looked like he was always trying to push out a pooh. And when he smiled, his poor dental hygiene was evident. Clyde had a few black teeth in a mouth full of crooked, yellow-stained teeth, which is what happens when you use too much of the product you sell.

Morris, on the other hand, was handsome. I was young, so I didn't fully understand the concept of attractiveness at the time, but I knew how I felt when I saw Morris: excited. I wanted to follow him around everywhere he went. I liked it when he hung out with my mother because I got to be close to him—to smell him. I would take in his aroma delightfully, filling my nose with his mixture of

Old Spice and teen sweat. The air tasted so much better when Morris was around. I would have licked every part of him if given the opportunity back then — a lollipop I could never have.

Morris was shorter than Clyde, but Morris's body was all muscle. He took his physique very seriously and knew he looked good. He flaunted his beauty as often as possible, usually going shirtless, weather permitting. His skin was slightly tanned and as clear as freshly fallen snow. Even his smile was perfect: no messed-up teeth. He was the opposite of Clyde in every possible way, yet they were best friends, having been so since Morris moved to Vermont.

Morris had beautiful eyes — sultry, hazel eyes that were mesmerizing when they caught your attention, which they did often. He had short, dirty-blonde hair that always looked disheveled, as if he had made it look that way on purpose. He had a thick trail of the same color hair running from his adorable, tight belly button knot, which swam in his sea of chiseled abs, down into his pants, which hung low off his lean waist. I wanted to suck on that belly button like it was my mother's tit. Not that I was still suckling my mother's tits at that age. Come to think about it, I am not sure I ever enjoyed her milk. Maybe she might have loved and connected with me more if I had.

When Morris was in our trailer, he was often naked — I don't think he enjoyed wearing clothes. He could not have been more than 16 years old, but he enjoyed pumping my mother with drugs and semen. They were both teens, clumsily trying to behave like adults. Neither did an outstanding job. When Morris would come over, I would be inside watching television or playing — anything so I could be close enough to see his sculpted body. I did not understand everything that was going on around me at that young age, but I did know that the dead girl, the bloody dog, and a naked Morris excited me—made my body tingle in ways I lusted after for years. I still lust for that feeling today.

08

Before I turned six, I witnessed a lot of drug use, death, and loss. Anyone growing up in a stable, loving household would never have experienced the pain and suffering I did, but I don't hate my parents for giving birth to me—for bringing me into this world. I hate them for not loving me—for abandoning me. They were kids themselves when I was born, teenagers thinking they were on top of the world and ready to be adults. They were so wrong.

I cannot imagine what my parents saw in each other or why they ever loved each other, assuming they did. I do not recall seeing them show loving affection towards one another, unless you consider throwing a punch as a way of showing affection. If they were not screaming at or hitting each other, they were sleeping beside each other, drooling, lost in some Morris-supplied drug cocktail, completely oblivious that they were next to each other or that they were parents. They could barely take care of themselves. I am not sure how they ever thought they would be able to take care of me.

I often found them in bed with other people. I did not think anything about it. I ran around our trailer naked a lot, too. My parents were not very good about keeping me clothed. Even Mrs. Rattleson had been naked with my father on more than one occasion in our trailer, and Morris and my dad swapped fluids a few times when my mother was not around.

On my sixth birthday, I woke to the sound of my parents yelling. Nothing new, but they were not singing Happy Birthday to me, as any child might hope on their birthday. I am pretty sure they did not even remember my birthday. They were too busy screaming at each other again. Morris was there, too. The three were in my parents' room—Mom and Morris under the sheets and Dad standing at the edge of the bed with his back to me.

My father had come home in the early morning hours after being out all night. I did not hear him come in or know where he had been, and it was apparent that my mother did not care either, since she and Morris were playing their naked game in her room again. As usual, my dad came home smelling like a brewery, which should have been alarming considering he was a teenager. But in that part of the world, it was too hard to keep tabs on people. Drugs were plentiful, and underage access to illegal substances was too easy. I could tell from my father's tone that he was not pleased to find my mother and Morris in his bed. I couldn't know if he was angrier with my mother or Morris.

I remember it all so vividly—my father standing at the door of the bedroom holding a big gun. Until that point, I had only ever seen the little guns that the police carry; enough police officers visited our trailer park in my younger years for me to see more than my share of pistols. But that morning, my dad was holding a rifle. It was big, shiny, and almost out of place in his tiny hands. My dad's body looked more like Clyde's than Morris', so he appeared awkward wielding the large metal object.

My father did most of the yelling. My mother fired some words back, but mostly, she was crying, begging my father not to pull the trigger. Morris was not crying. He was not arguing, either.

He was mute, interested only in getting dressed and out of the trailer alive. He behaved as if this were a routine matter, as if he were often caught in bed with another man's wife.

I sat in the living room with a direct line to all the action. I watched Morris jump off the saggy mattress on the floor—my parents' version of a bed with no frame and no box spring. Their room was depressing, but our entire home was a mess— mismatched furniture and dirty clothes covered everything, including the floor. You could tell the trailer was lived in by teenagers. I'd say that no right-minded adult would live in that filth, but our entire trailer park was dilapidated. I had only been in a few trailers in our park, and they were all depressing, just like ours. Even Mrs. Rattleson's was in some form of disarray. Living in filth must be the mindset of people experiencing poverty.

When Morris stood up, I looked at him. I remember drooling at the sight of his lean, naked body. His skin glistened with sweat. I wanted to dry him off with my tongue. I noticed that Morris' dick was thicker and longer than my dad's. My dad was not naked then, but I had seen his dick enough times in the past when he would walk around our trailer in the nude and flaunt a body not worth flaunting. Maybe that is what angered my father that morning—perhaps he was intimidated by Morris' big dick, or at least the idea that Morris was sharing it with my mother instead of with my father. I never did learn the truth about why my parents fought that morning, but that was the last time I ever saw my father.

My parents continued to yell at one another while Morris got dressed, and then, almost surprisingly, my father pulled the trigger. No one knows whether it was intentional or an accident. The gun made a loud bang sound as a bullet skimmed Morris' bare right shoulder before escaping through the thin wall of the trailer. Fortunately for Morris, his shoulder bled only a little. Unfortunately for Tommy Little, the ten-year-old punk who often tortured us smaller kids, the bullet entered the back of his skull and went out through his left eye socket. He was dead before his body hit the ground.

As strong as Morris looked, he behaved quite differently when the bullet grazed him. He screamed at my father and cried — it sounded more like whimpering. He stood in the bedroom wearing dirty jeans that hung low off his tight, thin waist. Morris held his t-shirt against his shoulder to stop the bleeding. We all heard Tommy Little yell and hit the ground, but we did not know what was happening outside at the time. We were too engrossed in our drama. My mother yelled louder at my father and thrashed at him. That was her way of punching, I guess. She looked ridiculous. The whole scene was ridiculous. The entire morning was laughable. It was fucking birthday, after all.

In all the chaos, my father panicked and dropped the gun, and as it hit the floor, it fired off another round, putting a hole in the ceiling. He did not care; he turned around, ran out of the bedroom, and right past me as if I were invisible. My father pushed through the flimsy front door and ran away quickly.

I looked back towards the bedroom to see my mother tending to Morris's wound as best she could. She was not a nurse and had no fundamental motherly skills. I watched two teenagers make a big mess, secretly wishing an adult could help. Eventually, Morris slipped his beautiful, large, bare feet into his boots, walked past me shirtless, and out the door. He held his t-shirt against his arm to keep from bleeding more. Unlike my father, though, Morris smiled at me and stopped to pat me on the head as he fled. He even whispered 'Happy Birthday' to me as he walked out. I couldn't believe Morris knew my birthday; his acknowledgment gave me goose bumps. I hugged him — tightly grabbed his leg and took in his aroma before he pushed me away and walked out the door.

My mother sat on the bed crying, oblivious that I was even in the trailer. I walked into the bedroom and looked at the two holes. Light forced through them, trying to brighten the dimly lit, filthy room. I saw the rifle on the floor and touched it briefly. It was hot.

My mother jumped out of bed, put on shorts and a T-shirt, and then grabbed my arm, pulling me through the trailer. We walked out the door and over to Mrs. Rattleson's. By now, the area around our trailer was bustling with activity. Tommy Little's mother was screaming and crying as she rocked back and forth on the ground, holding her dead son. We could hear sirens in the distance.

When the police finally arrived, Morris was long gone. So was my father. Mrs. Rattleson made the call when she heard the gunshots and then watched my father run away. I don't think she tried to stop him or Morris, but she was able to calm my mother to get part of her version of events before the police arrived. I pretended to sleep on Mrs. Rattleson's couch while the police interrogated my mother.

*   *   *   *   *

"Ma'am, can you tell us what happened?" one officer asked.

"Come on, Lori," Mrs. Rattleson kept saying. "You need to tell these nice officers what you told me."

"She is right, ma'am," a second officer said. "You are not in any trouble. We are here to help you."

"He does not love me," my mother finally said through tears. "He was trying to kill me. I am sure of it."

"Who was trying to kill you?" the first officer asked.

"My poor Morris," my mother said almost under her breath.

"I am sorry, ma'am, but who is Morris?" the second officer asked.

"Is Morris your husband?" the first officer asked. "Is this Morris here?" He asked, pointing at me.

*   *   *   *   *

The police made little progress with my mother. She was in shock and still coming off her high, so she did not make much sense. Mrs. Rattleson finally chimed in and told the police officers what she knew: how my father returned from an all-nighter to find my mother in bed with her drug dealer again.

Mrs. Rattleson informed the police officers that my mother and I required assistance. They interpreted that to mean that my father was a threat. What they did not know was that both of my parents were a threat to me, that I was going to grow up just like my parents if I did not live somewhere better, safer.

Neither of the officers heard the plea for help. Instead, they took statements, removed the rifle from our home, and set out to locate Morris and my father.

09

Finn fled the trailer and ran across two counties before stumbling upon an old sugar house abandoned years earlier. It was the perfect hiding spot, or so he thought. Soon after Finn arrived, Clyde walked through the door. Clyde had not yet heard that Finn shot Morris or killed Tommy Little. Clyde was at the sugar house to meet Morris, but was just as happy to see Finn. The two got high together and talked about nothing in particular. Eventually, they passed out beside each other, sleeping through the night. When Clyde woke the following day, Finn was gone. Morris never showed up.

A couple of weeks after Finn accidentally shot Morris, a different sheriff in a different county on a completely unrelated case discovered the sugar house and what would later be identified as Finn's left shoe and t-shirt. In addition to Finn's clothes, the sheriff found a baseball cap that belonged to Clyde. He also found a bong painted with both boys' fingerprints.

The sheriff finally tracked down Clyde at his parents' trailer. Almost three weeks had passed since Finn fired the rifle, so the sheriff was feeling less and less confident about finding Finn. The sheriff believed that Clyde was his only lead—possibly the last person to see Finn, but when a deputy went to retrieve Clyde, the boy was so high that he had to sit in a jail cell for 24 hours before he was clear-headed enough to talk with the sheriff.

The sheriff questioned Clyde for as long as he could, given that he had no real reason to detain Clyde, but the sheriff did not get any helpful information. Clyde said very little, admitted to nothing, and was eventually released, and the sheriff was still no closer to finding Finn.

A day after Clyde was released, the sheriff received a call about an accident at the Deerfield Inn along Route 116. When his team arrived, they found Clyde and an older gentleman. Clyde's body was lying on the floor, face down, in a pool of blood and vomit. He was naked. Shit oozed out of his ass, and his brains bubbled out of the hole in the back of his skull.

According to his driver's license, the older man was Steve Shapiro from New Jersey. The sheriff eventually learned from Mrs. Shapiro that Mr. Shapiro was a retired fireman who had traveled to Vermont for a two-week hunting excursion. He was celebrating the start of his retirement, and it was hunting season. Mr. Shapiro had never held a gun before buying the hunting rifle and pistol he had acquired three weeks earlier.

Mr. Shapiro's body lay across one of the motel beds, face up, fully dressed. He left a detailed note about what he had done and why he had done it. That letter sat on the desk across from the bed, and it had some blood splatter from when Mr. Shapiro put a pistol to his mouth and pulled the trigger. Bits of his brain covered the faded print of a forest that hung framed above the bed.

If it had not been for the note left by Mr. Shapiro, the sheriff might never have found Finn. The letter was more of a novella, detailing how unhappy Mr. Shapiro had been, how unfulfilled he felt after forty years of working as a fireman and fifty years of marriage to Mrs. Shapiro. The Shapiros never had children. He wrote about a long and lonely life. He confessed to the various affairs he had had over the years—the boys and the women. In his eloquent dissertation, Mr. Shapiro never apologized to his wife for the affairs. Instead, he apologized for killing Clyde and Finn and for not ending his marriage to Mrs. Shapiro sooner or in a better way.

According to his confession, Mr. Shapiro was hunting alone. He should have had a hunting partner, but he was unfamiliar with all the rules and regulations. This trip was his first time hunting—a bucket list item he needed to check off. One that he was ill-prepared to complete. As Mr. Shapiro sat quietly in the forest, completely camouflaged in his newly acquired name-brand hunting attire, he grew tired of waiting. He did not realize how much patience was needed when hunting. Exhausted and bored, Mr. Shapiro decided to pack it up for the day, and as he did, he finally saw movement in the forest. Without thinking, he aimed and fired.

When Mr. Shapiro reached his target, he found Finn shirtless, missing a shoe, and with a bullet hole in his head. The bullet was a direct shot into Finn's forehead, and miraculously, he was still breathing when Mr. Shapiro reached him. Being a retired firefighter, Mr. Shapiro should have called for help; he certainly should not have been alone. Instead, Mr. Shapiro wrote in his letter that he witnessed Finn's death. He spoke briefly with Finn and wrote that Finn's final words to him were, "Tell my son that I love him." Of course, that meant nothing to Mr. Shapiro.

Mr. Shapiro went on to write that he was sorry for shooting the stranger in the woods and for killing the boy in the motel. Spooked from killing Finn, Mr. Shapiro went to a bar for a drink. It was at that bar that he met Clyde. Clyde flirted with Mr. Shapiro the way that Morris taught him to flirt. Mr. Shapiro, still in a state of shock after killing a man, drank his fear away with Clyde before inviting Clyde back to his motel room.

Once in the room, Clyde got naked quickly — the very thing Morris told him never to do. When Mr. Shapiro saw the skinny, tattooed teenager standing before him naked, he felt sick. Mr. Shapiro vomited, covering Clyde with chunks of hamburger and a waterfall of vodka and beer. Clyde screamed at Mr. Shapiro, who stood motionless, unsure what to do. Then, panicking, Mr. Shapiro wiped his mouth and grabbed his pistol from the dresser. When Clyde turned away for a moment, Mr. Shapiro pulled the trigger, and Clyde fell to the floor.

Mr. Shapiro was quite detailed in his suicide note. He was also quite methodical. While Clyde lay on the floor bleeding to death, Mr. Shapiro showered, got dressed, and sat at the desk. He wrote his novella and then moved to the bed, where he sat on the edge, looking at himself in the mirror on the wall above the desk. He wrapped his mouth around the metal barrel and pulled the trigger.

The first gunshot — the one that took down Clyde alerted the motel staff. The girl behind the front desk counter called the police immediately. The police were knocking on the motel door when Mr. Shapiro fired the gun a second time. He was dead before the police could get the door open.

10

My mother spent even less time with me after my father died. Free from the shackles of the Fastiggi family, my mother fell deeper into the world of drugs, leaving even less time for me. Morris stopped coming around. I assumed that he blamed my mother for his gunshot wound—his scar, and for Clyde's death, too. While my mother seemed unfazed that Morris no longer visited, I was distraught. I missed seeing him walk around shirtless. I missed his smile. I missed his laugh.

My mother moved on.

She met other sketchy boys who were only too happy to have sex with her in exchange for a quick high. She forgot about me, assuming she ever remembered me. I was six years old, and I recall waking up hungry almost every day. Our trailer only had one bedroom, so I usually slept on the couch at the front end of the trailer. I did not have a proper bed until I moved into the orphanage. If my mother and her sleazy guys were drinking and getting high in the living room, I would retreat to her bedroom.

While sitting outside on a picnic table one day, I heard yelling. It sounded like people arguing, so I jumped off the table and walked around to the front of our trailer, where I found Mrs. Rattleson yelling at a couple of boys who had recently started hanging out with my mother. I noticed that the front door of our trailer was open, and one of the boys kept going in and out. He was not taking anything. He just looked confused. He was high. A second boy, Petey, stood outside the trailer shirtless and barefoot, threatening Mrs. Rattleson, but she seemed unfazed. She was a strong woman—you had to be to run a strip club. Petey was not hitting Mrs. Rattleson, but he kept lunging at her as if he wanted to hit her, to punch her in the face. However, each time Petey jumped forward, he lost his balance. He was high, too.

Petey wore a large creature, a full-color minotaur, across most of his tiny chest. I remember thinking that it looked ridiculous. It was out of place on his skinny, pale frame. Various shapes and random designs engulfed his slim arms, some in color and others all black. They did not make sense to anyone but him—maybe not even him. The strangest one was the tail of the minotaur—it wrapped around Petey's waist and up his back to fan out into a wild pattern, almost kaleidoscopic. He showed his colors like a proud peacock.

*   *   *   *   *

"I called the police," Mrs. Rattleson said. "You boys are in big trouble."

"Fuck you, bitch," yelled Petey. "You don't know shit. Just mind your own fucking business, you whore."

"You can cuss all you want, you little brat," Mrs. Rattleson fired back at him. "But you and your little friend are going to jail."

"That is funny, old lady," Petey yelled. "Don't you know who I am?"

"He is the Sheriff's kid," the first boy said as he exited our trailer again. "Ain't nobody never goin' to give him shit."

Mrs. Rattleson huffed and rolled her eyes, which fueled Petey's rage.

"I have had it with you," the Sheriff's son said to Mrs. Rattleson as he picked up a metal baseball bat. "Bitch needs a beating."

"Put down the weapon, Petey," said one of the deputies who had arrived moments earlier and had his gun raised and pointed at Petey.

"No!" Petey yelled back to the Deputy. "This bitch is accusing me of doing some bad things, and ain't nobody going to accuse me of shit and get away with it. I don't care who they are."

*　　*　　*　　*　　*

I remember hearing Petey scream as a bullet lodged into his bicep, creating a red explosion in the swirl of black psychedelia. Petey dropped the bat, hitting his left foot as it fell. The Deputy spoke into his shoulder, asking for backup, explaining that he just shot the Sheriff's son.

The other boy came running out of our trailer when he heard the gunshot. When he saw Petey on the ground, instead of helping Petey, the boy picked up the baseball bat and started running toward the Deputy. Two bullets were lodged into the boy's chest before he got close enough to hit the Deputy.

By the time the ambulance, Sheriff, and other Deputies arrived, the first boy was dead. I never learned his name. Petey survived, but his father locked him up for a week, hoping it would teach Petey a lesson. It didn't. Petey was back to his shenanigans days after his release.

The Sheriff called Social Services when he found my mother passed out on the living room floor. She had a lethal dose of meth flowing through her bloodstream, and I was, as usual, hungry, dirty, and alone.

That was the last day I saw my mother. I watched her get placed onto a gurney and hauled away in the back of an ambulance. As far as I knew then, she died. I did not realize that she was being taken to the hospital and then to jail, where she would live for another six years before hanging herself in her cell.

As for me, I moved to the orphanage where I would live, on and off, for the next 12 years. To the best of my knowledge, my mother never asked about me or to see me. I was nothing more than a crutch to her after my father left, and I believe that she was secretly glad that I went to the orphanage. It meant that she was free of motherhood. She no longer had to worry about caring for me—not that she did when we were together.

At age six, I was old enough to know I had a mother and a father and that my father was dead, so I kept asking the nuns when my mother would come to get me—bring me home. They usually avoided my question, then one day, after being at the orphanage for almost six months, one of the nuns pulled me aside and told me that my mother was never coming for me—that she was gone. To me, that meant she was dead, not two counties over, enjoying a childless life in jail. The nun, Sister Ruth Anne, said to me that I would be getting a new family any day and that I would be happier in my new home. She could not have been more wrong.

11

By the time I was seven years old, I had already been in my first foster home, the Cattleman's, and, like every foster family after, the whole arrangement started perfectly but ended disastrously.

When I first met the Cattleman family, they seemed nice enough. The whole family came to the orphanage to pick out a new child as if they were picking a puppy from a pet store window. I was not keen on living with another family, but the nuns did not give me much choice. I had grown comfortable living at the orphanage. I had a bed, three meals daily, and plenty of time to play. I was not looking for another family, after all, my first one did not turn out so great. Unfortunately for me, the nuns were always looking for an opportunity to get rid of another one of us boys.

I remember my excitement when I saw the Cattleman's house for the first time. It looked like a mansion, but anything would look big considering where I lived before the orphanage. Their house had two floors and a carport big enough for two cars. There was a massive tree house in the backyard and a full basement. I remember thinking that I would get lost walking the halls. The home was overwhelming at first, and it took me some time to get used to having my own bedroom. Even in the orphanage, I shared a room with 19 other boys.

Life at the Cattleman's was completely different from life in the trailer park or the orphanage. Mrs. Cattleman was a stay-at-home mom to their two children, Stevie and Sandy. Stevie was 12, and Sandy was 11. Unlike my parents, the Cattleman family was too attentive, and not just to me, because I was the family's newest member. Mr. and Mrs. Cattleman were affectionate with each other. They kissed and spoke lovingly to each other. No one raised their voice. No one hit anyone. Stevie and Sandy, who could have been furious at the idea of a ready-made, temporary brother, welcomed me with open arms. We went to church on Sunday and said Grace before each meal. Every room had a bible, so we would always be close to the 'Word of the Lord,' according to Mrs. Cattleman. It was all surreal to me, but perfect to anyone looking in from the outside.

The Cattleman family was as religious as the nuns at the orphanage. And, like the orphanage, I learned over time that, as much as everyone tried to portray that everything was good, evil still lurked in the shadows. I quickly realized that nothing was what it appeared to be, which played well into how I shaped my life — how I became a chameleon.

As picturesque as the Cattleman's life appeared, it did not take me long to see the darker side of a family that portrayed itself as picture-perfect. I should have known, but back then, I was young. I was naive to pleasantries. I was used to chaos, drugs, and violence. The idea that people lived double lives or pretended to live one way only to live another behind closed doors was new to me until I moved into the orphanage and saw the two sides of the nuns. I saw the same two-sided life in the Cattlemen and many other foster families throughout my childhood.

What I did not know — what nobody knew before I moved in with the Cattleman family was that Stevie and Sandy liked to get naked and play together. On more than one occasion, I walked in on them to find Sandy with Stevie's penis in her hand. It was not long before Stevie had it in my hand, too. I didn't entirely understand what was going on. I had seen my parents and Morris play this game many times, but they were bigger than I was. They seemed excited. We were confused little kids, clueless about the problems we were creating.

Stevie never grew as big as my dad or Morris. I remember thinking that maybe they only grow big at a certain age; mine certainly did. When Stevie put himself in my mouth, I liked how it felt—like I was chewing on a gummy bear. It was not until Stevie put mine in his mouth that something changed for me. The sensation: the tingle I felt was indescribable, especially at that young age.

Stevie was the epitome of the perfect child, the perfect older brother. He helped his mother clean up dinner. He kept his room clean. He always looked out for his little sister. To the outside world, Stevie could do no wrong, so when his parents walked into my room one day to find Sandy and me naked and my tiny penis in Sandy's mouth while Stevie took pictures with his parents' Polaroid, all hell broke loose.

Mr. Cattleman picked Sandy up and handed her to Mrs. Cattleman, and the two girls left the room. Mr. Cattleman grabbed the camera out of Stevie's hands and threw it against the wall with such force that it broke into three pieces. Stevie yelled at his father, but his father shouted back louder, hitting Stevie in the face almost as hard as he yelled. Stevie cried as he spat up blood.

Mrs. Cattleman heard all the screaming and hitting from the other room and was afraid that Mr. Cattleman would kill or at least seriously hurt her little boy, so she called the police after putting Sandy in the bathtub. She wanted to scrub the evil off of her.

While Sandy played in the warm tub of bubbles, Mrs. Cattleman returned to the bedroom to try to get Mr. Cattleman to calm down and not hurt her baby boy. He would not listen. Mr. Cattleman continued to scream and try to hit Stevie, but Stevie was running around the room, trying not to get caught by his father.

I moved to a corner of the room and watched my new, temporary family fall apart. I watched Mr. Cattleman swing to punch Stevie but miss and hit his wife instead while she tried to protect her son. The punch to his wife's face broke her nose and pushed her body. She smacked her head against the metal door handle before collapsing onto the floor, motionless. Mr. Cattleman did not notice. He was too focused on catching Stevie, who was nimbly bouncing around the room to avoid his father's wrath.

Even the knocking on the front door did not distract Mr. Cattleman from his mission. He and Stevie continued their dance around the bedroom. Mrs. Cattleman was lifeless on the floor, so I stood up and walked through the house, still naked from our fun game. I opened the door and looked up at two officers. They started to ask questions, but before the first one could ask much, they heard Mr. Cattleman violently yelling. The two officers pulled out their guns and walked past me and into the house. I walked out the front door and sat on the front step of the porch. The wood felt cold against my bare bum.

When the officers reached the bedroom, they found Mr. Cattleman pinning Stevie to the floor. He finally caught Stevie, who was still naked. Mrs. Cattleman's body was on the floor, but now her head was basking in a pool of blood from the impact of the doorknob that split her skull open.

The box of Polaroid photos that Stevie had been collecting of us was tossed around the room during the fight: pictures of children in compromising positions with each other littered the room. The images included more children than just the three of us. Until that day, I had not fully comprehended the evil Stevie was capable of. No one had.

From the perspective of the officers, they caught a pedophile in the act. From out on the porch, I heard the adults yelling, and then I heard two gunshots. As Stevie later told the story, his father, still completely enraged, let go of Stevie and lunged at the police officers. They each fired their gun to protect themselves. Upon hearing the gunshots, Sandy panicked, hid under the bubbles, and accidentally drowned in the tub.

By the time Social Services arrived, the police had convinced Stevie and me to get dressed. I knew at that moment that I was going back to the orphanage. I watched my temporary family unravel before me in just a few months, just as my real family had. I was beginning to understand just how messed up people can be. It wasn't just my parents or the trailer park. Stupidity was a disease that had spread far and wide. As I got older, I would use this realization to lure my victims.

With Stevie's sister and parents dead, he had nowhere to go but to the orphanage. I was excited that Stevie would join me there and was hopeful we could continue playing our game together. We didn't.

12

Stevie ignored me at the orphanage. Initially, he blamed me for unraveling his perfect life, but he moved on. At the orphanage, Stevie made new friends, including new boys who were willing to play inappropriately with each other when the nuns were not around. Stevie and his friends were found in compromising positions on more than one occasion by the nuns, and they received quite a few lashings from those nuns in the six years he spent at the orphanage. Naively, the nuns believed they could reform Stevie — make him a better boy that God would be proud of — but they were wrong. Because Stevie was such a troubled kid — a troublemaker, he never had the benefit of being placed with a foster family. The nuns and other orphans were his only family — the orphanage was his only home until he aged out.

When I was 17, on the cusp of turning 18 and aging out of the orphanage myself, I followed Stevie to a bar on the outskirts of a town fifty miles from the orphanage. I knew that when Stevie aged out of the orphanage, he didn't move far away. Most boys didn't.

In his last year at the orphanage, Stevie began hanging out with several local kids who were not a good influence — the Clyde and Morris of Stevie's generation. By this time in my life, I was mingling with the wrong crowd of kids, too, but for me, it was about having new experiences — to see how far rules could be bent or broken without consequence. For Stevie, it was for survival — he needed friends on the 'outside' to help him once he aged out. I kept tabs on where Stevie went after he aged out, not because I was infatuated with Stevie but because I had unfinished business with him. I never forgave Stevie for ignoring me at the orphanage, and I was determined to find a way to punish him.

He often hung out at a dive bar on the north side of town. I knew Stevie would not recognize me when I walked into that bar. I had grown into my man body by then. I no longer looked like the small kid that Stevie molested years earlier. I walked past Stevie, who was busy flirting with a group of guys, none of whom seemed remotely interested in what Stevie was selling. I noticed that Stevie had grown into an awkward young man who had not taken care of himself. He looked beaten and battered.

This was not my first time at this bar, although it was my first visit to it. I had frequented the area around the bar since turning 16. I had discovered it was a great place to meet older men who liked the taste of teen skin — an easy way to make some quick cash. As I looked around the room, I noticed a few familiar faces, some smiling back at me. I could have made some money that night, but I was not there to satisfy anyone's thirst but my own.

Sitting in a booth on the wall opposite the bar, looking handsome and innocent — an act I had perfected by then, I caught Stevie's eye, who immediately ditched the group of guys, ignoring his scripted performance. Stevie slid into my booth with a couple of beers, unaware that I was underage. Stevie began telling me a series of lies about his past to sound worldly and experienced, clueless to the fact that he was talking to someone he had molested a decade earlier.

The pedophile that I knew as a child had grown into an experienced hustler. He was saying all the right words to make himself sound like the perfect man to take home. I had assumed the act sometimes worked, since it sounded so well-rehearsed, but it wasn't working on me. I knew the truth.

I let Stevie touch my knee and even run his hand through my hair. I wanted Stevie to get his whole routine out of his system. I found it too entertaining to ignore. After he had had a few more beers, I let Stevie believe that we would leave the bar together and that he would score. Excitedly, Stevie grabbed my hand and headed for the door.

We walked out of the bar and around to the backside of the building—a familiar place to me. It was dark except for a single-bulb streetlight across the parking lot. I allowed Stevie to pin me against the building, letting him feel in control. We kissed. Stevie was a lousy kisser—rushed, sloppy, and uncontrollable tongue action. It was as if he were kissing for the first time. I eventually pushed Stevie to his knees. He smiled as he started to unzip my jeans. Stevie was clumsy and awkward, so I pushed him to the ground and zipped up my pants. Stevie got angry. He stood up and charged towards me with his fist in the air as if he were going to hit me. Instead, I swung a right-handed punch, knocking Stevie to the ground. As he wiped blood from his lip, he looked up at me, cursing.

I grabbed a cinder block that was on the ground next to Stevie and told him what an asshole he had been to me when we were younger. I told him I partially blamed him for how I turned out, which I knew was not entirely true, but it sounded convincing. Stevie did not understand any of it. Even when I told him who I was, he had a look of confusion on his face. Eventually, I gave up trying to explain everything to him, and so I smashed his head in with the cinder block. It was not the first time I killed someone, but it was the last time I ever visited that bar.

13

My second foster family experience was quite different from Stevie's family. The Wheeler family was not a close-knit one. The only child, Sarah-Beth, was in college. The parents, Martha and Samuel, were older: empty-nesters looking for something or someone to fulfill their empty lives. Where Mr. and Mrs. Cattleman reeked of affection and love, the Wheelers stunk of loneliness and sadness. I honestly wanted to kill them both the first week I moved in — to put them out of their misery and out of mine.

But alas, I did not.

The Wheelers had lived an empty-nester life for almost a year before pulling me into their depressing world. Mrs. Wheeler missed her daughter — missed smothering a child with love and affection. Mr. Wheeler missed his single life. Of course, he never told me that, but I could see it in his eyes. He spent almost every waking moment in his woodshed. At first, I thought he was working, but I quickly learned it was his hideaway. The shed was heated and equipped with power, so Mr. Wheeler spent his days drinking beer and watching sports on a large television. Mrs. Wheeler yelled at and to Mr. Wheeler often — from the back porch, in the house, pretty much everywhere. They did not fight like my parents, although they were like my parents — two people who wanted to be anywhere else and with anyone else.

As much as Mrs. Wheeler loved and missed her daughter and wanted a child in the house again, I was treated more like a prisoner. Mrs. Wheeler wanted to do everything with me — spend every waking moment I was not in school with me.

My freedom was school. I was the new kid, yet again, but by now, I had become adept at socializing when needed, either to get what I wanted or to give the illusion that I cared. Soon after starting my new school, I met Emily and Jason. They weren't twins, but they could have been. Both were androgynous, and both took to me like fish to water. Maybe it was because I was the new kid in town. Perhaps it was because they had no friends of their own aside from each other. Whatever the reason, the three of us became besties, if that is the right word to use when describing our odd dynamic.

Emily and Jason were inseparable. They lived next door to each other and just a few doors down from the Wheelers. The two spent almost every waking hour together. When they pulled me into the mix, they expected me to be as committed to the bond as they were. I was not. Emily and Jason knew the Wheelers well. Sarah-Beth had been their babysitter. They liked the Wheelers, and the Wheelers liked them.

But when Mrs. Wheeler learned I made new friends so quickly, she became jealous. She would not let me go out and play with Emily and Jason as much as they wanted. Many days, the two would knock on the front door with some excitement in their breath as they begged me to come out and play. Mr. Wheeler would let Emily and Jason into the house and my room if he answered the door, but if Mrs. Wheeler answered, she always said the same thing: 'Adam cannot come out and play today.'

Three months into my stay with the Wheelers, Sarah-Beth came home from college for a long weekend. She knew her parents were fostering me, and she assumed they were happy because they had a child in the house, just as they had been when she lived there. However, Sarah-Beth was just as clueless about how unhappy her parents were. Sarah-Beth was glad to hear that I had become friends with Emily and Jason—much happier than her mother was about the news, but she warned me to be careful. She never said why. She spoke to me as if I knew something I did not, but I let it go. Then, I learned about what Emily did to Jason.

I never witnessed it, but I overheard Sarah-Beth and Mrs. Wheeler talking about the most recent incident where Emily became very jealous of Jason or mad at him for something he did or said—it was all vague. And, apparently, in her rage, Emily stabbed Jason's arm with a pocket knife before pushing him off her porch, breaking his arm. Then Emily was the first person to sign Jason's cast, and she did so with a big red heart.

*   *   *   *   *

The Wheelers had a few acres of land stretching into a forest behind their house. In the rare moments I would be alone, I explored those dark woods, killing squirrels and rabbits. Emily, Jason, and I occasionally played in those woods together—usually when Mrs. Wheeler was not home. One day, I looked out my window and saw Jason heading into the woods without Emily—without me. He was still wearing his cast, but it was covered in colorful words and graphics. It was dirty, stained, and fraying at the edges. I ran outside to follow him.

When I caught up to Jason in the woods, he was peeing on a dead squirrel I had killed a few days earlier. I stood behind a tree and watched. Jason was tall for a nine-year-old boy, and he was lanky. Before he finished peeing, I said 'hello,' startling him enough that he jumped and peed on his jeans.

I walked towards Jason, and he frantically put his little penis back in his underwear and zipped his jeans, embarrassed to have been caught in the act. He had no reason to be ashamed. I thought it was fantastic. I did it all the time. Boys love to pee outside. I remember standing so close to Jason that I could almost taste his urine—the stench permeated from his jeans. I remember asking him why he was alone. He gave me some lame answer about his independence; then he started venting about always being associated with Emily and never getting to be his own person.

I was fascinated by how much Jason ranted—trash-talking his parents, his teachers, Emily, and Mrs. Wheeler. Jason showed me a side of himself I had not seen. I saw that he was not as clean-cut and innocent as he and Emily led everyone to believe. No one ever is.

"Shut up," I remember saying. "And stop talking like that about Emily."

I don't remember having feelings for Emily like I did for Morris. Still, I remember not liking that I never had alone time with Emily; I never really got to know her. I remember thinking that Jason stood in the way of me getting closer to Emily, and as I looked at him that afternoon in the woods, I realized that I had the power to change that—to take him out, to be with Emily more.

So, almost instinctively, I picked up a baseball-sized rock with a slightly pointed edge on one side and held it in my hand. I juggled it a little so that it felt comfortable, and then when Jason looked right at me, I swung, slamming the rock into the side of his head. I had not killed a person before, so I was not sure if the impact would be as brutal as when killing a squirrel or rabbit.

The rock cut through Jason's skin, lodging in his frontal lobe. Seeing all the blood ooze out reminded me of the day Chester bit off the little girl's arm. I was older now and still liked the feeling I got from seeing all the blood, from watching someone die.

Jason stood before me for the longest time. His eyes were swirling around in their sockets as if his brain was slow to register what had just happened and even slower to relay the damage report to the rest of his body. All the colors vanished from his skin, and as the river of red ran down his face, he finally tried to reach out to me or punch me; I will never know. I knew it was a delayed brain reaction. He barely got his arm to move before his body gave out, and he fell to the ground. Just before he started to tip over, I leaned in and kissed him on the lips; they were softer than I expected. When Jason's small body fell to the ground, his head crashed onto a pile of smaller rocks, cracking more of his skull. I watched as the ground around his limp body soaked up all the blood oozing out of him.

Quite unexpectedly, there was an intense sensation and explosion in my white briefs as Jason's body hit the ground. At that time, I did not understand what had happened to me—why my body reacted in that way. All I knew was that I liked that feeling. I stood above Jason, enjoying the wetness in my underwear for a few moments before I turned around and walked away, thinking that I would have Emily all to myself.

*   *   *   *   *

The following two weeks were chaotic. First, Jason was reported missing, then kidnapped, and eventually, his body was discovered in the woods. No one ever solved the mystery of what happened or who killed Jason. A few people were arrested, but no one was ever charged with Jason's death.

Everything was different after Jason's funeral. Emily was different—distant. I know she did not assume I had anything to do with Jason's death, but she looked at me differently. Emily looked through me as if I were invisible. She had never really wanted to be my friend—she had been because of Jason. I remember thinking how much that bothered me and how mad it made me feel—to be so quickly rejected by someone I thought was a friend. Luckily for Emily, I was gone before I could punish her.

The disruption to our otherwise quiet neighborhood—the police, the news reporters, the rumors, and the funeral—was too much for Mrs. Wheeler. She cried to Mr. Wheeler for weeks, and the next thing I knew, I was back at the orphanage. I remember overhearing Mr. Wheeler tell one of the nuns about Jason's gruesome death and that his wife was afraid that a serial killer was on the loose—by returning me, they were trying to protect me. What they could not know was that a serial killer was in the making.

14

I thought about Emily for weeks after the Wheelers dumped me back at the orphanage. I remember being mad, not necessarily because I wanted to stay with the Wheelers, but because I wanted to spend more time with Emily, especially with Jason out of the way.

Years later, when I was on the cusp of becoming a teenager, my body began to take on a new shape; my voice changed. I had not been fostered during those years, so I finally experienced some consistency in school, where I thrived academically.

Middle school was different. The kids were ruthless. Almost everyone was labeled, and groups were formed. There was a group for the Jocks and one for the Nerds and Theatre Geeks. There was even a group for the gay kids. What there was not was a group of awkward, loner boys who liked to kill things — kill people.

I had not killed anyone other than Jason by that point in my life, but I never forgot that feeling — total euphoria. I had not found another person worth killing. Even with the animals I killed, there was a purpose — a reason. In middle school, even though everyone was a prick, no one stood out to me — threatened my space in a way that had me think that they needed to die. That all changed when I met Susie and Rob.

Susie Chu was the first girl I can recall ever having a crush on. Emily was more of a fascination — a curiosity, but something about Susie intrigued me from the very start. She did not look like all the other kids, and she always smelled like vanilla and roses with a hint of lavender. I don't think it was perfume. I think that was just how she smelled. You could smell her coming around the corner. It was one of those smells that just stuck with you—something I could never forget, like the smell of Morris.

I was hurt when I heard that Susie was dating Rob Long, the captain of the middle school Football, Hockey, and track teams. Not in the 'oh my god, I think I will just die' kind of hurt, but more in the 'why him and not me?' kind of way. I mean, I get why she would want to date Rob. He was the all-American jock. He had good looks, he was athletic, and his family had money. Who wouldn't want to date Rob?

However, I did not believe Susie should have dated Rob, and I certainly did not think he deserved someone as wonderful as Susie. But they were in love, so she said. Susie talked about growing old together with Rob and possibly even getting married. We were in middle school. Who talks like that in middle school with any amount of seriousness? Susie did.

The more I saw them together, the angrier I became. I don't think I loved Susie. Maybe I did. It was one-sided love, if it existed at all, but that did not change the fact that I did not like the two dating. So, one day, I took a leap—stepped way out of my comfort zone and told Susie how I felt.

*   *   *   *   *

"Do you love him?" I asked. "Are we even old enough to know what love is?

"Of course I do," Susie said, smiling. "I think."

"Well, I like you," I said. "Like, like like you. And if you are unsure if you love Rob, you should stop dating him and be with me."

*　　*　　*　　*　　*

It all sounded so logical in my head, but as our conversation ended and Susie walked away without saying she liked me the same way I liked her, I felt rejected. I knew there was only one thing left for me to do: kill Rob. I knew that taking Jason out of the picture didn't bring me closer to Emily, but in my mind, this was different. Taking out Rob would make Susie run into my arms—pull me into her heart.

It was the first time I thought about killing someone. When I killed Jason years earlier, it was in the heat of the moment. I had not gone to the woods to kill him. It was just what I did once I was alone with him. But with Rob, it was different. I found myself thinking about all the ways I could kill him and not get caught.

I spent weeks watching Rob, following him from afar. I took mental notes of his schedule and discovered that he had a fairly routine schedule. In the years after, when I studied other victims, I found the same thing: Humans are predictable. We fall into a routine that brings us comfort, and we stick with it. Sure, there are variances, but for the most part, humans are not complex creatures. This discovery served me well for many years.

Rob enjoyed walking to and from school. He did not live far from the campus, and I noticed he walked the same path every day, usually alone. So, one day, after school, I followed him, expecting to watch him go home. Instead, he turned down an alley, going off course. I followed only to discover him waiting for me once I entered the same alley.

He looked right into my eyes and smiled when I noticed him. He had that look I have had many times over the years when my victim was right where I wanted them. Rob did not say anything. He stood there waiting for me to say something or freak out and run, but I did not. I just continued walking down the alley —our eyes locked on one another. I walked straight towards him with the confidence of a lion attacking its prey.

Once I was within reaching distance, Rob grabbed both of my shoulders, spun me around, and pinned me against one of the buildings. Our faces were within inches of each other—I could taste his breath. I remember he held me in that position for longer than I expected. For the longest time, he said nothing. He stared at me as if trying to read my mind or freak me out. His intimidation tactics were weak. I stared back at him, never blinking.

Then, entirely unexpectedly, Rob leaned in closer and kissed me. It was not a quick peck, either. He went in hard, and while I pretended to resist to make him work harder, I eventually pushed my tongue into his mouth. That must have freaked him out because he stopped immediately and pulled back. He let me go and stepped back a few feet as if a cobra had just bitten him. I stayed silent, watching Rob self-analyze his actions.

"Say something!" he yelled as if my words were the Holy Grail that would make his actions acceptable. I said nothing. I was not about to tell him that what he did was okay. After all, I had been following him to kill him so that I could be with Susie.

After a few more minutes of silence, Rob pulled a gun out of the back of his pants. I was surprised and wondered how often he carried a gun. As he held it, I thought about my dad and how awkward he looked holding a gun. Rob looked the same. It looked like a squirt gun, but I knew it was a real one.

Rob pointed the gun at me. The barrel was so close to my head that I could see the sweat oozing down his fist as he tightly held the grip.

"Say something!" he yelled again. I stood silent, staring back at him, unnerved by the nervous teen before me. I remember being surprised at how calm I felt at that moment. I had a gun pointed at my face at close range.

"What do you want me to say?" I finally asked Rob. He was becoming more upset about the kiss and the whole scenario. "You pinned me down. You kissed me. I am the victim here."

"Faggots" someone yelled from the end of the alley. A group of boys had been watching us the entire time. "You gonna kiss him again, you fag?"

Rob turned and fired the gun three times in the direction of the boys. I watched one of them fall to the ground. The others scattered. Then Rob turned towards me again and pointed the gun back at my head.

"I like you," Rob replied. "Like, really like you."

Then Rob pointed the gun at himself and pulled the trigger again. He collapsed, and his blood splattered all over me. I remember standing there for a few more seconds, taking in everything that had just happened. I was supposed to kill Rob that day. He was not supposed to kill himself.

I licked some blood that was dripping down my face and smiled before running away. I was not about to be caught and blamed for something I had not done. I remember cleaning myself up in a gas station bathroom before returning to the orphanage and getting an earful from the nuns for missing dinner. I was angry with Rob for taking away my fun.

15

I never forgot the hug Morris and I shared the morning of my sixth birthday. It was the only real present I received that day, and it was the last time I saw Morris for almost a decade.

*   *   *   *   *

The bullet that grazed Morris' arm was not the only time Morris had a close call with death, not that he was in any real danger of dying from that flesh wound. But that morning was a wake-up call for Morris, and when he ran out of the trailer, jumped on his BMX bike, and pedaled into the distance, he thought about his life and what he needed to change.

Morris was the youngest of six children, all of whom were significantly older than he. His drug-addicted mother gave birth to Morris when she was in her mid-40s, and Morris did not share a dad with his other five siblings. Three different dads had once called Morris' mom their wife or girlfriend. All three dads were gone now — dead, not that they were around much when they were alive.

Although he was gone before Morris was a teenager, Morris remembers his father — he remembers the drunk who would hit him at every possible opportunity, who would beat him with a belt until he bled. Morris remembers the man who punched him in the face on his 10th birthday when Morris yelled at his mother because she dropped cigarette ash all over his birthday cake while trying to light the candles. The only real gift his dad gave Morris that year was a broken nose.

Morris resented his mother for allowing his father—her boyfriend—to beat him. Truth be told, Morris' mother was more afraid of her boyfriend than Morris was. She tried defending Morris when he was young, but her efforts were futile. Morris' dad would beat Morris' mother anytime she interfered with Morris getting a beating. Morris' only salvation was his friendship with Clyde.

Morris met Clyde when they were both in elementary school. Morris and his parents moved into the same trailer park where Clyde's family lived, and the two boys became inseparable almost immediately. Morris' dad would tease and hit Morris—call him a 'sissy' and 'fag' because Morris and Clyde spent so much time together, but that was not what their relationship was about. Morris and Clyde loved each other as much as any two guy friends could love one another without being sexual. Morris's dad never grasped that level of modern thinking and had never formed a bond with a male friend himself.

Neither Morris nor Clyde cared for school much by the time they were in middle school, and once in high school, they skipped more classes than they attended. Morris was book-smart—he read a lot. Clyde was not, but he was more street-smart. Together, they made a great team, so it seemed natural for them to start selling drugs together as they entered high school. Clyde's cousin introduced the boys to the world of sex and drugs. They began as mules and quickly rose to distribution.

Clyde had the connections. He had a vast family network, so Clyde was welcomed with open arms everywhere the boys went.

But it was Morris who did the talking—the selling. He was the outgoing, attractive teen people wanted to know, wanted to buy from, and wanted to have sex with. Clyde was the sidekick.

Morris became a great hustler at a young age and enjoyed it. He liked the attention. He wanted the money. He loved the sex. It did not matter to Morris, man or woman, old or young. As long as he got paid, he would do almost anything with almost anyone. And along the way, he sold a lot of drugs. But with this high-on-life lifestyle came consequences. On multiple occasions, Morris had to call his mother to bail him out of jail with money she did not have. More times than he would like to admit, Morris found himself sitting in the E.R. waiting for someone to explain the latest STD running through his body, weakening him, his business.

Eventually, Morris met Lori and Finn. He met Lori first. She was hanging laundry to dry when Morris and Clyde arrived at her trailer park to make deliveries. Morris flirted first, but Lori flirted more. She wanted what Morris was selling and was ready for anything other than Finn.

Lori was a loyal customer—paying her debts with sex more than cash, which at times landed Morris in trouble with his 'boss,' but Morris made up the cash difference in other ways—with other customers. Morris thought Lori was the prettiest girl around. Adam was almost a year old when Morris and Lori first slept together. He was unfazed by the baby in the next room, apparently watching the pretend adults have sex.

Morris did not know about Finn immediately—he didn't know that Lori had a husband. He assumed the baby daddy was gone, like so many in that area. When delivering to a customer in the Lowbridge Motel, Morris ran into Finn, physically colliding with each other. Finn caught Morris from falling backward as the two bodies crashed. Finn held Morris for a few moments, and then Morris pulled himself closer to Finn. Without thinking, he kissed Finn, then pushed himself back and apologized.

Finn pulled Morris closer again and kissed him back. It was the first time Finn kissed a guy, and it felt natural. Morris was the only guy Finn ever kissed — the only guy he ever had sex with, and that first kiss led to many days and nights when Clyde could not find Morris — no one could because Morris and Finn were hiding out at a different motel, enjoying each other.

*   *   *   *   *

As Morris stood in his living room, still bleeding from his flesh wound, he looked at his mother and knew he was ready for a change, so he ran to his room, gathered what few drugs were left in the trailer, and flushed them down the toilet. He was done with this lifestyle, and he knew he would be in trouble for destroying the drugs, but he did not care. He stuffed as much clothing as possible into a backpack and walked out the door.

"Good-bye, ma," he said to his sleeping mother as he walked out the door, knowing she did not hear his words.

He never kissed his mother goodbye, woke her up to tell her he was leaving, or even tried to find his best friend, Clyde, to share the news or invite him on a new adventure. Morris needed to do this alone.

Minutes later, Morris found himself standing on the side of the road. He looked left and then right. Not a car in sight. He was about to take his first step when a car appeared on the horizon.

Morris turned and extended his thumb. He thought that if the vehicle stopped, he would be heading left, moving West.

Morris spent the next ten years in upstate New York working on a farm. He kept to himself, not making any new friends. He was focused on cleaning up his life—staying clean. He enjoyed the farm life. He worked long days. The farmer and his wife took Morris in, giving him food and shelter in exchange for his work on the farm. They became his new family.

His new life was going well. He felt refreshed, reinvigorated, and happy for the first time in a long time. Then, his mother died of an overdose. Morris had not spoken with his mother since he left Vermont, but one morning, he woke from a bad dream and was compelled to call his mother. When he did, his aunt, his mother's only sister, answered the phone. She cried the news through the phone, and Morris was on the next bus back to Vermont.

16

By the time I turned 14, I no longer looked like a little kid. I had grown up—I matured faster than others. While the boys in the orphanage wanted to run into the woods and smoke or drink or wank together, I wanted to hone my killing skills. After Rob killed himself in front of me, I felt cheated. He was supposed to die by my hand, not his own, and out of frustration, I later killed two random people. It was the first time I killed blindly—not knowing my victims. I did not like it at first. It felt so impersonal, but rage had built up inside me, and it needed to be set free at any cost.

I had been walking in the park across from the high school when I heard two girls walking behind me. They were giggling about something I didn't know, but they seemed happy and distracted. I recall saying hello to them as they walked past, but they ignored me. Without thinking, I pulled out my pocket knife and quickly stabbed them both in the back. By the time they both hit the ground, I had stabbed each of them about 15 times.

I stabbed the one on the right, then the one on the left. Then back and forth, equally distributing my anger and their pain. Blood fired back at me, but I did not mind. I enjoyed it. I only got a few stabs in each before they turned around to face me, at which point I grabbed one by the hair and pulled her down to the ground while I continued to stab the other. Once the second fell to the ground, I resumed stabbing the first. One died quickly—bled out all over the ground. The second put up a bit of a fight—she was thicker than the

91

other. Eventually, I grew bored, and I jammed the knife into her neck. When I pulled the knife out, I knelt close to her so I could be showered red as she fell to the ground. Then I calmly stood up and walked away as if nothing had happened, like it was any other day.

I was in the wooded part of the park by the time I heard screams over what I assumed to be the pile of red-stained white flesh in mini-shirts that lay on the path. I could no longer see my creation, but I sat and enjoyed the cries of people attempting to save the dead. I listened as the police arrived, and then I left. No one saw me kill the two girls, and I later read in the newspaper that they were two cheerleaders from that high school — the very high school I was slated to attend a month later.

I never got to walk those halls. A week after I killed those girls, the Robinson family arrived at the orphanage. At first, I thought the Sheriff was there to arrest me — maybe someone saw me murder those girls in broad daylight after all. Thankfully, I was wrong. The Robinsons wanted to foster me — possibly adopt me.

*   *   *   *   *

The Sheriff and Mrs. Robinson wanted another child, and after a few miscarriages, they decided adoption was the best option. They already had one son, but he was in his 20s and no longer living with them. The Robinsons wanted another young son to give Mrs. Robinson a do-over. From a very young age, their adult son disappointed the Sheriff and Mrs. Robinson. When anyone asked about their son, the Robinsons had very few kind words to say about their only child. Fostering, or adopting a new son, was supposed to be their chance to do it right—to be better parents. It did not work out so well.

*   *   *   *   *

A few weeks after I moved in with the Robinsons, the three of us were enjoying a family dinner when their adult son walked through the front door. I had no idea what their son looked like or what he did. There were no photos of him around the house, and they never spoke about him to me. It was as if the kid never existed. But when he walked into the dining room that night, I almost dropped my fork. Standing across the room from me was Petey, the asshole who fucked with my mother after Morris vanished. I couldn't believe my eyes, and I couldn't believe my luck. He had treated me and my mother like shit, and now here he was, older, dumber, and still a pain in the ass. Even his parents didn't like him. I could not believe that the people fostering me were the parents of one of the people I wanted to kill.

Of course, Petey did not recognize me. I had grown into my young adult body. Few people from that trailer park would recognize me. They might remember my name or my parents' story, but they would not know the grown person I had become—the devil in sheep's clothing.

Petey stood in the dining room. He ignored me while he and his father argued about money or responsibility—something Petey did wrong or was looking to his parents to fix. The details are vague, but watching Petey struggle to beat his father in their verbal fight was entertaining. The sheriff was bigger and louder. Petey eventually accepted defeat and walked out of the dining room and into what he remembered as his room, but had become mine.

* * * * *

"What the fuck?" we all heard Petey yell. "What happened to all my stuff?"

"It's all boxed up and in the shed," the Sheriff yelled back, still trying to eat his dinner.

"Who the fuck do you think you are?" Petey yelled, standing back at the dining room door. "That is my stuff. You have no right to touch it."

The sheriff stood up, towering over his son, and pointed to the front door. "Get out of my house before I pick your sorry ass up and throw you through the front window, you fucking prick."

"Stop all the cussing." Mrs. Robinson screamed as she walked back into the room. "I am tired of all this yelling.

"You broke my heart one too many times, Peter," she said quietly to her biological son. "I cannot take it anymore. Please leave and do not return until you have cleaned yourself up and gotten your life together. You are too old to behave like this anymore."

* * * * *

I remember the look on Petey's face. He had no remorse for his behavior. Instead, he just looked at me as if I were the one to blame for everything that had unfolded. His behavior outside our trailer all those years ago got him shot and jailed, and now his same childish tyrant was getting him kicked out of his own home, with me being his replacement. Petey left, but not without throwing a few things — breaking some of his mother's trinkets on his way out the door.

That was not the last time we saw Petey. He came back a few more times when his father was not around. He tried repeatedly to win his mother over — to convince her that he had changed. She knew he was lying. She remained steadfast and strong-willed, but you could tell it was killing her on the inside. She would not cave to her only son's plea for help. She knew he was nothing more than a Siren who would lead her back to disappointment. Eventually, Petey stopped coming around. Months later, after the Robinson house felt calmer and more stable, Petey made one more visit.

The sheriff was working late that night. Mrs. Robinson and I had just finished dinner. For giggles, I laced her wine with a pile of crushed-up sleeping pills I found in her bathroom one day while snooping around. I thought it would be fun to knock her out, maybe even torture her a little, without her understanding what had happened. She drank more than expected that night and never got up from the dining room table. One minute, she was talking, and the next minute, her head went down, smashing into her dinner plate. She cracked the dinner plate and knocked her wine glass over, spilling what remained all across the table and onto the floor. I thought about tying her hands behind her while she sat in the chair, maybe even tying her upright so I could have some fun, but I never got the chance. My fun was interrupted by a loud bang.

Petey smashed through the front door with a sledgehammer, taking it off the lower hinge. Before he reached the dining room, I ran into the kitchen and around the house so Petey wouldn't see me when he walked in, and found his mother slumped over in the dining room.

I heard him yelling at his mother, who remained silent, her face still swimming in pasta sauce. That was when Petey should have shown remorse—the minute he should have called 9-1-1 and saved his mother. Instead, he went towards her bedroom to look for money. I knew long ago that Petey should die, and that night was my chance.

I grabbed a broom from the kitchen and walked towards Mrs. Robinson's bedroom. I could hear Petey making a lot of noise, making a mess of his parents' room. I stood in the doorway and watched him ransack the room. With his back to me, I could see a gun in the back of his pants.

"Whatcha doin'?" I asked calmly.

"Who the fuck do you think you are?" Petey yelled as he stood up, spun around, and pulled the gun out of the back of his pants. He pointed it at me and started crying—ranting about everything and nothing simultaneously. I could tell that he was high —pretty fucked up, really. His words were slurred, and his sentences made almost no sense—rambling sounds. I remember thinking that killing him would be too easy, and at the same time, a blessing to everyone he had been an asshole to over the years.

Petey got very close to me, still pointing the gun at me. I could have grabbed the gun out of his hands, but I did not. I knew enough not to touch it. I stood there, eye to eye—I was not the little boy he yelled at all those years ago. Before Petey could pull the trigger, if he ever were going to, I swung the broom handle up off the floor and into his crotch with great force. He dropped the gun and grabbed his crotch as he fell to the floor.

I stood above Petey, contemplating how to embarrass him. He was rolling around, screaming at me—cussing at me through his pain.

"My balls!" Petey yelled. "What the fuck do you think you are doing? I am going to fucking kill you, you little prick."

I said nothing.

I knew he would be upright again soon, so I kicked his gun into the hall and grabbed a belt I saw on the dresser closest to me. I thought about strangling Petey right then as he lay on the floor, but that seemed like an easy out for him. Instead, I pulled his arms behind his back and wrapped his wrists with the belt. It was not a super secure way to hold him, but he felt trapped enough to stop struggling.

I helped Petey stand up and walked him into the dining room, where I sat him in a chair close to his mother. Once in the chair, I removed the belt from his wrists, put it around his neck, and pulled it tight until he passed out—his head hit the table.

I felt invincible at that moment. For the first time, I was able to subdue two adults, but since I had done very little killing up to that point in my life, I was not sure what I wanted to do next—how I wanted to kill them.

Using Petey's gun would have been an easy way, but it would have been too loud, and I don't like guns. I don't like how quickly and cleanly they take a life. I wanted blood—and I love a slow death. I always have, so the more blood I can see, touch, and taste, the better.

Without overthinking it all, I went into the kitchen, grabbed a butcher's knife, and put it through the back of Mrs. Robinson's neck. Not realizing my strength or the length of the knife, the blade went through her neck and out the front. Blood oozed all over her back and the table; it was a glorious sight. While deciding what to do with Petey, I heard Sheriff Robinson's car pull into the garage.

I ran back to the hall, grabbed Petey's gun with a hand towel, and quickly returned to the dining room. When Sheriff Robinson walked into the dining room, I pulled the trigger three times — one bullet entered his skull, and the other two went into his chest. I did not know what I was doing. I hated guns, as I have said before, and I had never fired one, let alone held one, before. I did not like it.

The Sheriff fell to the floor before he could reach for his gun. I knew the loud noise would alert neighbors, so I placed the weapon in Petey's hand, pointed it at his skull, and pulled the trigger one last time, in an attempt to make it look like Petey killed his parents and then killed himself. I liked the blood splatter everywhere, but I did not like using the gun. It felt too easy and impersonal, but I had no choice. If Sheriff Robinson had not come home, I might have had more time to have fun with Petey — to kill him the way I like to kill people — slowly.

I went into the main bedroom and called 9-1-1 and told them that I heard shots and that I was hiding in my parents' room. I did not need to complicate the story for the 9-1-1 operator. It was a small enough town — they knew I was calling from the Sheriff's home. They knew that the Robinsons were fostering a 'lost' child, and they all knew what a pain in the ass Petey had been to his parents through the years.

I staged such a beautiful scene that no one ever questioned my involvement. However, it did mean that I was sent back to the orphanage. I was not destined to have a full-time family. I am sharing this level of detail with you now so that the police will know it was me all those years ago. I never wanted the attention or the fame, but as I tell this story now, as I fear my life is going to end soon, I feel compelled to come clean — to admit to all of my crimes.

17

The Robinsons were the last family to foster me. Most families do not want to foster or adopt a teenager, certainly not one so close to becoming an adult, so close to aging out of the system and being on their own. So, I spent my final years in the system before becoming a free man, finally on my own for good. This meant more time with the nuns and more time with idiot orphans asking stupid questions about random shit all the time. It meant being a big brother to the younger orphans who needed help. I did not volunteer my services—no, that would be too easy. The nuns always made the older kids look out for and help the younger kids, and there was never a shortage of kids flowing into the system, needing guidance. I was supposed to get the same sort of guidance when I arrived, and I am sure that I did, but I ignored it. I kept to myself, hoping no one came running toward me, trying to include me in anything, to try and fix me.

I hated high school. I found it boring—too structured and repetitive, and I knew all the answers to all the questions. I learned more than the teachers—for as fucked up as people might think I am today, I was a smart kid back then. The problem was that what I wanted to learn was not something they were teaching in school— there were no classes on how to murder. I learned about the human body in Biology and the dangers of various chemicals in Chemistry, but those courses only sparked my interest to a certain extent. So, to fill my time back then, I often skipped school. I forged nuns' signatures on notes so the school would not call the orphanage looking for me. I was pretty good—still am good at forgery, among many other misdeeds.

On those days when I would skip class, I would go around town watching people—looking for loners, anyone who could be an easy target. All I wanted to do in that chapter of my life was to kill —to take a life. It was around that time that I met Lucas. He was a senior and often skipped class, too. We met when he found me hiding in the bed of his pickup truck one day: To avoid the campus officer making his rounds, I jumped in the back and hid, but Lucas was also leaving campus thanks to a fake note from his mother. He was good at forgery, too.

Lucas was cute and rugged. He pulled off the aloof, stoner farmboy look in his tight-fitting jeans, flannel shirts, puffer vest, and cowboy boots. It was a look that lured me in, and I found his aloofness attractive. Lucas did not necessarily like people. He wanted to be alone, so it surprised me when he took me under his wing; he made me his buddy. We both took a shine to each other, and we spent a lot of time together—much more than I had anticipated back then.

It was Lucas who introduced me to the world of drugs and hustling. I knew about drugs—I grew up surrounded by them. Drugs were the reason Morris had been in my life. But before hanging out with Lucas, I did not comprehend the plethora of drugs available and the effects they had on a person, but I thought I knew enough. Lucas taught me so much more. Thanks to Lucas, I experimented with acid, mushrooms, cocaine, pot, heroin—you name it. Lucas had access to it all, and I really liked that he stayed in control when he got high. He did not abuse or overuse the way Clyde had.

Don't get me wrong, Lucas loved taking drugs. We got high a lot—always experimenting with some new cocktail. He said it was so that we knew what we were selling, which made sense at the time. I realize today that it was just an excuse to get high. We were kids and did not know any better. Through it all, Lucas taught me a valuable lesson about the use and abuse of power. We never abused our drug use. We had fun, but we never went so far that we could not stay focused on making money. We both wanted out of Vermont—desperately. That was a lesson I cherished—learning control. I have Lucas to thank for that skill, and I learned a lot about control when it came to my victims, but through the years, I have had some trouble with keeping my drug use in control. Some drugs are just so good that I could kill for another hit, and that is when I realized I lost control of my drug use. Honestly, I am surprised to be here to tell this story. I went through a few years of horrible drug use. I am not sure how I still managed to kill without being caught when I was so high.

Hustling, on the other hand, was something I loved. I was amazed at how much money people would pay me to have sex or even get naked and let them look at me or touch me. Sometimes, I didn't even have to do anything but lie still while my client fulfilled their sexual desire. It was ridiculous, easy money. Many guys liked to suck my toes while they stroked themselves until they exploded. I will admit that it made me explode, too, a few times, but it was crazy to learn about the shit people would do, and how much they would pay me in the process.

Sometimes, I would be the third for a guy and his girlfriend, looking for some excitement in their relationship. Those experiences taught me how to satisfy both men and women in ways I had not known were possible—I was barely 17 years old at the time. What I found most astonishing about the early days of hustling was how little people seemed to care that they were violating or being violated by a minor. Maybe they did not know. I certainly looked mature enough, and no one ever asked for identification, but looking back at it all now, I realize that those people, and even I, could have gone to prison.

It was the money that I made dealing drugs and hustling for a couple of years that helped me get out of Vermont after I aged out of the orphanage. If it were not for that money and Lucas, I might never have left Vermont or the Burlington area, but I am getting ahead of myself.

One day during the summer after Lucas graduated high school, he and I were making some deliveries when he told me two things: he was finally leaving Vermont, and he loved me. We had been friends for almost six months by then, and he taught me a great deal about life during that time. We made dozens, if not hundreds, of drug drops all around northern Vermont. We spent a lot of time together. He was like the older brother I never had, so I was surprised to hear those words come out of his mouth—the ones about loving me. I was not surprised that he was leaving Vermont. We both talked about that dream—our shared dream, a lot. As for the loving me part, Lucas did not make a big deal about it—the words just fell out of his mouth like he was talking about the weather. I was not sure what to make of it all. I remember us driving in silence for a little while afterward, and then, for giggles, I said the words back to him. He smiled and reached over to hold my hand—something he had never done before that moment, and never did again.

Our last stop that day was at a house party, and Lucas suggested that we hang out there. It might have been his way to avoid being alone so soon after telling me how he felt about me, but I did not get to ask him—we never had the chance to talk about it again. The house party was packed with dozens of people of all ages. We were the farthest I had ever been from the orphanage, so I did not recognize anyone at first. After a while, though, I started to notice different drug and hustling clients. It was almost like a reunion—a bad trip down memory lane. Many of the tricks I had hoped never to see again were at the party, and looking at me through drug-laced eyes as though they were going to have sex with me again. I remember holding Lucas' hand tightly. I cannot recall if he grabbed mine or I grabbed his, but he held tight, too, until he didn't.

Lucas dropped me off in one of the bedrooms on the second floor and told me to wait for him. He had to take care of some "unfinished business." Surprisingly, I listened—I was, after all, still the student, and he the teacher of life. I sat on the unmade bed and looked at the filth around me. I remember wondering if the entire house was as messy as that room. The bedroom door finally opened after what seemed like a really long time. I am sure I said something snarky, thinking Lucas was coming to retrieve me. It wasn't—Lucas. Instead, the man who stood at the door was Morris. To complicate things further, it was his room that I was sitting in—his bed. I had not seen Morris in over a decade, and he still looked as dreamy as he did when I was four. I stared in awe—in shock.

Morris did not recognize me; if he did, he played dumb. He aged well. He looked fantastic, but tired. We shared a lot of small talk about why I was in his room and how the party wasn't his. He was renting out the room and did not really know the owners. He was not planning to be in town for much longer, and I recall him explaining why he felt the need to justify himself. Like me and Lucas, it turns out he had plans for a life outside of Vermont. He had one and was trying to get back to it.

*　*　*　*　*

"There you are, babe," I heard Lucas say as he opened the bedroom door almost an hour later to find Morris and me sitting on the bed talking. "I have been looking all over for you."

"You left me here," I said.

"I told you I would be in my room," Morris said, almost over my words. "But look who I found in here." Morris pointed to me as if I were a door prize.

"Yes, I left him in here," Lucas replied. "He is my gift to you. Happy Birthday."

"Gift?" I asked.

"You are so sweet," Morris said, again over my words, as he leapt off the bed to hug and kiss Lucas.

"What the fuck is going on here?" I yelled. The two stopped kissing and turned to look at me. Finally, my words were heard.

"Sorry, Adam," Lucas said to me. "This is my dear friend, my mentor, Morris. He has been back in town for a little while, and I thought it would be fun if the three of us hung out and maybe played together."

"Played together?" I asked. I suddenly felt like that six-year-old boy, clueless about what was happening around me.

"Yeah. I've taught you how to be a great hustler, so I thought it would be fun if you and I had some fun with Morris before he left town again."

"Are you tricking me out to your friend?" I asked, furious at the idea that Lucas would treat me like that after telling me that he loved me, while excited at the thought of finally having a chance to be with Morris—something I had dreamt about for more than a decade.

"Don't think of it as tricking," Lucas started to justify his words. "Think of it as three dudes exploring each other's bodies."

*   *   *   *   *

I am pretty sure that Morris had no idea I was only 17 years old at the time. I am not even sure he was excited at the idea of me being in the room, of having to share Lucas with me. He seemed to be very focused on Lucas, which quickly irritated me. Lucas and I were not dating—hell, Lucas just told me hours earlier that he loved me. Maybe I read that wrong. Perhaps he liked me, but didn't truly love me. I was still learning to read people, so perhaps I had misread Lucas.

Lucas took off his shirt, displaying his many tattoos—a heart with his 'mom' written in it, a shamrock, a butterfly, some tribal pattern, and the word 'love' written in cursive over his heart. It was an odd collection, and I knew that if we had more time together, I would have learned what each meant, but that never happened.

Then, unprovoked, Lucas punched me in the chest. It was not a hard punch, but he was clearly trying to show dominance over me — to show me and Morris that he was the alpha dog. I did not flinch. I remember Morris being impressed that I could take the punch, but before Morris could commend me, I swung back at Lucas, knocking him to the floor.

Morris jumped up from the bed and grabbed me as if he thought I was going to attack Lucas after the punch. I wasn't. I just wanted to let him know that he could not push me around, even if he thought he was playing. I pushed Morris off of me and punched him in the stomach. He fell to the floor, too.

Lucas held his jaw as he stood up, surprised at the strength of my punch.

"I was only kidding about the tricking," he said, coughing. We were having a little fun and hoping to have a lot more fun if you are interested. You can leave, if you want."

Of course, I was not going to leave. I had not been this close to Morris in a long time. He smelt a little differently — older and cleaner — but I was still hoping to get a taste of him.

"What do you mean, kidding?" Morris said, laughing. "He'd better be staying." Then he stood up and grabbed me, pulling me closer to him. I will admit I was enjoying the attention. Two good-looking guys, both wanting to touch me — to taste my underage juice.

"Of course I will stay," I told them as I pulled at Morris' belt. "But I like it a little kinky. I hope that is okay."

The two smiled worryingly as they quickly removed their clothes. Morris was closest to me, so I used his belt to tie his wrists behind his back and sat him on the edge of the bed. Once Lucas was naked, I did the same to him with his belt. I stepped back and looked at the two hustlers sitting side by side in their birthday suits. Both had stunning bodies — the right balance of fat and muscle — but I was more fit than either of them.

I took Lucas' t-shirt, stuffed part of it into his mouth, wrapped it around his head, and tied it in the back — a make-shift gag. His eyes looked back at me with trepidation.

"Don't worry, everything will be okay," I assured him with a lie and a smile.

Then, I put Lucas's boxers over his head so he could not see what was happening around him. I did not completely cover his head. He tried to resist, but I grabbed his shoulders and reassured him again that it was all okay. Morris watched me closely, probably worried I would do the same to him. Neither of them knew what they had gotten themselves into.

I grabbed Lucas' pants from the floor and fumbled through the pockets until I found the bag of cocaine he told me about earlier. I wet my finger and stuffed it in the bag, coating it like a chicken tender about to be deep-fried, and then I shoved my finger up Lucas's nose. He happily inhaled the powder, his nose hairs licking my finger clean.

I then poured more of the cocaine on the back of my hand and put it up to Morris's nose. He was very hesitant to sniff it in. I did not know it, but he had been trying to stay clean on some self-proclaimed program, and he knew the spiral he would fall into if he inhaled. With my free hand, I grabbed his balls and squeezed them tightly. Morris flinched, then reluctantly vacuumed the white powder through his perfect little nostril.

I wanted both boys on the brink of overdosing, so I gave them both a few more lines of cocaine. When I could see in Morris's eyes that he was well on his way to heaven, I knew Lucas was, too. I wanted them both to feel so happy, so at peace—so numb. That is when I took out my pocket knife and quickly stabbed Lucas in the neck. As I pulled the knife out, blood ejaculated all over Morris and me. It was so exciting to me, but Morris was petrified. I remember laughing as I smeared the blood on Morris' face, shoulder, and chest. Lucas eventually fell off the bed and onto the floor, where he bled out. I was never going to know if he really loved me, but that was okay. He was not my focus—never was my focus. Morris was the one I always wanted.

Morris tried to get up and run, but I pushed him back onto the bed. He was no longer saluting—any excitement he felt earlier had gone limp. You could see in his drug-laced eyes that he was afraid for his life—afraid of me.

"Please don't hurt me," Morris begged as tears rolled down his face, swirling with Lucas' blood.

"You don't remember me, do you?" I asked calmly.

Morris shook his head, no.

"Do you remember a girl named Lori?" I asked, a little hurt.

Morris shook his head no again.

"Seriously?" I asked, getting annoyed with Morris. "What about Finn?"

Morris shook his head no, yet again, and that pissed me off. I spent the better part of a decade remembering his smell, his smile —everything about him, thinking, no, hoping that he remembered us—remembered me. All the love or lust that I felt I had had for

Morris up to that point in my life vanished as if a spell had been broken—I had been set free.

I held the bloody knife close to Morris' face. I wanted him to remember, but he didn't, couldn't—wouldn't. So I sat down next to him and lowered the knife. I put my arm around him—he flinched again.

"It's okay," I said as more of his body was covered in blood. "I wish you remembered me like I remember you."

"I am sorry, but I do not know you," Morris said through tears.

At that moment, I looked at his shoulder, saw the scar, and smiled. That badge he wore on his skin all these years should have reminded him even a little. I leaned in and kissed that scar.

"Finn did that to you," I said. "My father gave you that scar with a bullet. I cannot believe you could forget something like that so easily."

"Adam?" Morris asked as I slit his throat with the pocket knife.

Then I leaned in and kissed Morris. His lips were as soft as I had always thought they would be. I held my lips against him with my free hand, holding his head close to mine as blood rushed down his neck. Then I pulled away.

As I stood back, I watched Morris grab his neck with both hands, thinking he could stop the waterfall. Within minutes, he collapsed onto the floor next to Lucas. Two secret love birds lying in each other's blood. I threw the pocket knife on the floor near them and left the room. Bathed in their blood, I went in search of a bathroom.

18

As kind as Mrs. Rattleson had been to me when we lived next door to each other, I resented her for not doing more to save me, to help me have a normal upbringing. I did not necessarily blame her for my misfortunes, but eventually, I did hold a grudge against her for not taking me in, for not reporting my parents for neglect. I was too young when I first went to the orphanage, but by the time I was a teenager, I started having thoughts of punishing Mrs. Rattleson.

*　　*　　*　　*　　*

For the first few years after Adam arrived at the orphanage, Mrs. Rattleson mailed a birthday card to him, but the nuns did not deliver it to Adam. They did reach out to Mrs. Rattleson repeatedly and asked her to stop trying to communicate with Adam. They wanted Adam to start a new life — to leave his old life behind, and to do that, they did not want Adam reminded of the life he had lost. They were naive to think that Adam would forget his past — forget where he came from and move on towards a new life. He was smarter than that and learned to hold quite a grudge about it all.

A month before Adam turned 18, with several murders staining his hands, he returned to the trailer park he called home as a child. He never forgot. He had been there a few times prior with Lucas, but during those visits, Adam avoided being spotted by Mrs.

Rattleson. He was not quite ready to see her. The trailer Adam once called home had been abandoned for many years. The sides were engulfed in weeds taller than a toddler, and the roof above the living room was missing. An electrical fire destroyed most of that end of the trailer.

Across the yard, Mrs. Rattleson still lived alone in her trailer and was still working at the club. If she was not working at the strip club, she sat alone in her trailer, drinking and crying herself to sleep, wanting desperately to reconnect with her own son — her only child.

*   *   *   *   *

Earl Jr., Mrs. Rattleson's son, was happily married and living in California. After high school, he enjoyed a full scholarship at UCLA and ultimately became a successful entertainment lawyer. He and his wife had two children, and as far as all his West Coast friends were concerned, Earl Jr. had no family other than his wife and children. He created a new life for himself after leaving Vermont. Earl Jr. hated his mother for his deprived childhood. He refused to give her any credit for his ability to learn easily, to stay out of trouble as a teen, and to graduate from college. Those accomplishments were his own and were made possible by his resilience, given his challenging upbringing.

Mrs. Rattleson would have argued that case with her lawyer son if he ever gave her the opportunity, but he did not. The fictional backstory Earl Jr. told his wife about his new life would never reveal the truth. All they would ever know was that Earl Jr. grew up outside of Burlington, and his parents died shortly after he started college. He even changed his name. In his new life, Earl Jr.

was EJ Rattleton. There were no names behind the E or the J. He was just EJ. He had a story for that simple naming, and it was often buried in the short story he shared about his childhood.

Mrs. Rattleson tried to find her son a few times—she even hired a private investigator, who, at a considerable cost, provided her with a phone number. Mrs. Rattleson called that number many times before Earl Jr. finally answered for a brief conversation. The call was only long enough for Earl Jr. to tell his mother that she was dead to him—that he was no longer her son. The next time Mrs. Rattleson tried to call that same number, it had been disconnected.

Mrs. Rattleson contemplated hiring another private investigator, but she did not have the money. She thought about flying to California, but having never been anywhere outside of Vermont, she was afraid of the journey—fearful of what her son might say to her face if she ever found him. So, she never went.

* * * * *

After many months of stalking Mrs. Rattleson, I finally decided to visit her. I knocked on the door, and the two of us stood looking at each other through a flimsy screen door. Mrs. Rattleson looked the same to me—older, and more worn, but basically still the same person wearing too much makeup and not enough clothing. She still had a cigarette hanging from her lower lip and a faux crystal glass filled with vodka in her hand. For Mrs. Rattleson, it was not as easy to identify me. I had grown up, after all—I was almost a man. When I finally told her who I was, she was thrilled to see me and very happy to know that I was still alive. She invited me in, and we sat in the dark, dirty trailer for hours, discussing my

113

parents and life. As much as Mrs. Rattleson enjoyed the stroll down memory lane, she was more interested in what I was doing with my life as a grown teen on the cusp of becoming a man. I am sure she hoped I was living a great life with a great family in a great home. I lied and told her that I was living my best life.

*   *   *   *   *

"Why didn't you take me in?" I asked.

"It's not that easy, darling," Mrs. Rattleson said, taking a big gulp of her third glass of vodka.

"Yes, it is — was," I continued. "All you had to do was come to the orphanage and bring me home — bring me here."

"I know you don't want to hear this, darling, but I did visit you at the orphanage more than once," Mrs. Rattleson began.

"Bullshit!" I interrupted, irritated.

"No. It's true. I did," Mrs. Rattleson continued. "But the nuns did not think that I would be a good foster parent for you, darling. They would not even let me see you."

"That is bullshit!" I yelled, getting agitated at what I believed to be lies.

"Darling, I don't know what you know about me, but I own a strip club," Mrs. Rattleson confessed. "I could not even keep my own child happy. There was no way social services was going to let me take you home, especially with the tumultuous upbringing you had."

"Excuses, excuses!" I yelled. "You are no better than every other adult who has fucked me over — who helped fill me with anger — with evil."

"Darling, you are not filled with evil," Mrs. Rattleson said, trying to reassure me that he was a good kid who would grow up to be a great person.

"I could have been a better person if you had taken me in," I lied as a tear escaped my left eye.

*   *   *   *   *

I stood up abruptly and began pacing the small trailer, which frightened Mrs. Rattleson. The more I paced, the more I yelled — cussed. I blamed Mrs. Rattleson for everything that went wrong in my past. Mrs. Rattleson tried to respond, to justify her actions, but it was wasted breath. After yelling a little too long and too loud, I walked up to Mrs. Rattleson and punched her in the face. She screamed, so I hit her again.

Mr. Rattleson was known to hit Mrs. Rattleson now and again, but never as hard or with as much venom as I did that night. By the time I stopped, I had punched Mrs. Rattleson ten times, breaking her nose and crushing her cheekbones. Her face was swollen and covered in blood. She tried to speak, but couldn't get her words out clearly.

"You could have saved me," I yelled at her every few minutes. "You *should* have saved me."

I felt more tears stream down my cheeks. I could not recall the last time I cried — if I had ever cried since moving away, but as I beat Mrs. Rattleson and yelled at her, I felt a lifetime of built-up anger, frustration, and resentment escape me. It felt so good.

Mrs. Rattleson never got another word out. As she lay back in the recliner in her living room, covered in blood and crying from all the pain, she watched me go to the kitchen and come back with a dull kitchen knife. I stabbed Mrs. Rattleson 14 times: she had slashes in her arms, legs, chest, and stomach. When I finally stopped stabbing her, I left the knife in her stomach, and I fell back into the chair across from her, exhausted. I grabbed the bottle of vodka that sat on the floor next to Mrs. Rattleson's chair. The bottle was splattered in blood and was slippery when I grabbed it. I drank the clear, stinging liquid directly from the bottle as I watched Mrs. Rattleson bleed out and take her final breath.

I could have walked out and left her body to rot, but instead, I turned on the propane stove, grabbed a dish towel, stuffed it into the open vodka bottle, and placed the bottle on the counter. I lit the other end of the towel and held the flaming bottle for a moment before dropping it into Mrs. Rattleson's lap. I watched the flames engulf and burn her body before I walked out of the trailer and towards the road. The fire destroyed more of the trailer, and eventually, the entire trailer was engulfed in flames.

By the time I heard Mrs. Rattleson's propane tank explode, I had stopped an approaching car on the main road, several hundred feet from the trailer park

Instead of getting in the passenger side, I pulled the driver out of the car and punched him in the throat before smashing him against the side of the car and letting him fall to the ground. Then I slipped into the driver's seat. As I sped away, I came close to running over the driver, but I managed to miss.

*   *   *   *   *

The driver finally stood to see the fire through the trees, but before he could do anything about what he saw, another vehicle—a truck came speeding down the dark road. The large pickup truck struck the man, severing him in half with the large, sharp bumper guard that housed a snowplow in the winter months. Adam was out of sight by then, unable to witness another death caused by his actions.

19

On my 18th birthday, I did not get a cake. I was not surrounded by loved ones singing 'Happy Birthday' to me. Instead, I woke, showered, and went to the dining hall as I did most mornings at the orphanage. After eating runny eggs and fatty bacon, yet again, I returned to the boy's hall and packed what little I had into a duffel bag. I remember sitting on my bed, looking around the room at all the other beds. They were empty. Everyone was still eating breakfast or had already left for school. I remember thinking the room looked as depressing on that last day as it had on the first. I had seen other kids age out, and they all cried — some because of sadness and others because they were not ready for the real world. Others tried to seek out and hug other boys or nuns — making a big deal about their final day. I did not do any of that. There was no one I wanted to hug. There was no reason for me to cry. The orphanage was always a warm bed for me. I never connected with anyone — never bonded or formed long-lasting friendships. Anyone I got remotely close to was usually adopted soon after, and I never heard from them again, so I stopped getting close to anyone — to everyone.

On my 18th birthday, I received one gift, but it was not wrapped in shiny paper. It did not have a big bow. The gift was my freedom — freedom from the grasp of the nuns, the orphanage, and the state. I was free to do as I pleased, whenever I pleased. After packing my duffel bag, I walked to the front office of the orphanage — a place I had avoided as much as possible over the previous decade. The front office was where you went to get scolded or shipped off to a new family. No good ever came to me when I went to the front office until my 18th birthday. With the stroke of a pen, the nuns handed me $1,500 in cash. Everyone who aged out received a small sum of money, as if that were supposed to be enough for an 18-year-old to survive on as they ventured into adulthood alone. Fortunately for me, I had saved all the drug and hustling money I earned from hanging out with Lucas. Unlike most kids who aged out, I was heading into adulthood with almost $9,000. I knew I was not rich, but I knew I had enough to get far away from Vermont, which is precisely what I did.

I walked to the bus station, clueless about where to go next. I just knew I wanted to be as far away from Burlington and Vermont as possible. The man behind the ticket counter told me that I could take a bus to Boston that day or wait two days for a bus to New York, so I bought a one-way ticket to Boston, and two hours later, I was sound asleep in the back of a bus that smelled a lot like an old folks' home. I didn't know anyone in Boston, and I wasn't sure what I would do once I arrived. I just wanted to get out of Vermont.

I slept through most of the almost seven-hour journey to Boston, despite the numerous stops. I probably could have slept the whole way had it not been for the old lady beside me, who kept nudging me every time she moved in her seat. Every time I woke, she started talking to me, almost picking up where she left off the last time I fell asleep. She was lonely and excited to travel to Boston to see her grandson. I reminded her of him—so she said. She even insisted that I meet him when we both got off the bus in Boston. I must have been having a weak moment—a rare act of kindness for me, because when her grandson was not at the bus station when we arrived, I sat with her until he arrived 45 minutes later. He blamed the traffic, but she did not care. She was thrilled to see him and couldn't wait to hear about his first year in college.

His name was Liam, Liam Bracket, and he was just who I needed to meet on my first day in Boston. Liam took me in when he and his grandmother learned I had nowhere to stay. Liam's grandmother was only in town for three days, but Liam still put her in a quaint bed & breakfast on his street. Her only grandson, the son of her only son, Grandmother Bracket, was very well pampered by Liam.

With his grandmother tucked into the B&B, Liam invited me to be his guest. He offered me his couch for as long as I needed, which turned out to be only a week. I think by day two, he was ready for me to leave. He was young and in college, living alone in a lovely city apartment paid for by Daddy, and I am sure I was cramping his style. At least, that is what I thought until the fourth day after his grandmother was safely on the bus heading back to Vermont. That is when Liam invited me to join him at a friend's house.

*　*　*　*　*

"This is the guy I was telling you about," Liam said to the older man, who opened the large, heavy door and led us into an equally significant foyer wrapped in shiny brass and mahogany.

"Welcome to my home, Adam," Charles said to me just before he leaned in to kiss Liam, something I was not expecting. "Hey, babe, how was school?"

"I told you not to treat me like a child," Liam said as he pulled away so Charles could not kiss him.

"I am paying for that fucking education, so I can ask anything I want, you little prick," Charles yelled into the air while smiling at me.

*   *   *   *   *

I had heard about situations like the one I found myself in. Lucas told me about sugar daddies and how profitable they can be if you don't mind shacking up with an old dude. For me, it was never about gender or even age. It was always about how I felt in the moment.

I was a guest at their argument, foreplay, or whatever they wanted to call it. I did not know Liam well enough to care about his feelings, and I knew nothing about Charles other than the obvious as I looked around. The guy was loaded. My next thought was how to kill Liam so that I could get in on the kept-boy cash machine.

Charles took Liam and me to dinner at a restaurant that was too fancy for me. I couldn't decide whether he was showing off for my sake or if he lived like that every day. We ate too much food, and they drank a lot. I did not drink—could not drink on account of my being only 18 years old. Charles offered me some wine—almost forced me to drink some wine, but I was hell-bent on not drinking. I was in the middle of a situation I knew nothing about in a city I knew nothing about. I was not about to blur my thoughts or my vision. I needed to stay clear-headed—stay in control. For all I knew, the two of them were serial killers, and I was their next victim. Of course, that is all quite humorous now, considering how things turned out for me.

After dinner, we walked the three blocks back to Charles's townhouse. They wanted me to come in, but I told them I needed to explore the city and walk off the heavy meal we had just finished. Neither of them argued. I think they wanted to be alone but were being polite. I bid them farewell and walked away. Before I left, Liam handed me his house keys and told me he would see me in the morning.

I walked away and quickly realized I had no idea where I was or where I was going. I did not even know Liam's address, but thankfully, he was a good Boy Scout—his keychain had an "if lost" tag that included his address and phone number. I wandered the city for hours. I was in awe at how alive the city was at all hours of the night and into the morning. I had walked for miles, zig-zagging through the dark and seedy streets of Boston, yet I still found my way back to Liam's apartment long after sunrise.

I was not expecting him to be home—he surprised me when he opened the door as I fiddled with the key. He stood there, holding my packed duffel bag in his hand.

"I think it is time for you to find your own place," he said to me nonchalantly, as if it had been something we had actively been discussing. "I cannot have you here anymore."

I did not care. I had no investment in Liam. He was a gentle soul who offered me his couch—probably because his grandmother made him do it. I thanked him, traded his key for my bag, and walked away without any questions.

"Don't you want to know why?" Liam yelled at me as I walked down the hall and back towards the stairs.

"Nope," I said as I vanished behind the door that led to the stairwell.

I knew why he kicked me out, or at least I thought I knew. I saw the way Charles looked at me the night before. I knew that old man took one look at me and thought, 'Fresh meat.' I also knew that I was a whole lot less maintenance than Liam.

When I walked out of Liam's building's front door and started down the front steps, I heard him yelling. I looked up and saw Liam hanging out of his window.

"You cannot have him," he yelled. "He is mine."

I contemplated engaging with him, but I walked away, not even looking up at Liam. He continued to yell, but the farther I walked, the harder it was to make out what he was saying. I knew then that Liam needed to die.

20

I walked all around Boston that day. I was exhausted from not sleeping the night before, but I did not want to spend any of my money on a hotel—not yet, anyway. I stumbled upon the Granary Burying Ground. Fascinated by the old tombstones, I sat down near one, and before I knew it, I felt someone shaking my body.

"Son, are you okay?"

It took me a minute to realize that it was a police officer. I jumped.

"Don't be startled, young man," he continued. "You cannot sleep here. You need to move on."

Eventually, I stood up. The officer was holding the reins of his horse, and another officer, still on his horse, was looking down at me. I did not want to be arrested, so I apologized, grabbed my bag, and walked away. I turned around a few times, and the two officers and some onlookers were watching me each time.

That was the first time I had ever been in a cemetery, and aside from the altercation with the police officers, I was fascinated with the place—not necessarily *that* cemetery, but cemeteries in general. The old stones, the architecture, the quietness—all of it was hypnotic. I walked across the street and turned to look back at the garden for a little while, admiring the deathly beauty of it all.

Then I turned and unintentionally collided with a man. Before I could apologize, he pushed me down to the ground and started yelling at me for not watching where I was going, as if the entire collision was my fault and my fault alone. Then he walked away, cussing into the air. He needed to be added to my list, but everything happened so quickly that I couldn't care about him. After a few minutes, I saw a hand reaching down to help me up.

"Are you okay?"

I told the angel I was fine—emotional bruising more than physical, and he laughed.

"You don't remember me, do you?

I didn't, to be honest. I was tired and a little bruised, having been kicked out of an apartment and a park, and suddenly realized that I was pretty hungry, too.

"It's Adam, correct?

I finally looked at the man and realized it was Charles—Liam's Charles from the previous night. He was in a suit and his hair was slicked back—a very different look from the night before.

"You're bleeding," Charles said, grabbing my arm. Blood was staining the elbow of my shirt. I had not noticed it until Charles pointed it out, and then suddenly I could feel the pain—feel the warm blood oozing out.

"I live on the other side of the park," he said, pointing into the air as if I knew exactly the direction he wanted to go. "Come with me and let's get you cleaned up."

I should have declined the offer. I should have ignored the pain and the blood and found another cemetery to nap in, but I didn't. I took Charles up on his offer to help me as he hailed a cab.

"I normally walk, especially on a clear day like today, but you are hurt, so let's get you home quickly and safely."

I liked that he said 'get you home' as if to indicate that his home needed to be my home. Once in the cab, Charles gave the driver an address and then returned to tending to my elbow as if I had a bone sticking out of my skin, or something. I kept telling him that it was no big deal, even if it was. I was uncomfortable with all the attention he was giving me. I was accustomed to having the attention of a trick, but not of someone sincerely concerned about my well-being. It was disconcerting. Every time I tried to pull away, he would pull my arm back towards him so he could look at it.

When we finally arrived at Charles' home and were safely inside, we quickly moved to the kitchen, where he had me remove my shirt so he could apply creams and bandages to my elbow. His hands were big and soft. He was very gentle and kept asking if he was hurting me as he tended to my wound. He was quite the father figure in that moment—tender and loving.

I thanked him and let out a really earned, but exaggerated, yawn. I realized just how tired I had become, and before I could say anything, Charles asked if I had slept at all. Of course, I told him that I had not, and so he led me into a spare bedroom and told me to take a hot shower and rest.

The next day, I woke to the sun kissing my face. Birds were chirping, and as I adjusted my eyes, I took in the beauty of the room and the comfort of the bed I slept in for 18 hours. I had not realized that I had slept so long, and was amazed that Charles never interrupted my sleep to put me back on the street. Once fully awake, I headed towards the kitchen, where I heard noise.

"Good morning, sir," said a young Mexican woman. "Would you like some breakfast?"

I looked around to make sure she was talking to me. I had not seen this woman before and wondered why she was in Charles's kitchen.

"Mr. Charles had to step out," she continued. "But I made breakfast for you." She proceeded to show me to the dining room, where she had a fantastic spread. It looked like enough food for a family—eggs, pancakes, bacon—I was in heaven. I had not eaten that well in a long time, like a really long time. Although I never figured out how she knew to prepare all that food so timely.

Her name was Luna, and she was Charles' housekeeper. She cooked and cleaned for him. She ran errands for him. I never heard of such a job, and I certainly had never met anyone rich enough to have someone do all these things for them. I began to understand the appeal Liam had for Charles, despite being older.

Charles returned home while I was still eating, so he joined me for breakfast. He apologized yet again for the man who knocked me down, as if he needed to be that man's proxy. I thanked him for taking care of me, for providing me with a bed to sleep in, and for the generous meal he had prepared for me. He asked a lot of questions—questions about where I was from and what brought me to Boston. He wondered how long I would be staying in town and if I needed a place to stay. He asked a lot of questions about me, but did not offer much information about himself. I didn't ask either.

While we were eating, Liam walked through the front door. He slammed the door and was complaining loudly about what I cannot recall—just yelling about it as he walked through the house towards the dining room. He went silent, briefly, when he saw me sitting at the table.

"What the fuck is he doing here?" Liam yelled towards Charles in a fit of jealousy.

"I found him bleeding on the street, so I brought him home to get him cleaned up—not that it is any of your business," Charles replied with the stern tone of a father scolding his child.

They exchanged a tirade of words, and eventually, Charles took Liam into another room, where they continued to yell at each other. I quickly learned that Liam was a pretty demanding diva, and he was extremely jealous of me—probably of anyone being in the house—being anywhere near Charles. After a while, they went silent, and then I heard the front door slam. Moments later, Charles returned to the dining room and apologized for Liam's behavior.

I was having a hard time adjusting to Charles' kindness. I had not experienced anything like it before. Maybe Mrs. Rattleson had tried to do what Charles was doing, or at least she thought she had, but not really. When I was a toddler, she tried, but did not come close to Charles. I felt guarded and relaxed at the same time, if that was even possible.

Charles told me that I could stay with him for as long as I wanted and to let him know if there was anything I needed or wanted. Luna was not in the room when he told me all of this, but I heard him tell her later that I was moving in for a short while. She did not seem happy or upset about the news, which made me think that this was something that Charles did often. I felt like I was just the next one in a line of many who had the temporary privilege of living in the house of Charles Brandenstock, III.

*   *   *   *   *

Before I knew it, a week had passed. I did not do much of anything—did not try to figure out my future. I fell into the same pit that all the boys before me probably did. I found myself lying around the house being waited on by Luna during the day and joining Charles out on the town at night—sometimes with his friends and sometimes just the two of us.

Then a month passed, and I was enjoying the wardrobe that Charles had bought for me when he took me shopping. I found myself walking down the street looking posh—feeling rich. I felt on top of the world—untouchable. But then it happened—he touched me. Almost five weeks after arriving in Boston—after being brought home by Charles to stop my elbow from bleeding out, Charles tried to cash in on his investment—on me.

First, it was a flirty touch—a caressing of my knee or arm as we sat at the dining table. Then it was hugging me—holding me on the couch while watching a movie. Then one night, after a bottle of wine—yes, by now I was drinking with Charles he leaned over to kiss me. He was drunk, or at least I think he was intoxicated. He always drank so much that it was hard for me to tell. I could have fought him off—should have fought him off, but I let him kiss me. Hell, I had let men who paid a lot less do a lot more to me in Vermont, so the least I could do was let this older man get his rocks off, at least once.

I played along, then he paused to drink more and pulled out a bag of drugs, and before I knew it, I woke up the next morning completely naked in his bed. Of course, he was gone—he was gone a lot, actually. I could have lain there and soaked up what had happened the night before, but I could not remember it all. I could not remember what drugs we took—what he sedated me with, and that bothered me. It made me realize that he could do that to me again. I could black out again. My thoughts were interrupted by Luna walking into the room carrying a breakfast tray. To her, all of this was normal—something she had seen time and time again, I am sure.

Charles would then go weeks without trying any stunts like that one. He would be the Charles I first met—the gentleman, the dad figure looking to take care of a wayward boy. We would have platonic fun; then he would be gone again for a day or two. This rinse-and-repeat formula started to get old for me. I fell into this pattern and stopped going out on my own and exploring the city—instead, I was staying in and killing time in the city. Suddenly, he started going out of town for weeks at a time. Those were the times when I pounced.

*   *   *   *   *

One time, when Charles was out of town, I went to one of the bars that he had taken me to a few times. While sitting at the bar by myself, minding my own business, Liam walked in with a group of guys. He saw me and came over to me with a look of fury on his face.

"What the fuck are you doing here?" he yelled, trying to be louder than the deafening music blasting through the speakers.

I tried to ignore him.

"This is the prick I was telling you boys about," Liam continued, now speaking to his entourage. "I gave this little fucker a place to stay when he first arrived in town, and how does he repay me?" He asked rhetorically. "He moves in on my sugar daddy, and I get kicked to the curb."

The boys surrounding Liam were fuel for his fire. They gasped and threw their hand over their mouths in awe and disgust, surprised that a young handsome man would dare steal another man's man. I could see all their mouths moving, but they spoke too quietly to hear.

"This is my club, bitch!" Liam shouted. "First my man, and now my club? I don't think so!" He waved his finger in the air as if that made his statement more commanding. It just made it all the more dramatic — silly.

I tried to explain to him that I did not steal his man or his club. I tried to explain to him that he fucked up his deal with Charles by being a total bitch diva, but he did not listen. He was only interested in one narrative, and that was the one that portrayed him as the victim.

Eventually, Liam and his boys walked over to a high-top table and ordered drinks. Some started dancing. One started making out with someone I assumed he knew. I was not drinking. I was underage, and even though I had a fake ID. I was not in the mood to drink. I was on a mission that night. I was not sure who I was going to kill, but I knew that I was going to take someone's life that night. I sat at the bar, looked past the bartender into the mirror behind him, and watched Liam and his friends get sloppy drunk. Now and again, Liam would look towards the same mirror and see me looking at him. He would mouth 'fuck you' or flip his middle finger at me like he was twelve or something. I ignored him.

As the night went on, Liam came up behind me and spilled his drink all down my back, purposefully, of course. He tried to apologize, as if it truly was an accident, but I knew better. I ignored him and didn't react. I sat there on the barstool quietly and calmly.

Eventually, I grew tired of Liam's protagonist behavior, so when he and his friends were on the dance floor, I walked out of the bar. I walked across the street from the bar and leaned up against a lamp post, and I waited. I watched as people came and went from the bar. A line had formed to get in, a long line that wrapped around the building. I watched a boy with two girls, both wearing skimpy outfits, each holding on to the bulging arms of the jock they were both hoping to score with that night, jump up and down like cheerleaders. I saw two girls making out. I watched a group of young guys watching the two girls kissing, whistling, and howling like teenagers seeing porn for the first time. The line to get into the bar was long and eclectic. Funny, it didn't seem that diverse when I was inside, but then I wasn't really paying attention to anyone but Liam.

Eventually, I saw Liam come out of the bar, alone, and walk away. I did not remember where he lived, so I was unsure if he was heading home or somewhere else, but that did not matter. I picked up my pace and started following him. After a short while, mostly because he was drunk, I caught up to him—took him by surprise.

"Fuck, dude!" Liam yelled. "What the hell are you doing? Are you stalking me?"

I did not respond. There was no point. I did not want to get into an argument. I put my arm around his shoulder and led him down the sidewalk and then into an alley. It was dark, but then they always are—dark. He continued to yell at me and even tried to wiggle out of my hold, but he could not. I was stronger than him. Much stronger. That and I was sober. I knew exactly what I was doing while he was having trouble figuring out where we were.

I stopped in front of a dumpster and pushed him up against it. I was finally showing him my angry side—the side of me that I think he was trying to unleash since that day he kicked me out of his apartment. I did not say anything to him. I was not looking to lecture him. To me, he was not worth the words. Instead, I punched him in the stomach, and while he was leaning over, I punched him again and again. I wanted to see blood—to taste his blood.

Liam tried to fight back—to punch me, but the alcohol had taken over his balance control. He swayed too much to throw an accurate punch, but he tried and tried, and tried. He hit the dumpster with his fist a few times, and each time, he let out a scream. A fist into a metal dumpster can never feel good. Frustrated that he was unable to punch me, Liam pulled out a switchblade—something so out of character for the Liam I knew. It was easy to knock it out of his hand. It fell to the ground, and that is when I grew tired of Liam. I opened the dumpster, lifting the heavy metal lid as high as I could with one hand. With the other, holding Liam, I propped him up and rested his neck on the edge of the dumpster. Then, with all my might, I pulled the lid down, smacking his head. I did it again and again and again until I saw blood start oozing out of his ear. Then I lifted the lid one last time and, with both hands now, pulled it down with all my might. I heard his neck crack.

I picked the switchblade up off the ground and then went in to almost hug Liam's dead body, and as I did, I forced the switchblade into his back and then licked the blood from his ear. The warmth tasted so good. It had been too long since I last tasted blood. As I stood there, wrapped around his body, licking his ear like a kitten cleaning its paw, I felt a warm explosion in my pants. I clung to Liam for a little longer, enjoying the various sensations that ran through my body, then, as quickly as it all began, I walked away, out of the alley and back to Charles' house. My shirt had some blood on it, so I took it off and dropped it in a trash can a few blocks before reaching Charles' house. As I walked back to Charles' shirtless, I thought about how good it felt to kill Liam. I wondered why he left the club alone and why he felt so much anger towards me. For a brief moment, I felt sad for Liam, but I got over that before I reached Charles' house.

*   *   *   *   *

Charles returned home the day after I killed Liam, and two days later, he received a visit from the police. Liam's body was found quickly—I really did not hide it. Fortunately for Liam, the Boy Scout, he had emergency contact information in his wallet. Unfortunately, Charles's name was on the card. He did not know that Liam had done that, and he was even less pleased about having the police arrive at his house, lights flashing.

I did not hear what Charles told the police, but it was a convincing performance because they did not stay long. A week later, Charles told me that he needed to go to London for business. He would be gone longer than he had been anytime since I moved in. I couldn't tell if he was telling me this because he wanted me to move out, or so I wouldn't worry or wonder where he was or why he would be gone for so long. I only told him that I had never been to London. Perhaps it was my good looks or maybe it was my aloofness; I am not sure. All I know is that a few days later, his lawyer dropped a passport off at Charles' house for me, and the two of us were packing for London.

21

We were in London for a month before I grew bored with Charles. I finally started seeing the side of him that I am sure Liam and endless others saw—the controlling side. Sure, his giving side was pretty cool—my private fairy godmother, but it got old at some point. Without asking for anything in return—aside from the occasional blacked-out sex—Charles was giving me clothes, jewelry, and even cash. It was the unexpected perk of meeting Liam entirely by chance. Liam and I never discussed how he came to know Charles or how he was aware of Charles' willingness to pamper young men. And I never understood why Liam felt threatened by me or what Charles might give me that he hadn't provided to Liam. From what I could tell, Charles spoiled more than one young man at a time.

I had the misfortune of sitting around a table at a nightclub in London one night. Charles had wandered off to the bathroom or to make a call. I did not pay much attention to his movements in the clubs. But the collection of young boys sitting with me each had an opinion about how displeased they were with the others sitting around the table. They all believed that each should be the only boy Charles pampered. A group of young, eligible men who probably could go off and have a healthy, sexual relationship with someone closer to their age did not care or want anything like that, or maybe they had it but did not disclose such secrets for fear of no longer having access to the endless diarrhea of cash and gifts from Charles.

A couple of the boys revealed to me that they were boyfriends, but they continued the charade with Charles so that they could each score big. I was a ruthless person—still am, but even these guys disgusted me. They had no code, no set of morals, and I know that sounds like the pot calling the kettle black.

I never asked for anything from Charles, but I never rejected anything he gave me. I never had anyone spoil me the way Charles wanted to spoil me, so I was not going to give that up; well, not until it got old, which happened a lot faster than I thought it might after listening to the table of bitchy twinks.

I kept waiting for Charles to cash in—to want me to perform some weird, kinky sexual act on him or lie quietly while he raped me—taking what he believed he deserved for all of the gifts. But other than that one time, none of that happened, and I am not 100% sure anything happened that one night I blacked out. Charles never suggested—never even used the word sex around me, not even jokingly. Sure, he was controlling, especially once we arrived in London. He was in meetings most days, leaving me to wander the city—to explore. He would ask me a million questions, wanting to know my every move—my every stop. Each time, my story was boring—uneventful—at least, that is what I told him. My days were filled with excitement and wonder. I ventured down every street— every alley, taking in the largeness of the city. I definitely was not in Vermont anymore.

Charles would take me out at night—first dinner, then drinks or dancing. I think he just wanted to feel young—to be seen with a handsome young man. He certainly attracted enough of them while we were out. He could have taken any boy home that he wanted, and yet he chose me. Of course, I would eventually learn that was not entirely true. I thought I was special. I thought I was Liam's replacement. I did not get to know Charles well enough in Boston to know that was a lie, but with our extended stay in London, I got to see the true Charles — the self-righteous, narcissistic, ego-driven man who demanded a lot from his boys. I learned that he liked to have many boys around — but all separate from one another, as if that helped make each one feel more special. But sometimes, and not necessarily by Charles' choosing, we would be at a club frequented by his little boy toys, which is how I found myself at a table with several of them that one night.

One day, while walking around London, I passed a restaurant. I had stopped to look at the menu outside the door when I noticed Charles eating inside. He was not alone. He was with a dark-skinned boy. The boy was hanging off Charles, kissing him — they were kissing each other. From outside, I could see the boy fondling Charles under the table. Another time, I returned to the rented apartment earlier than he told me to be back, and I found Charles in bed with two Asian boys.

So it was not that Charles was averse to sex; it was that he was averse to sex with me, which was fine by me. I did not find him particularly attractive, but I would bet that most of these boys did not either. They were in it for the money, the connection — maybe the attention. Charles was in it for power. I could relate to that because I often put myself in situations so I have the power — the control.

So, as I said, I grew tired of Charles. I never found out exactly why he had brought me to London. Perhaps it was because I didn't care. He could have his boys, but then I was always there for a night on the town. I was his backup plan for those days or nights when he could not buy some cheap whore for a few hours.

Whatever the real reason, it did not matter. I was tired of playing his game. I wanted him to play mine, and that meant spilling blood — his blood.

I realized that killing Charles was outside my code, not that I had a defined code this early in my killing career. The few people I had killed up to this point were all deserving participants. Charles never hurt me. He saved me — picked me up off the pavement that day and then showered me with gifts. So, if anything, Charles deserved to live a long life — to die some way other than by my hands.

And maybe that is why I killed him — he didn't deserve to die. Perhaps that was my whole point of killing, after all. It was with Charles that I realized that my reasons for killing — my purpose did not need a code or a scenario to play out or not play out. With or without Charles, I would accept that I liked blood — the sight, the taste — everything about it, and I especially liked it when it came out of other people. I had a thirst for blood — a need to kill someone, and Charles happened to be right there with me when that desire intoxicated me most.

*   *   *   *   *

When I walked through the door of Charles's London flat one afternoon, I was stoked — ready to end his life. I had spent the day wandering the city, spending a lot of time in Brompton Cemetery — one of the more beautiful places I stumbled upon soon after we arrived in London. I sat in that garden of death for hours, watching people come and go. Some stopped. Some cried. Some walked through only to take advantage of this shortcut between two neighborhoods. I loved everything about that morbid garden. Anyway, as I sat on the ground, leaning up against a tombstone for a man named Charles Dixon—a father and a husband who died in 1876, I contemplated ways to kill my Charles. Well, he was not 'my' Charles. If anything, I was his Adam—his kept boy, even though I didn't feel like I was being kept or trapped. I did not feel like he was suffocating me. I was just bored—ready for a new chapter.

When I believed I had it all planned out, I leapt up and walked the thirty minutes it took to get back to Belgrave Square. I had a confident strut—excited to be able to kill again, to get blood on my hands. With a smile on my face and the taste of blood in my mouth, I walked through the front door of Charles' flat and heard moaning—not the suffering kind of moaning, but the ecstatically sexual moaning that one lets out when they are on the cusp of orgasm—when they are so close nothing could keep them from exploding; erupting.

I quietly walked through the flat, getting closer and closer to the source of the noise. It was an extended climax—the moaning continued. As I opened the bedroom door, I found Charles and one of the two Asian boys he had been with in bed before. Charles's back was to me. He was thrusting into the backside of the Asian kid with a great deal of force as the Asian kid bent over the bed like a cheap whore. My entire plan—the one I conceived in the garden of death was killed, and I had to compromise. I quickly grabbed the porcelain statue of David from on top of the dresser—all 18 inches of solid, heavy stone- and swung it down on Charles, splitting his head open as he collapsed onto the Asian twink.

The kid went from moaning to muffled screaming. Charles was a much heavier figure, so he pinned the Asian kid down on the bed and covered the kid in blood. I loved the juxtaposition of the heavy white man crushing the tiny Asian boy—watching Charles' body wiggle as the Asian kid struggled to break free. He could not. As Charles suffocated the Asian boy, I smashed Charles's head a few more times with the statue. Each blow opened a new gash, letting out more blood. I found myself laughing at the absurdity of the situation: me beating a naked, older man to death with a statue of a nude, ageless man while he crushed a naked young man.

My final swing jammed David into the back of Charles' head; I heard the crushing of his skull and watched the smooth white statue drown in a pool of red. I stood back and watched until Charles' body stopped moving—a sign that the small boy beneath him had finally stopped breathing, too. He was a casualty of sex— an unexpected kill—not by my hand; that honor fell to Charles. As I sat there watching the bodies stacked, tasting the blood and watching it flow away from Charles, creating various rivers across the bodies and the duvet, I wondered if the kid climaxed—if Charles climaxed before they took their last breath, or did I rob them of that moment.

I knew that when the police would eventually arrive and find this work of art, they would discover that Charles had been killed. They would learn that all the blood belonged to Charles, which would support a theory of jealous rage.

I knew the asian kid—or at least I knew of him. I had seen him in the bedroom before with Charles, and I saw him at the nightclub on more than one night. The kid who lay lifeless in Charles' bed was one of the two boys I met who were dating each other. Once I made that connection, I knew that the boyfriend would be blamed for the mess I had made, and I was okay with that. I did not need — and I did not want — the credit or attention for it. I left millions of little bits of me behind, swimming through the red river of Charles. That is all I needed — wanted.

After I exploded, I lay on top of Charles, feeling the warmth of his blood. I remember being so relaxed in that moment that I actually fell asleep. I woke up only because I heard the doorbell ringing. I quietly slipped off of Charles and into the bathroom, ignoring the bell. I showered, got dressed, collected what little I brought with me to London, and slipped out through the service entrance. I never looked to see who was at the door before I showered, and they were gone, or at least stopped ringing the bell by the time I was cleaned up and ready to leave.

Once back on the ground level, I walked into the back garden, jumped the privacy fence, and down the back passage before turning onto Lyall Street and then into Eaton Square.

22

I woke to the sound of the train racing along the track. It startled me. I was not in my bed—Charles' bed. I was not in the quiet, comfortable Belgrave environment. The man next to me was not Charles. I looked at the back of his head and traced the tattoo lettering from his neck and down his exposed, smooth back. Every few seconds, he would exhale, and his body would rise and fall. He was alive. The duvet ate the rest of his body—I could only make out the contour until it faded to his feet and then the bed. Everything moved in rhythm. I wanted to touch him, but for the longest time, I just watched, quietly.

Eventually, I had to pee, so I slipped out of the bed as stealthily as I could. I wandered around to find the toilet. I could have explored the entire flat—rummaged through everything —but I didn't. Instead, I peed, flushed, washed my hands, and was back in the bedroom as quickly and as quietly as possible. I stood at the edge of the bed, almost afraid to get back under the duvet for fear of waking Murray. I watched him—watched the duvet rise and lower. I watched the muscles in his back flex as he took a breath. I could have stood there all morning watching him silently move, but he did not allow that. A few minutes into my peaceful moment, Murray turned, and as he did, I jumped back into bed, taking advantage of the disruption. By the time I got back into bed, Murray had rolled over and flung his arm over my body, almost locking me in the bed with him. I smiled again. The calmness, the warmth, the comfort of our position lulled me back to sleep. When I woke again, I was alone.

I sat up in the bed, staying under the warmth of the covers. I listened for any movement, but I could not hear anything. I thought about calling out, but I wasn't sure if he lived alone. I did not know anything. As I sat there, I realized I knew nothing about Murray beyond his name and where he worked. I was not even sure where he lived. I was not paying attention the night before. I was too busy living in the moment for a change—engrossed in his attention; his smell—his smile. It was not like me to overlook the other details. I should have panicked. A younger version of me might have, but I stayed calm. After all, I was the serial killer, not him—at least I did not think he was one, but then again, no one ever thought I was one; at least not until they learned that I killed a lot of people.

Drowning in my self-imposed rabbit hole of thoughts, I suddenly heard a door open and close. I did not know if someone was coming or going. I wanted to yell out, but I stayed quiet. Then, moments later, Murray walked through the bedroom door carrying two coffees and some muffins. The smile on his face as he walked in washed over me—engulfed me. I suddenly remembered I was naked under the covers.

*   *   *   *   *

That is how it was the first morning I woke up next to Murray. It's been weeks since, but the feeling I felt that morning had to be love. It certainly was happy; blissful. I could not ever recall having that feeling for anything or anyone, including Morris. The feeling I felt when I killed was different—almost distant. The emotion I felt when I was near Murray after that first night was virtually indescribable. The time I spent with Murray was magical. When we were not together, which was often, I found myself thinking about him—his smell, his taste, all the time. I could be stalking someone or even killing them, and yet I would still have happy thoughts about Murray. When we were apart, I was almost consumed with a desire to be with him again. It had to be love. I tried to convince myself that it was nothing more than infatuation, but I knew I was lying to myself. It was more—so much more.

When we were together, and I looked into his eyes and felt how he held me—how gentle he was with me, I was convinced that he was experiencing the same feeling. But neither of us put the feeling into words. It was as if we were both afraid that if we said the words—said the feeling out loud, that the entire fairytale would crumble. So we stayed silent.

I did not move in with Murray. He never asked me to move in either. I could tell he was guarded, like me. He told me he was guarded—never hesitated to share that detail about himself, eventually. The one feeling he did share was how nervous he was about how serious he felt we were getting, and how quickly we were getting serious about one another. It scared him. It scared me, too, but I never told him that part. I smiled and hugged him, reassuring him that everything was okay—that we were OK.

He never asked where I went when I did not sleep over, and I never offered. He never asked to stay with me at my place. I never offered, mostly because I didn't have a place to call my own. If I was not crashing at Murray's, I was sleeping on a bench or in a park. Sometimes I would spend a few pounds on a hostel so I could shower, but I lived on the streets—something I thought I wouldn't have to do once I met Charles. I was wrong about that—about him.

No matter where I slept, I made it a point to go to the pub almost every day that we were not together. I cannot say whether I did that in hopes of Murray inviting me back to his place or if it was because I really wanted to see him. Each time I walked through the doors of The Drunken Unicorn, I felt a little weak in the knees. Do you know that feeling I am talking about? It was like seeing Murray for the first time, each time—like falling in love all over again. It was not lust. I knew that feeling. Lust was a feeling that drove my killings—powered them. Lust was reserved for blood.

23

Brompton Cemetery was one of my favorite spots to visit when I wasn't with Murray. I spent time in other cemeteries around London, but I always found myself back at the one on Old Brompton Road. There was something magical about it. Its size, for one thing. The place was massive—so easy to get lost among the tombstones, and trust me, I got lost often. It was a maze of old paths and dark corners.

It was in Brompton Cemetery where I first saw her—saw Catherine. I only knew her name because a man yelled out to her once as they walked through the cemetery to get to Chelsea. They were moving quickly, or at least he was trying. She kept stopping to look at the tombstones. Together, the cemetery was a shortcut, but when I saw her on her own, the cemetery was something entirely different for Catherine. It was a place of peace. I could see that in how she walked and sat alone. I could see that in how she took her time, like me. She enjoyed the serenity of that garden of death, maybe even more than I. I'll never know for sure because I never asked her.

I did not see her often, and she was not the only person who walked through the cemetery, admiring its architecture, history, and the lives of those who had passed away. Many did the same thing, but there was something about Catherine that caught my eye. She was pretty—not model-pretty, but pretty. She was not flashy. She did not draw attention to herself. If anything, she tried to blend into the air so as not to be seen, much like me.

I know many of the same people walked the cemetery repeatedly, but Catherine was the one whom I remembered the most—maybe at all. I saw her many times, and each time, I thought about walking up to her and saying hello—sharing our similar interest in the peaceful space—but I never did. I always stayed in the shadows. I am unsure what I was afraid of with her, or if it was even fear that stopped me from saying hello.

It's not like I was stalking her or anything. I did not go to that cemetery in hopes of seeing Catherine or anyone, for that matter. The cemetery was a place where I felt a sense of peace. It is also where I found anger. Sitting in a cemetery, I would sometimes think about the nuns and the way they treated me and the other orphans—the scolding and the beating—the hanging on the cross in the courtyard.

For as much spiritual mumbo jumbo as the nuns spat at us day and night, they were surprisingly quite devilish. They would yell if we stepped out of line, even a little bit, and they would punish us for the slightest infraction. Those nuns ran a tight ship and took great pleasure in making an example of anyone who stepped out of line.

They would not let you eat if you arrived one minute late to the dining hall. Instead, they would make you sit in a chair along the wall and watch the other kids eat—your punishment for being tardy. Few kids made that mistake more than once.

If you spoke out of turn or talked back to the nuns, they would grab you by your ear and drag you down to the nurse's office, where you would be forced to drink shots of liquid soap. I made that mistake once, and surprisingly, many kids made this mistake quite often.

If you did not complete your chores, if you hit back when a nun hit you, or if you did anything where they felt they needed to make an example of you, the nuns would strip you down to your underwear and tie you to the large wooden cross that stood tall in the center of the courtyard for all the other kids to see. You would hang there, rain or shine, as an example of what happens to children who disobey the rules. Depending on the severity of your crime, you could be hanging on that cross like Jesus for hours, sometimes even days, like Damian.

*   *   *   *   *

It was a summer month, so this one boy, Damian, did not have to suffer through rain or cold weather, but still, he hung with his arms spread wide, tied tightly. He looked like a tiny Jesus.

I would sit in the courtyard and watch Damian hang from the cross when I was not eating, sleeping, or doing chores. I loved watching him there, helpless. His wrists and ankles were bound tightly to the wood with thick boat rope. He would squirm to try to get free, but it was useless. He and others who tried would get rope burns and splinters. Some, like Damian, would bleed. I liked that part the most.

Damian's underwear was stained yellow, soaked in urine, so much so that you could easily see the outline of his penis. It looked big, but back then, I was a little kid — probably nine or ten years old, so everything looked big. You could tell, even from a distance, that he worked out. Muscles in all the right places defined his athletically thin body.

Seeing Damian tied up excited my body in ways I was still discovering at the time. It was not necessarily sexual for me, not then. For me, it was seeing Damian restrained — helpless. I got excited seeing him trapped and bleeding from the rope burns. It would be years later before I understood the sexual desire Damian, Morris, and many others stirred up within me.

Damian was 16 when I first saw him hanging on the cross. Like me, he spent more than a decade at the orphanage. Unlike me, Damian never spent time with a foster family, which was understandable. He was always mouthing off to the nuns. Whenever I heard the nuns yelling or running around frantically, I knew Damian had to be at the center of whatever chaos the nuns were trying to subdue. He spent a lot of time hanging on that cross.

I remember that Damian always had a big grin on his face as if he were thinking evil thoughts. I loved that grin so much that I often found myself emulating it. The day before the nuns strapped Damian to the courtyard cross for the last time, I watched him and a girl do things to each other that I had seen my parents and Morris do together. It all started when I followed Damian into the woods behind the orphanage — something we all did back then.

After a few hundred yards, I stopped when I saw Damian leaning; his back was against a tree. His pants were at his ankles, and the girl, on her knees, had Damian in her mouth. From my perspective, she looked much clumsier than Morris had been with my dad. After a few minutes, the girl stood up, pulled her skirt down, and took Damian's spot against the tree so he could enter her from behind. For the first time, I got to see how big he was as her ass swallowed him. My body tingled. Both were particularly quiet. I recall that my parents and Morris made a lot of noise when they performed similar acts. It took me years to understand why.

Minutes after Damian entered the girl, the two of them were interrupted by Sister Mary Susan, who appeared almost out of thin air. Fortunately, she did not see me hiding in the bush, so she was unaware of anyone witnessing her wrath. That day, I learned just how evil some nuns could be when they believed no one was watching.

At first, Sister Mary Susan looked to be lecturing Damian and the girl. The teenagers, still with their clothes around their ankles, stood before Sister Mary Susan, each cupping their crotch. I watched Damian while Sister Mary Susan lectured them both about her Lord. I waited for her to demand that Damian and the girl cover themselves up, but she didn't. Instead, Sister Mary Susan pushed the girl back up against the tree, then I watched Sister Mary Susan swing her wooden walking stick into the air before repeatedly bringing it down on the girl's ass. I could not believe that a nun was being so violent. It excited me to see the girl's blouse stain red with each loud smack the cane made against the girl's bare bottom. The pain the girl wore on her face was erotic to me. I was wet with excitement, especially as I watched her fall to the forest floor, crying and begging for Sister Mary Susan to stop.

Before Damian could pull his pants back up, Sister Mary Susan smacked his crotch a few times with her walking cane, tearing his sack. He got blood all over his underwear as he got dressed.

After caning the girl almost to her death and leaving her half-naked and bleeding on the ground, Sister Mary Susan grabbed

Damian by the arm and pulled him back to the orphanage. He was much bigger than Sister Mary Susan and could have easily overtaken her, but he let himself be dragged, entirely defeated by her. I watched the girl lie still on the ground for a few minutes, but she never moved. I should have called out to her or run for help, but I watched her bleed. I watched her irregular breathing eventually normalize, and then I watched her finally stand up and pull her underpants back over her bruised ass. She saw me looking at her. She knew I could see her tears and her fear, but instead of reacting, she turned her back to me and began walking away — limping. I watched until I could no longer see her, and then I turned and ran after Sister Mary Susan and Damian. I never learned what happened to the girl. For all I know, she died before she could get out of the woods. To this day, I still wonder who my worst role model was: Sister Mary Susan or my mother.

*   *   *   *   *

Damian and I were not that different — we both liked torturing people. We just did it in various ways. For Damian, it was all about the moment and the attention, almost trying to embarrass or overpower his enemy. For me, torture is personal and private. It is not something I intend for the world to see, even though I know that eventually, someone will stumble across my creations. But, unlike Damian, I never stuck around to get attention from the mess. Damian loved the attention, which ultimately worked out in my favor years later.

24

I never took Murray to any of the cemeteries I visited around London. They were my sacred space—my place to be spiritual in my way. And the people I met at the various cemeteries never knew about my life outside the gates. Few of them ever lived long enough to see the next sunrise. There is something erotic about killing someone in a cemetery, for me, at least. The idea of being so bad in a place that is supposed to be so good, so sacred—so Holy, excites me in ways that are difficult to describe.

One of the more colorful people I met was Archie. His girlfriend, or friend who was a girl—he never really clarified—caught my attention one afternoon, not long after I killed Charles.

I was sitting on a low wall in the cemetery—something I probably should not have been doing, but I did it anyway. The grounds were not policed very well, so if I had been breaking any law, no one was there to scold me—no nuns around to slap my wrist or tie me to a cross.

I sat thinking about Charles and the Asian boy who died and about the Asian boy who lived. I wondered what he was going through—if he missed his boyfriend or Charles more. Since killing Charles, I had been thinking about the living Asian kid a lot. Still, I could not decide if I was thinking about him because I wanted to kill him, too, or because I was curious about his new life as a single man—possibly an incarcerated man.

As I pondered, I heard a laugh—one of those loud belly laughs you know has to be genuine—sincere. There is no way to fake that kind of laugh. Trust me, I have tried. I looked up, and this girl, whom I would soon learn was named Chloe, was trying to get away from a boy, whom I would soon learn was named Archie. He attempted to tickle her—he was only partially successful, as she laughed deeply. I watched them for some time. They were like little kids having fun without a worry in the world—ignorant of everything around them. Just two people having a good time. You don't see that a lot. You really don't. If you don't believe me, stop and watch people. Everyone is on a mission—some place to be, something to do. Few people live in the moment, thoroughly enjoying what or who is around them. It was refreshing to see these two playing in a cemetery, of all places. I watched them as they walked through the garden, heading toward Chelsea.

I am not sure what it was about seeing Chloe and Archie that made me think of Damian and that girl from the woods, but I did, and then I couldn't get them out of my head. As I said, I have no idea what happened to the girl, although I didn't really care. I liked watching her get beaten by Sister Mary Susan, though, and only wish she had bled more that day so long ago.

I do know what happened to Damian. He died as Jesus had, hung from a cross. I know that sounds so apropos. The kid spent so much time hanging from one at the orphanage that I thought it only fitting that he hang from one when I killed him.

I did not set out to kill Damian. It was just one of those things that happened. He aged out of the orphanage, and I assumed that was the last of him—he vanished into the real world like so many before him. I had forgotten all about him and his pee-stained undies. Well, that is not entirely true. Every time I looked out into the orphanage courtyard and saw some other sucker hanging from the cross, I thought about Damian.

After Damian left, no one tied to that cross was nearly as good-looking as Damien. Everyone was either fat or too bulky. Some were so skinny I thought they would slip right out of the rope knots. So, yeah, I watched the cross to see who was being punished, but I never gave it the attention I did when Damian hung from it. I know I am rambling. I do that sometimes—deal with it.

As I said, I had forgotten all about Damien until I ran into him during one of the many drug drops Lucas sent me on alone. Believe it or not, one of our drops was in an old abandoned church outside of Colchester. I could not tell you how long it had been abandoned or why. A few of the stained glass windows had holes where kids had thrown rocks through them. The inside of the church was surprisingly well-maintained. There was graffiti and broken glass on the floor, but nothing else inside was damaged.

I remember the inside so vividly. When you walked into the main room, a large cross hung above the altar, the focal point. I arrived early and explored the building, tugging on the cross, feeling its weight and strength—almost comparing it to the one back at the orphanage.

While I was fiddling with the cross, a guy walked in quietly, almost startling me.

"You with Lucas?" he asked, almost in a whisper as he stood just a few feet behind me.

"Yeah," I replied, aloof, stepping away from the cross.

"Cool. Right. So, um, how does this work exactly?"

That question took me aback. I was supposed to be the newbie in that scenario, but it turned out Damian had only ever purchased drugs at house parties. He knew Lucas, or knew of him well enough to trust the remote meeting.

I was a dick. I toyed with him—making him question whether I was being honest, or if I was some undercover officer, which did not go as I anticipated. Damian got spooked and pushed me against the wall where the cross hung.

"Don't fuck with me, dude," I remember him saying. His breath was warm, filled with the odor of old cigarettes as it swam around my face. I cringed. I wanted to throw up, but instead I pushed back, sending him to the floor. He looked up at me with some trepidation—unsure what I might do to him.

"Wanna get stoned?" I asked with a huge smile on my face. I extended my arm to help him up.

"Fuck yeah!" Damian yelled.

I pulled out a baggie filled with colorful pills from my backpack and handed Damian two big pink ones. I told him they would make him feel like he was king of the world. He believed me and tossed them into his mouth. I pretended to grab two more for me. He was clueless.

We both smoked a joint while we waited for the pills to take effect. Soon, Damian stood and danced around the altar. The effects

155

of the drugs took over his body, and then he collapsed, almost unexpectedly. I had wandered around the sacristy. When I heard him hit the floor, I smiled. I remember smiling and dancing around the sacristy, excited to have another victim within reach. My excitement was heightened when I found a box of spikes and a hammer.

Back at the altar, I nailed a few of the spikes into the cross so that I could suspend Damian from them — something to support his weight. Thankfully, he was not a very large person. His drug habit kept him thin. It was a struggle, but eventually I managed to spread Damian's arms over four spikes that I nailed into the cross. He never woke up, even when I dropped him a few times while trying to lift him onto the cross.

I stepped back and looked at the lanky, young man. He did not look like the image I remembered from my early days at the orphanage, so I pulled out my pocket knife and started cutting all of his clothes off of him. When he was young, he hung in nothing but his underwear. The problem I discovered as I started cutting into all of his clothes was that as an adult, he was not wearing any underwear, so by the time I finished cutting everything off of him, he hung naked. I walked back into the sacristy to find something that could be a loincloth, and luckily, I found a small tablecloth. It was bigger than I wanted, so I cut it down to size with my pocket knife and wrapped it around Damian's waist, then tied it in place. I used the rest of it to tie his wrists and ankles to the cross, tightly.

With Damian secured to the cross and still completely wiped out from the drugs, I took one of the spikes and nailed his right palm to the cross. That jolted him awake, and man, did he scream. I am sure it hurt, but that was the point. Before he could truly comprehend what was happening, I nailed his other palm to the cross, pinning him in place. Then, of course, I nailed his feet to the cross. It was all very biblical—beautiful.

By the time I finished nailing his feet to the cross, Damian was yelling at me and struggling to get free. Every time he struggled, he tore more skin, which only drew more blood. I sat back and watched.

"What the fuck?" Damian yelled—more like slurred, still a little numb from the pink drug cocktail. "Get me down from here."

I don't remember really engaging with Damian after that point. I remember telling him who I was—that I remembered him hanging from the cross at the orphanage. I remember him pissing himself, soaking the tablecloth. And I remember his screams as I nailed four more spikes through his skin, eliminating any chance of him getting down. I put a spike in each of his thighs, and I put a spike in the middle of his chest. I loved how he screamed each time the metal pierced his skin. I licked the first few rivers of blood created by each spike.

The more spikes I put through him, the less he talked—yelled. As I prepared to put the final spike through his neck, I could hear his breathing getting more strained. He had lost a lot of blood by that time. I hugged him a few times, which only smeared his blood all over me even more.

As I stood on the chair that I had used to hang him originally, I was so close to him. Our chests touched, and I got goosebumps as his blood stained my shirt. I could feel it soaking through to my skin. In that euphoric moment, I put the final spike through Damian's neck, and I was splashed with more of his blood. I kissed his neck, close to where the blood gushed out.

I remember holding—hugging Damian for what felt like a long time. The rhythm of his chest slowed down—eventually stopped, so I let go of him, stepped off the chair, and started to walk out of the church. As I did, I heard the distant chatter of people. I slipped out the back of the church and across a small field before I saw three young kids, no older than me, walk through the front door of the church. I did not stick around to see what happened next.

25

Chloe was cute—pretty for a Brit. She wore excessive makeup, concealing her true identity, which made her look less attractive. You know those girls who try too hard, put on too much make-up, or wear too few clothes, all to impress someone. She was that type of girl. Every time I saw the two walk through the cemetery, which was probably five or six times before I finally saw Archie alone, Chloe appeared more trashy—probably trying too hard for someone, for Archie.

When I finally saw Archie walking alone one afternoon, I watched him walk through the cemetery much more slowly than when he walked with Chloe. He looked around as he walked. He was not interested in the tombstones. He was interested in the people hiding among them. I watched Archie sit next to another guy on a bench not far from where I stood. Archie sat down, and then the other guy slid close. Their bodies were practically touching. I could see them hold hands briefly, and then Archie stood up and walked away.

I watched Archie until I could no longer see him, and then I turned my attention to the other man on the bench. He sat there for over an hour, and five other men sat close to him. They touched, and then the visitor left. It took the third guy for me to realize that the man on the bench was selling drugs—more sins in the garden of death.

I contemplated going over and sitting on the bench and seeing what I might score for myself, but as I started to walk in that direction, I looked up and saw Archie. He was leaning against a tree, watching me. I walked towards him, and when I was about 20 feet from him, he turned and walked away, but he sauntered as if his plan was for me to follow him. So I did. I followed him through and then out of the cemetery and towards Fulham. I hung back about ten paces, following cautiously. It was the first time I had taken the bait—been the follower, not the leader. It felt a little weird—out of place for me.

Archie turned a corner, then I turned the corner. As I did, I watched Archie walk up some steps of a building of flats. The door opened as he reached the top step, and Chloe popped out. The two hugged, and she descended the steps and jumped into a Black Cab. Archie stopped at the top of the steps, looking back at me—for me. He stood tall and confident, holding the door open. He smiled, so I moved quickly, almost leaping across the street and up the steps. He did not say anything to me. Instead, he waved me in, and then, once the door closed behind us, he walked ahead of me up the stairs to a second-floor flat.

I kept waiting for him to say something, but he did not. I could have spoken up, but I thought it would feel like I was nervously trying to fill the silence, and that wasn't my style, so I stayed silent. I walked up the stairs behind him, almost too close to him. I could smell his cologne—he used a lot of it, but I couldn't identify the brand. I never could on him or anyone. He stopped and knocked at what I believed to be the door to his flat, which I found very peculiar. A shorter, less attractive young man opened the door quickly as if he had been waiting for us, like he knew we were coming. This second guy smiled and stepped aside to let Archie and me in. At that moment, I started to realize that the afternoon might not go as I had assumed. Once the flat door closed, I felt a heavy foot kick me in the back, sending me tumbling to the floor. I did not know which of the two had kicked me until he put his foot on my back, pinning me to the floor.

"You like it rough, you little fag?" asked the new guy. It was at that moment that I realized I had been played. These guys, and probably Chloe, were in it together. They set me up. Then I felt a kick to my head, and I heard Archie laugh.

My head was pounding, but I was more focused on when I got duped and lost control of the situation. I asked myself if it had been that day or some other day. I wondered if they had been stalking me more than I had been stalking them. Not knowing when I got duped hurt me the most at that moment, even though I could taste the blood in my mouth from when one of them kicked my face.

Above me, I could hear the two guys laughing and goofing around, pleased that they had managed to catch someone to beat up. I listened to the new guy call Archie by his name and eventually heard Archie call the new guy Russell. They let me lie on the floor for a few minutes, and Russell took his foot off my back and yelled for me to stand up, which I did without hesitation. I knew what I would do—have done to someone who did not stand as quickly as I wanted when I was beating them up, and I did not want any more bruises. I needed to let these two idiots continue to think they were in charge and in control.

When I stood and turned around, both boys were standing a few feet away, side by side, just looking at me like a caged animal at the zoo. They both had thick Essex accents, making it difficult to understand every word. I knew that specific accent well. Many of the twinks at the club who hovered around Charles, looking for a free handout, had similar accents.

I licked my lip, drank the last of the blood from it, then asked the two guys who wanted to go first. The two of them looked at each other, perplexed by my question. Thinking I was making a sexual advance, Russell sprang towards me, fists up. Before he could swing, I swung low and hard, punching his balls with extreme force. He fell to the floor, gripping his crotch, moaning. I looked up and smiled at Archie. "You ready?"

Archie looked at me with a scowl and leapt towards me. I twisted and raised my leg, kicking him in the chest. He flew backward, slamming into the wall next to the front door.

"I am going to suggest that you both stay down," I told them harshly. "The next time you go down, you will not be coming up. And if you think I am kidding, go ahead and stand up."

I heard a lot of moaning and groaning echoing along the base of the floor, but neither got up. Russell eventually stopped moaning and proceeded to yell up at me, still cussing and talking as if he were in control of the situation. Archie lay on the floor quietly. I am sure I broke a couple of his ribs.

"I am going to walk out of here," I told them. "And if I ever see either of you out on the street, I promise you that with every fiber of my being, I will kill you, and not in a quick, painless way. I will make you regret ever luring me up here. I will make you beg for your life, and then once I kill you, I will hunt down the other one of you and Chloe and make sure that the three of you never see another day. Have I made myself clear?"

I remember the two of them moaning in agreement. I looked toward the kitchen and noticed a few knives suspended along a wall—magnetically hanging. I reached across the counter and grabbed one without paying attention to which one I clutched in my hand. Then I turned and shoved it into Russell's leg. He screamed.

"That is my only warning and the least amount of pain you will feel from me if you don't take my words to heart," I said as I opened the door and walked out. I did not even bother to close the door behind me. I was hopeful that a neighbor would walk by and see the two pathetic boys down and wounded.

As I walked out the front door of their building, I noticed Chloe getting out of a Black Cab. She looked up and saw me—noticed me. As I walked past her, I grabbed her, holding her captive while I whispered to her: "Do that again, and you die."

She looked at me like I was nuts and tried to wiggle herself free of my grip.

"Who the fuck do ya think ya are?" she asked me. "Let fuckin' go of me before I fuckin' beat the shit outta ya."

I laughed.

"Your boys thought they were tough, too, you bitch. But let me be fucking clear. You are picking a fight with the wrong guy. No matter how you think this will play out in your favor, you are wrong, and if you don't believe me, ask those two punks upstairs."

I let her go, and she ran up the stairs and into the building. I turned and headed back towards the cemetery. I will admit I was nervous that day. When I felt the first kick to my back and was pinned to the floor, for a moment, I thought my time had come—the

Grim Reaper was there to collect on my debts. To make matters worse, it was not the last time I felt I had lost control.

26

I stayed away from Brompton Cemetery for a few weeks. Not because I was afraid of running into Chloe, Archie, or even Russell, but because I wanted them to think they won. I wanted them to go back to their routine and let their guard down — let them think I went running off, never to return. Little did they know that I had every intention of hurting them again, maybe even killing them — most definitely killing them. I did not know when, and neither did they.

Instead, I walked around the city, crashing parties and going home with new strangers. I found myself back at The Drunken Unicorn every few days only to see Murray. I don't know why I didn't tell him I had no home; I roamed the streets like a lost puppy, looking for anyone to take me in. I don't know why I continued to put on a charade for him, especially if I thought I loved him, but something about him made me act this way — behave ridiculously — totally not me.

One day, when I stopped by The Drunken Unicorn, I discovered that Murray was not working. He had called in sick. For a brief moment, I thought about leaving — running over to Murray's flat to comfort him, but the narcissist in me did not want to get sick, too. So I stayed at the pub and flirted my way through a few drinks. I was running out of money by this time — all my savings from Vermont and what little I managed to steal from Charles only took me so far, so drinks were something I needed people to buy for me, and as much as I wanted a hostel for the night, just for a warm shower, I knew I needed to find someone to go home with—possibly someone from the pub since Murray was not there.

I chatted with a young couple who mistakenly stumbled into the pub. I watched them enter and almost immediately turn around and leave, but the girl stopped the boy. It was mid-afternoon, so the pub had not turned into the wild dance club that it did after sunset. The pub retained most of its old English charm at this early hour.

The couple looked around, seemingly befuddled, as if they had never been in a pub. They sat at the bar instead of sitting at a table, taking the two seats next to me. Eventually, the girl turned to me and asked what I would recommend from the menu. She spoke in beautiful, broken English. I was not worldly enough to know that the undertone of the accent was French. Menu recommendations turned into pub and club recommendations, and before I knew it, I was her live-version 'Time Out' guide. She was cute and funny as she struggled to say words in English. Her male friend was not much help. He spoke less English. I was able to learn their names—Didier and Corinne. Nice enough people, but dreadful to listen to as they butchered my native tongue. Fortunately for all of us, one of the twinks who clung to Charles and me when we used to come to the pub together, Pierre, was 'working' the room and heard the three of us struggling. Pierre was a French National but had been in England for most of his life. He spoke beautifully in both languages. For all the time he spent trying to impress Charles, I was surprised that Pierre never spoke French. Of course, I had no idea if Charles spoke French.

Pierre once saw me as a roadblock on his journey to Charles, but now that Charles is gone, Pierre is quite friendly with me. He tried to go home with me a few times with no success. When I suggested that I go home with him, he panicked and changed the subject. I later learned that Pierre still lived with his parents, and according to another twink, Chad, who often hovered around Charles, Pierre's parents were unaware of their son's interest in male anatomy.

For all his flaws, Pierre was invaluable to Didier, Corinne, and me that afternoon. After about an hour, he all but pushed me out of the conversation, which was fine. I had no use for Didier or Corinne, at least not until I overheard Pierre mention that he would be happy to go back to their hotel with them as he kissed Didier on the cheek.

Unfortunately for Pierre, Didier and Corinne were only interested in his ability to translate and give them tourist tips. Pierre read the room wrong and had been flirting with Didier, who had no interest in Pierre. Corinne got annoyed with Pierre's flirting, so she stood up and headed for the door, pulling Didier. I watched Pierre turn and follow them with his eyes for about three seconds, and then he moved on, continuing his hunt for attention.

I ran out after Didier and Corinne, hoping to convince them that I was a nice enough fellow and that they would want to hang out together. They agreed, but they said they wanted to go back to their hotel to change and freshen up. I offered to walk with them, and after a bit of convincing, I agreed to follow them to their room.

The three of us sat on the bed in the small hotel room. We muddled through some conversation, and eventually, we fell asleep. I was more tired than I thought, and when I woke to find the two of them still sleeping — the three of us still clothed, I felt a sense of relief that the foreigners had not robbed or hurt me. They were kind enough to leave those destructive behaviors to me.

With the two of them sleeping, I thought it was a good time to use their shower, so I went into the bathroom and took a long, hot shower. My moment of peace was interrupted by Corinne as I watched her come into the bathroom naked and step into the shower with me. I will not lie; it was a little cramped, but I welcomed the company. Corinne had a beautiful face and figure. Her skin was olive and smooth, and her boobs were small — they fit perfectly into the palm of my hand. I was surprised by the sunflower tattoo she wore on her inner left thigh, but it was hard to miss as she walked towards me in her nude state. With our bodies melting together under the hot water, I struggled to stay focused — not to get aroused, but then I heard a noise and turned around to find Didier entering the bathroom, also naked. He was skinny — much skinnier than he looked with all the layers of clothing hanging on him earlier. His dick stuck straight out in front of him — not big enough to hang down. I was taken aback at how small it looked — how small it was.

Before I could truly understand what was happening, Didier was in the shower with Corinne and me. It was very cramped by then. One minute, Corinne was between Didier and me, facing Didier, and the next minute, I was in the middle, facing Corinne. After about ten minutes of cramped fidgeting in the tiny shower, the three of us escaped the hot chamber, limp and unsatisfied. Neither of them said anything the entire time they were in the shower. I was silent, too. I thought the shower was erotic enough that maybe it was a teaser of what the two of them were into, but I could not have been more wrong.

They dried off faster than I did, leaving me alone in the bathroom. When I finally did emerge from the bathroom, I was surprised by Didier as he tackled me to the floor. With me pinned down, Corinne approached us with a rather large needle. I saw it only for a moment before she rammed it into my right butt cheek. It stung, I will admit. I have never been one for needles. Once Corinne pulled the needle out of my ass, Didier let go of me. He stood up, and the two of them stepped back from me. I tried to stand, but as soon as I was almost upright, I felt my entire body go numb, and I went crashing back to the floor.

When I woke up, I was sitting upright in a chair. My arms were pulled back behind me and tied at the wrists. Each of my legs was tied to the leg of the desk chair. I was still naked, and I was alone. I looked around the hotel room and even called out to Didier and Corinne. Neither of them answered because neither of them was in the room. Nor were any of their belongings in the room: no luggage, no rucksack. No clothes, no wallets. The room looked clean and ready for the next guests, except for me sitting in the middle of it, tied up and naked. From my perspective, all my belongings were gone: my clothes and my wallet. Even my passport was gone. I was trapped in the room — trapped in the country.

I had a gag in my mouth, but it was loose enough that I was able to wiggle my face and spit it out. It fell around my neck and hung like a scarf. I panicked. I had been in many precarious positions before, but this one was the worst. I tried to stand, but unlike the gag around my mouth, the ties around my wrists and ankles were tight.

Thankfully, the desk chair was made of wood and a little wobbly. I wiggled my body around a bit and eventually managed to tip the chair onto its side. As I fell to the floor, I snapped one of the chair legs, allowing me to angle my leg so that I could loosen the tie with my hand. Then, I snapped the other and repeated the process. It took a long time. I kept waiting for housekeeping or new guests to walk through the door and freak out at seeing me naked in the middle of the room. With my legs finally free, I was able to contort my body enough to bring my arms forward and use my teeth to loosen the ties. Once I was finally free, I managed to find a hotel bathrobe and slippers in the closet, and I walked out the door, through the hall, down the elevator, and through the lobby. No one asked me a question. No one stopped me. I walked out the front door, and once I had my bearings, I walked to Murray's flat. It took me three hours of walking down crowded streets and silent passages in nothing but a bathrobe and slippers, but I made it to Murray's only to find out that he was not home. He should have been home. He was supposed to be sick. But then I realized I didn't even know if it was the same day or if yesterday was the day I met Didier and Corinne. I had no idea how long I had been asleep in that hotel room, alone. I did not know what day it was or what time it was, so I sat on the front step of Murray's house and cried.

It was the first time I could remember crying in a long time. I was not sure if I was crying because I lost everything, or because I was cold and embarrassed for letting myself get robbed, or because I was going to have to explain to Murray why I was wearing a hotel bathrobe, and why I was in that hotel in the first place.

27

I am not sure how long I was sitting on Murray's step, alone in just that bathrobe, but I remember him calling my name — Murray cried out my name. I jumped up when I heard his voice, but no one was there. I rubbed my eyes and looked around again, thinking I was looking in the wrong direction, but I was not. I was still alone, and Murray was still not home. His house remained silent and dark. The sun was setting, and I realized I was having a dream. I knew I could not wait for Murray for much longer. I had been there for hours; it was getting dark, and I was still in nothing more than the hotel bathroom and slippers.

My back hurt — my ass hurt. I had been sitting for so long, at least it seemed, uncomfortably. I had pissed myself while I was sleeping, so now, on top of everything else that was going wrong with my day, I smelled like a roadside cafe urinal. I was hungry, too, and I had no idea where to get a hot shower, a meal, and clean clothes.

I walked away from Murray's house and wandered the city. I knew I could always find someone looking for a young, good-looking guy to take home, so I headed towards Camden Market. I knew the vendors would be closed up or closing for the day, but I was hopeful that I would find someone lingering around looking for a good time. That was not one of my prouder moments, but I was desperate — I was furious. Until that point in my life, I was proud of myself for never tricking because I needed the money. It had been because I needed a victim. Unlike many hustlers seeking attention, affection, and money, tricking for me was a way to find an easy target. But lately, I have had to resort to tricking for cash—for survival. I knew I was falling down a slippery slope and might regret some decisions, but tricking was my only option.

As I walked through Camden Market, I noticed a young vendor packing his tent. I stopped and pretended to be interested in some of the remaining handmade trinkets he had not yet sold.

"That one is hand-carved soapstone," he told me, ever the salesman trying to make an honest wage.

I had never heard of soapstone before, but I loved the smooth feel in my hands. It was surprisingly heavy for such a small object.

"It is a mother polar bear and her baby," he continued. "It is one of my favorites and is only 20 quid."

"It looks like two animals fucking," I said back, smiling as I handed the heavy carving back to him.

Twenty minutes later, I was stepping out of his tiny shower. The water pressure sucked, but I felt clean—I was clean. The stench of the street, of my piss, was all gone. His blood washed away the easiest since it was the freshest.

He gullibly invited me back to his flat as he packed the last of his carvings. He had a three-wheeled bicycle with a large basket in the back filled with boxes of his work, and we walked it back to his flat, which was thankfully only a few blocks from the open market. He parked the bike in a shed, locked it, and pulled me through a door and up two flights of stairs to a small studio flat that doubled as his work studio. It was a mess. He was a mess. He rambled on about art, about different stones—all nervous energy, I assumed. I was too focused on bathing and getting back to Murray, so I paid very little attention to the art history lesson he presented.

I remember picking up a larger sculpture from a shelf—it looked very similar to the small one from the market, but he told me it was something completely different. Clearly, I did not understand art, but it felt good in my hands—heavy. Solid. It felt even better when I turned around and lodged it into his skull as he approached me from behind, holding two cups of water.

He never said another sound, but the plastic cups clanked along the wooden floor in the puddles they made as they crashed. I pulled the sculpture back, and he fell to the floor. My hands were covered in blood. I put the bloody sculpture back on the shelf and rubbed my face, smearing warm blood over my eyes, nose, and mouth. I licked my fingers and then dropped the bathrobe, almost covering the artist. I stood in his tiny room, naked and bloody for a few moments, nearly forgetting why I was there in the first place, then I walked into his bathroom and cleaned up.

After showering, I went through his dresser and found some decent clothes. I found a rucksack and filled it with some extra clothes, a bottle of cologne, a toothbrush, and some biscuits. I left his wallet, but took the 673 pounds I found inside—probably his life savings, and then I walked out of his flat. It was dark by then. I was nothing more than a shadow—a dark figure on a night, unseen by anyone. I walked a few blocks and then hailed a cab and headed back to The Drunken Unicorn.

Murray was not at the bar when I walked in. I thought about going back to his house, but instead I stayed to have a drink. It had been a crazy day. As I sat at the bar, I saw Murray come up from the cellar carrying a case of beer. I saw him before he saw me, but when he looked up at me, his face lit up. A smile engulfed his face, and I knew I would be sleeping in a comfortable bed that night.

"Where have you been, love?" Murray asked me as he hugged me. "I was beginning to think you gave up on me."

"I am sorry," I said non-empathetically. "I've been busy working." I lied.

"Not working the streets, I hope," Murray said with a nervous laugh.

"No," I replied. He put the case down, and we hugged. I gave him a tight, firm bear hug. A hug that said 'I missed you' without needing to say the words. A hug that said, 'I want to be with you tonight.' He reciprocated.

"I am actually wrapping up my shift," Murray said. "Did you want to come back to my place?"

I smiled and nodded.

As Murray hugged me tighter, I looked over his shoulder and saw Didier and Corinne on the other side of the pub. They did not see me. I wanted to cut both of their throats and gut them alive. I could feel my heart pounding in my chest, so I knew Murray could feel it, too.

"Are you okay, babe?" he asked.

"Of course," I said as I let him go of him so he could go about the task of closing out his register and clocking out. "Do your thing. I am going to the toilet."

I walked up to the table where Didier and Corinne were sitting with another couple. I put my arms around their shoulders, standing between the two of them, gripping them tightly.

"My two favorite people," I proclaimed with a big smile on my face as if I were reuniting with my dearest friends. "What brings you two out so late tonight?"

They were silent. Their friends were silent. I kissed Didier and Corinne on their cheeks and rambled on about us all needing to get together soon. I kissed each on the cheek again and whispered into Didier's ear before releasing them both from my grip, and then I headed to the toilet.

A few minutes later, much to my surprise, Didier entered the toilets. I fully expected him and Corinne to make up some excuse to their friends and then run out of the club.

"It was all in fun, right?" Didier asked, laughing. "We were just playing with you back at the hotel." Suddenly, his English was so much clearer.

Before Didier could speak another lie, I slammed my fist into his stomach with every ounce of strength I had in me. He bent over, moaning. When he finally stood upright, he threw a punch at me. I ducked. He missed. I swung, drawing blood from his lower lip. He wiped his lip and swung again. He missed again.

I grabbed the back of his head, holding a big chunk of his soft blonde hair in my hand, and swung his head down onto the bathroom counter. His head put a crack in the countertop, and he fell back to the floor. A large gash in his forehead leaked blood. He was unconscious. We were the only two people in the toilets, so I picked him up and put him in a stall, sitting on the toilet seat. I pulled down his pants so anyone looking under the stall would see a man sitting on the toilet taking a shit. I cleaned myself up and walked out.

As I headed to the bar, I looked over and saw Corinne. She was not looking in my direction. It was clear that she was trying to ignore the situation — ignore me. Before I could sit at the bar, Murray told me he was done, so we walked out to the street and hailed a cab back to his flat, where I spent the next few days nestled under his duvet, enjoying his company when he was there, but enjoying the silence when he left me alone so he could go to work. I did not leave his flat for days. In fact, I couldn't recall even getting dressed for the whole week. I remember wanting to forget the rest of the world and revel in the comfort of being taken care of, yet again. Three days later, Murray broke the news.

"Someone was found dead in the club the other night," he said as he walked into his bedroom, finding me still under his duvet.

"Have you…" He started.

"Yes, I showered earlier today," I replied before he could ask me any incriminating questions. "Dead?"

"Sorry, yes," Murray continued. "They have no idea how long he had been dead, but the police say he died of blunt force trauma to the head. Can you believe that?

"Who was it?" I asked innocently.

"No idea," Murray yelled back from the bathroom, his pee hitting the toilet water as his backup noise. "Some foreigner — French, I think they said."

I tried to change the topic, but Murray was infatuated with the story—the death. He would spew something he had heard someone say, then go silent for a moment, and then regurgitate more second-hand information about Didier.

"And the worst thing about it, aside from the dead body, of course, is that The Drunken Unicorn is going to stay closed for a week while the police tear the place apart looking for clues."

"More time for us to be together," I said to Murray as I patted the space next to me in the bed. "Get in here and let's go to sleep. We can gossip more about your dead man in the morning."

*   *   *   *   *

We did not gossip about the dead man the next morning. Instead, we debated what to do with the week ahead, given that the Drunken Unicorn would be closed. Part of me wanted to stay close so that I could monitor the situation—to make sure Corinne didn't come forward and call me out by name. I did not want to get sucked into the investigation, after all, she did have my money and ID. I did not want to get caught.

That was the first time in my life when I felt that I was as close to being caught as I had ever been before. I know it was a sloppy kill. I know I should not have killed Didier in that bathroom, but I was so enraged, and I was not thinking clearly, and in all honesty, I did not think I killed him. I felt that he would wake up eventually and maybe remember what happened. The fact that he actually died was nice, considering what an ass he had been to me, but I did not like that Corinne was still walking around—still alive.

She would know I was the one who killed Didier. She had to know it was me. She had to know that I would come for her next.

Murray, on the other hand, wanted to get out of town—to take full advantage of the forced holiday. He wanted to go to the coast or to the mainland. I didn't have that kind of money, and I tried to make that clear, but he was insistent that we get out of the city for a few days. I made the case that I had not seen much of the UK countryside, so we agreed that a train ride through the center of the country would be a cheap and cheerful option.

28

The train ride through the countryside was nothing special. I am not sure if I was expecting it to be wonderful or if I had it in my head that being with Murray was wonderful enough. Still, as I sat in the train seat, looking out the window, watching England pass by at a crazy fast speed, I could not help but think that it all looked like rural Vermont. Murray was beside me, holding my hand, sleeping the entire train ride. He told me that trains always made him sleepy. To him, this adventure was nothing new—nothing exciting. As it was my first train ride, I was alert, excited, yet also a bit disappointed. I kept telling myself that being there with Murray and experiencing that for the first time with Murray was somehow special.

For the first time in a long time, I felt a sense of relaxation. Murray's head rested on my shoulder, and his snoring was quieter than a whisper. As the train slowed to stop at the next station, I looked up to see Corinne walking through the train. She saw me, and she looked right at me as she walked past. The serene feeling I had been feeling vanished, and I stood up to go after her, leaving Murray to sleep peacefully.

Corinne looked back to see that I was following her. She wanted me to follow her; at least, that is what I told myself to justify my ditching Murray. If I had not been so angry with Corinne and Didier, I might have stopped to think that maybe she was leading me into a trap and handing me over to the police. I hoped that was not the case. I felt pretty confident that she had been following me, hoping to punish me for killing her boyfriend or whatever he was to her.

When she got off at the next station, I did the same. I was sure I would have enough time to confront her, at least, before the train took off, but I was wrong. Corinne jumped out of the Northbound train, ran across the platform, and jumped into a Southbound train. I followed her, and just as I stepped onto the new train, I heard the other train, where I left Murray sleeping, pull away from the platform. I should have run after it—tried to stop and rejoin Murray, but I was too focused on stopping Corinne from doing something stupid—something we both might regret. I knew I would have to devise a good excuse for Murray, but I needed to follow Corinne at that moment.

I watched her enter the toilet at the far end of a train car, so I sat and looked at the door. She stayed in that small space for a long time. I finally approached the door and knocked. When she opened the door, she was holding a gun and pointing it right at me.

"Get in here now," she said to me with a wave of impatience in her trembling voice.

I half expected her to pull the trigger, but I knew she would not. The gun would make too much noise. She would be trapped and arrested too easily. Then again, perhaps she didn't care. I had killed Didier, and I assume she wanted revenge.

The bathroom was small. She tried to keep the gun pointed at me, but there just was not enough room for us both to move around comfortably, so she dropped her arm and started to whisper-yell at me. I found it funny that she was prepared to shoot me—make a lot of noise with the gun, but without the gun, she was focused on being quietly angry with me for fear of being heard.

I let her ramble on for a few minutes, allowed her to release all her anger and frustration as if I were solely responsible for the position we found ourselves in. She did not see that actions had consequences—that drugging me and stealing my things would result in the death of Didier or her.

I was beginning to realize that while I had thought Corinne was the smart one of the two—the ring leader in this disastrous adventure —Didier had to have been the brains behind their operation. With him gone, Corinne was grasping at straws, struggling to make sense of her life and what she would do next— without Didier. She tried to raise the gun again, but we did not have room. I grabbed the hand holding the weapon, keeping it pointing toward the train floor. With my free hand, my right hand, I reached up and punched her in the face, breaking her nose. The sudden burst of pain that filled her face forced her to drop the gun as she raised both hands to her nose. She was taken aback by my force, almost surprised that I would hurt her, which made little sense given what I did to Didier.

With Corinne focused on her nose, I took the opportunity to grab her neck, almost pinning her arms against her. The position made it impossible for her to wiggle free or fight back. I squeezed the life out of her slowly, tightening my grip. As I felt her start to go weak, I used all the strength I had left in me and snapped her neck, and then set her down on the toilet seat, slumped against the wall. There was some irony in my leaving both Corinne and Didier dead in the bathrooms after what they did to me.

As I emerged from the bathroom, the train slowed down and pulled into another station. I jumped off the train as soon as the doors opened, then I walked down the platform to wait for a train heading north. I had to figure out how to catch up to Murray, and I needed a good excuse. Even I was having trouble coming up with something that would explain why I got off the train at the wrong station without him. When I looked at the train schedule, I knew I had an even bigger lie to tell, since the next northern train was not expected to arrive at the station for another four hours. At that moment, as I stood alone on the platform in a strange town with just the clothes on my back and the money in my pocket, I decided I would have a better chance if I walked into town and hailed a cab.

As I walked through Coventry, I was struck by the cookie-cutter feel of the town. Every street looked like the last. The rows and rows of houses all looked the same. I found myself getting lost until I stumbled upon a cemetery. The London Road Cemetery was stunning and isolated. The large, thick trees created so many hidden corners. For a brief moment, I forgot that I was trying to get back to Murray. Instead, I found myself walking the paths of the cemetery, thinking about Corinne — wondering if she had been discovered yet and if she would get buried in a beautiful garden of death. As I thought more about Corinne, I started thinking about Didier and what the two of them did to me, and somehow, killing them both had not satisfied my anger towards them. I found myself wanting to hurt someone else — anyone else.

That is when I saw Olivia. I did not know her name, not at first, and not when I smashed her head in with an ancient, rusted cross that I tore off a tombstone. I only knew her name when I heard a frantic, motherly voice screaming, 'Olivia. Olivia, where are you?'

over and over again. The mother and I passed each other as I walked towards the cemetery gate. I still had blood on my hands, so I stuck them in my pockets. The mother stopped me and asked if I had seen her little girl. Of course, I said I had not. I did not even ask any questions — her age, hair color, anything that would show compassion or empathy towards the dead little girl I left slung over a tombstone. I shook my head and kept walking briskly towards the gate. I felt satisfied for the moment, but knew I needed to focus on getting back to Murray.

I had no luck finding a cab driver willing to drive me the distance to catch up with Murray, so I decided that sitting at the train station, waiting for the next train north, was my only option. That is where I met Callum.

*   *   *   *   *

Callum was older than me. Not as old as Charles, but close. He stood tall and regal, with just a slight hint of gray in his otherwise golden hair. I never asked him his age, and he never offered it to me. He was well dressed — not in a business suit, but in khakis and a polo. He wore a cardigan sweater over his polo and loafers with no socks. His hair was bright and thick, hanging down past his ears. He was well-groomed and had a beautiful smile — a mouth full of snow-white teeth. He spoke in a thick Scottish accent, making it almost impossible for me to understand the words he fired in my direction. However, that did not stop him from sharing a wealth of unnecessary information with me — the history of Coventry, the development of the train system, and the rationale behind the motorway numbering system. Callum was filled with useless factual information, or at least I assumed it was factual. Most of it sounded too preposterous not to be true.

Callum was heading north, too, to visit some family before he would make his way south again, back to his home in London. He clarified that his final destination was London — almost like he was inviting me to join him. It was clear then that Callum was not well-versed in how to pick up a stranger at a train station. I was no pro either, but I had spent enough time living on the streets to know how to make a proposition or get the stranger to propose that we go somewhere I wanted.

When the train finally arrived and we boarded the same car, I knew Callum was determined to spend as much time with me as possible. And don't get me wrong — the guy was nice enough to me and almost too kind. But, at that moment in my life, having just killed two women after leaving Murray on a train, I was singularly focused on getting back to him.

I sat in a window seat, and to no surprise, Callum sat in the seat right next to me. He continued spewing information at me as if he had an endless supply of facts within him that he needed to get out. He offered little personal detail and asked almost nothing about me. It was clear to me that Callum was trying to flirt or at least determine if I would accept his flirtations, however bad they might be. He never touched me, nor did he proposition me — at least not directly. As we approached what I believed to be the station where I would find Murray, and I excused myself to leave the train, Callum handed me a small card. His name, his address, and his phone number were on it.

"Call me anytime you are in London," he said as I stepped over him and headed for the door. The train slowed to a stop. I looked back to see Callum watching me as if to ensure I got off the train safely. I half expected him to follow me off the train, but he did not.

*　　*　　*　　*　　*

"What the hell?" I heard Murray yell as I spun around on the platform, looking in every direction in hopes of finding Murray. "What the fucking hell?"

"I am so sorry," I said, sounding as apologetic as possible. I got up to use the toilet, and then I got lost on the train. I could not find you, so I got off the train when it stopped, thinking it had reached our station. But you were not on the platform, so I caught the next train here. Please forgive me. Please."

Looking back at that moment, I thought it was one of my more award-winning performances. I might have shed a tear — probably not, but it was definitely a moment where I might have been able to shed a tear if I tried hard enough.

Tear or no tear, all that mattered was that Murray believed me, or at least forgave me. He went on to tell me how scared he had gotten — how he thought something horrible had happened to me. He was just glad that I was back. He gave me the biggest, tightest, longest hug I believe anyone has ever given me. Sometimes, I can still feel his hug if I think about that moment hard enough. I certainly long for it on some days.

29

Murray was different from every other guy — every other person I had ever met. He was a naturally kind person, and he liked me. I loved him, too, but I could tell, as time went on, that his love for me — his interest in me was far greater than anything I could give back. Don't get me wrong. He was a fantastic person, and he let me be me — well, at least the me I let him see, but I guess all couples do that, at least at first. Right? He asked me to move in with him several times, and I almost said yes each time. I wanted to get off the streets, and Murray was making it very easy for that to happen, but I worried that if I had moved in with him, he would end up like Charles.

Of course, Murray was nothing like Charles. I knew that almost immediately, but I did not want to look back and regret killing Murray. I did not regret killing Charles. He gave me a good life, but I wanted more, and believe it or not, I did think, at one point, that Murray could give me more — could be more for me and to me than Charles ever had been.

I appreciated Murray in a way that I never appreciated Charles, or any other person, for that matter. And every time he asked me — every time he tried to give me a key to his home, I made up some excuse for why it was the wrong time. I fell in love with Murray in a way that was uncomfortable for me. He sparked feelings in me that no one had ever done. Looking back, maybe he was meant to be the 'one' for me.

When he smiled at me, it was through his eyes, and my heart melted. His smile almost had me confess my sins to him on more than one occasion. It had me wanting to be completely open and honest with him. That was how intoxicating Murray was for me. Luckily, I stopped myself every time, but it was not easy. Love is not easy.

His touch. His smell. His voice. Everything about Murray made my body tingle — my blood heat up and my heart rate jump. Morris never made me feel that alive — that wanted. And even when I would disappear for days, Murray always welcomed me back into his flat as if I had been away on business — as if it were perfectly normal to be apart like that, and it was — normal for me. He never asked why we never slept at my flat — not after the first time he asked, and my excuse sounded plausible enough. He never asked what I did or where I went when I would vanish for days and sometimes weeks. He was just always grateful that I came back. And yet, that was not enough for me.

Murray was perfect by every definition of the word. He was the ideal person. My problem then and now is that I did not know how to accept that type of relationship. I have always been too focused on killing people, so I never contemplated what a great life I could live if I stopped killing people and just be with a fantastic person who thought I was really incredible, too.

Eventually, though, as expected, Murray reached his breaking point. He went months living a euphoric dream of a relationship. We both did. He continued to work and flirt with customers, but relished the idea that when he finished his shift, I would be there waiting to go home with him. And on the nights when I was not around, I assumed he just went home alone and went about his life as if he were single. I had no reason to imagine any other scenario until I saw it myself.

*   *   *   *   *

Murray did go home alone most nights when Adam was not sitting at the bar waiting for him to finish his shift. And sometimes he would leave the bar with whichever twink nagged him the most or left him the biggest tip. He had grown used to Adam's attention—his warmth, and when Adam could not be around, Murray eventually felt like he needed to fill that void for himself. It was never the same. They were never the same—those twinks. They were nothing like Adam—never could be. None of them could hold a conversation. They all just wanted sex, and while Murray wanted—needed that now and again, it was not what he wanted—needed. He wanted Adam. He needed Adam. After a few nights of not seeing Adam, Murray grew jealous of what he did not know—where Adam went when they were not together.

Murray had grown tired of their distant relationship. He grew weary of giving his entire being to what he thought would be his 'forever' relationship while never getting the same energy in return. After being together for months, Murray finally found the courage to tell Adam how he felt, what he wanted, and what he needed from their relationship.

*   *   *   *   *

I spent more time away from Murray than I had intended, which doesn't make sense when you think about it. I wanted to be with him—be near him all the time, but my craving to kill was stronger, and I found myself wanting to kill more often. This overwhelming urge within me was almost uncontrollable, and I feared I would burst while with Murray. I knew that if that happened, he would see the real me—the killer. I feared that he could potentially be the victim—my victim in those moments, and I kept thinking that I would kill myself if I ended up killing Murray. I loved him that much.

He knew something was different. He could sense it— probably smell it on me. The urge to kill seeps out of my pores, souring our relationship in the most painful way possible. He told me how much he loved me the last time we were together. He told me how much I meant to him and how important he believed I was to his future. He preached his everlasting love to me in a way that sounded like he was leading up to propose to me, and just as his speech was at its climax, he told me that we needed to take some time to be alone—be away from each other.

His words crushed me in ways I did not know were possible. Losing Morris and my parents had not crushed me like Murray's words that afternoon. I struggled to find words to defend our relationship and challenge him to continue this journey together, but he was steadfast. Nothing I could say then changed his mind. He told me it was not 'goodbye,' but just a little break— something we both needed to do to clear our heads and reflect on what we wanted.

I wanted him. He wanted me. The problem was that I wanted to kill more than I wanted to be with Murray. I never told him that, of course, but I eventually came to that conclusion on my own, and that is when I realized that it was 'goodbye.' I did not know it then. I loved him enough to agree to us taking time away from each other. I told him I would stay away from the pub and stay clear of his life so we could figure out what to do next separately. And I was true to my word.

I have not been in the pub, but I have lurked in the dark corners of the streets, hoping to get a glimpse of Murray now and again. Most of the time, he was alone. Many times I saw him crying. I saw him with a random stranger a few times, too, and then I stopped seeing him entirely. I am not sure if he quit his job or what, but the last time I saw Murray was a few weeks after our conversation—our 'goodbye.' I watched him walk out of the pub and get into a cab. I never saw him again.

30

I met Imogen the first time I sold my sperm—well, I did not really meet her as much as I saw her from across the room. She was so beautiful. He skin was flawless, and I wanted nothing more than to touch her—to feel what I saw as smooth, soft skin. She wore a name tag, and I remember thinking that she had a really cool name. I was not exactly sure how to pronounce it, but the way she had written it on her name tag with the 'o' in the shape of a heart and a flower bud above the 'i' was all quite cute.

I had reached a low point in my life and was desperate for money. Losing Murray crushed my spirit in ways I never thought possible—certainly not for someone like me who reveled in seeing people suffer. Without Murray, my life unwound. I slept on the streets more. I tricked more just so I could have a hot shower and make some money, but the problem with tricking is that the Johns are typically troubled. Hell, a number of the Janes were equally as challenging. I went home with an older woman who had been looking to fulfill some cougar fantasy. When we arrived at her flat, I was surprised to meet her two sons. They were both around my age, maybe a little older. One was passed out on a settee. He had no shirt on, so I could see all the needle marks on his arm. His hand still held a needle as it rested on the floor. A little drool seeped out of his mouth, and he stretched as if reaching for the needle.

The other son was making lines between him and his brother in a large pile of powder on the table. He had been tasting his product before we arrived—I could tell from how he was so focused on making the remaining lines match exactly. In the light of their flat, I could see that the mother, whom I thought was in her 40s, was clearly in her 60s. The makeup concealed quite a bit of her wrinkles in the dark pub. She was a big woman—someone I would struggle to get away from if she held me down, so I played along that night. I did some lines with her and her son, and I let her play with me in ways that I bet she probably wanted to play with her boys but feared crossing that line—at least sober. I fooled around with the second son a little that night after she passed out, but what makes that night so memorable—so worthy of me sharing with you is that it was the moment when I realized my life was falling apart. I liked how the drugs made me feel—how they shielded me from thinking about Murray, so I snorted more. I even found myself going back to her flat for days afterward to get high again. I knew it was a slippery slope. I knew I should have stayed away, but it was the only way I could cope with losing Murray.

Her two sons introduced me to selling my 'lads,' as they said. The two of them had been doing it for some time—wanking into a cup for cash. And it was that easy, eventually. The first time I walked into the office, I looked like shit. I had not showered in a few days and had been sleeping in a cemetery. The receptionist was about to call security to remove me when Imogen walked in and, I don't know… took pity on me.

She was pretty—stunning even. She could not have been much older than I was at the time, but she was years ahead of me in terms of her ability to speak and present herself well. I wanted to emulate her confidence—confidence I once had myself but had lost as the time away from Murray grew. Without Murray's love, which

I never needed until I had it, my life had no meaning. Seeing Imogen sparked some life into me—it had me wanting to be whole again. I tried to envision Murray when I was alone in the room holding the cup, but each time I cried. So, I started envisioning Imogen and how she would feel in my hands. I was filling cups every week thanks to Imogen.

The problem I still had back then was not thinking clearly. Come to think about it now, I am not sure I have thought clearly since Murray left me. I tricked for money. I wanked for cash. I got high with that money. I did not save any of the money. I did not eat or dress better, and I certainly did not think about working towards getting a regular place to sleep or call home. The only thing that kept me even remotely focused was killing, and even that started to get sloppy.

During one of my visits to the sperm bank, I saw Imogen walk in. She walked through the lobby, never noticing me, but she did stop to talk with another person—another guy. They hugged and shared smiles. He laughed. She laughed more. Their playful banter angered me. I was hungry. I was tired. I was desperate for money, so my head was not in the best place as I sat in that lobby, getting mad at a man I had never seen before, never met. I was oddly furious at this man because Imogen focused on him and not me. I had become that type of person—the needy, jealous type of person, fueled by petty, stupid things. I look back at that version of me now and hate myself. I hated what I had become—who I had become.

Imogen eventually left the lobby, and the receptionist called my name, along with Bernard, the other guy. We both walked to the counter together, smiled at each other, and grabbed our cups. He went into one room, and I went into another. That should have been the end of it. I should have wanked and walked out and never seen the guy again. I should have moved on and focused on something — anything more important than that guy. But I could not. He was all I could think about in that room. I was mad at this guy, Bernard, even though I never met him. I was upset that Imogen focused on him and not me. I should have been upset with or mad at Imogen, but it was he who got the brunt of my anger. I left the room with an empty cup. I left the bank with an empty pocket, but I left fueled with rage — the very rage that feeds my murderous behavior.

I remember walking out of the bank and sitting on the steps outside, waiting. I remember hearing the door open and close, and I remember his smell as he walked past me, down the stairs. I did not know if it was his cologne, or his body odor, or maybe even the glow he wore after wanking into a cup, but it was distinctively his. As he passed, I stood and followed him, hanging back only a few steps. At the base of the steps, he turned right, so I turned right. He picked up his pace, so I picked up mine. We maneuvered through the city, turning right and left for what seemed like forever. He did not stop. He did not run. He did not turn around. But I knew he knew I was following him — felt pretty sure he knew I was following him. Then he made one more turn, and when I looked up, we were both in Brompton Cemetery. Before I could truly comprehend how Bernard managed to lure me to my own feeding ground, he stopped and turned around. We collided as I walked into him.

I cannot recall our conversation, or whether we even had one. I do remember him punching me in the stomach for anyone to see. I do remember him lecturing me about following him — at least I think it was a lecture. It could have been praise or thanks for following him so that he could punch me. I remember letting him believe that his punch hurt—that he was overpowering me there in the cemetery. I also remember swinging my right arm and throwing an uppercut. He screamed as he bit his tongue as my fist made contact with his chin, tilting his head back before he fell to the ground. He started crying. I kicked him, grabbed his wallet, and took off running.

I was through the cemetery and out on the street before I stopped to tear through his wallet. I scored a few hundred pounds and his address. It was not a kill, but it was what I needed to set up one. I remember using that money to get cleaned up at a hostel near the cemetery, get a good night's rest, and fill my belly the next day before I bought a train ticket to Cambridge.

31

I had to get out of town. I should have gotten out of the country, but I no longer had a passport, nor did I have anything that could prove my identity; I had Didier and Corrine to thank for imprisoning me in this country. After stealing Bernard's wallet and underperforming at the bank, and being thoroughly depressed by the spiral I descended into with the cougar and her boys, I knew it was time for me to refocus — to recommit to taking care of me, and that meant killing.

During one of my last visits to the cougar's house, I found a book collecting dust on a shelf in her living room. She could not have read it in some time, if at all. The amount of dust covering everything on the shelf was mind-boggling. Neither of her boys seemed like the reading type, so I slipped the book into my backpack. I was not a big reader either, but this book was fascinating — a history of all the cemeteries in the United Kingdom. It was a menu of murderous locations neatly wrapped in a dark-colored hardcover.

The printing was once silver, or possibly gold. It was all so faded. I could not even make out the title on the cover. All of the pages were so thin — frail like my victims, and the smell, oh the smell was intoxicating. It smelt of a time long forgotten — a time I never knew. Snatching this book made my low moments with the cougar and her boys worth it in the end. The experience I had with them, while tragic and depressing, left me with a door prize that opened a whole new world of possibilities — of destinations for me to explore. I was determined to see them all, to murder in them all.

The first stop on my road to recovery, and one of the first cemeteries in the book, was Histon Road Cemetery in Cambridge. I used some of the money I stole from Bernard to buy a train ticket to Cambridge, and I will admit that the train ride was not as fun without Murray. I sat alone — the carriage was mostly empty. As I sat, watching the countryside whip past me through the window, I thought about Murray. I thought about how I really fucked up that relationship. Then, and even now, I do not regret my decision, but I still think about him and wonder if he thinks of me.

When I arrived in Cambridge, I was greeted by hundreds of students silently moving around the town on bicycles. I had never seen so many people on bikes before. There were cars, but very few of them were visible. The city appeared dedicated to the idea of exercise, or saving the planet, doubtfully both. I did not know that Cambridge was a college town — a town filled with people who are way smarter than I could ever conceive of being. Yet, for as smart as those people were supposed to be, none were smart about protecting themselves from deviant stalkers like me.

I wandered around the town for an entire afternoon, meandering up and down small cobblestone roads, being consumed by the hundreds of students walking or cycling, all on a mission to be somewhere — anywhere except where they were. It was easy for me to blend in — to be mistaken for a student. After walking most of the afternoon, I found myself sitting on a barstool, leaning against an old wooden bar, scanning the dark room of what I later discovered was a gay bar called The Glenfairy. The guy next to me, Jacob, was slightly younger than I at the time. He spoke first, asking me simple questions. We exchanged names. He told me he was studying Theology. I had no idea what that was—still don't, not really. He tried to explain it to me without my asking, but he got too caught up in it, losing me entirely. I recall that I had to interrupt him and tell him that I wasn't particularly interested in the subject. He could have walked away, maybe even cussed me out in the process, but instead, he apologized and changed the subject. He was a friendly enough kid—the first one in Cambridge to engage with me.

Nothing about Jacob stood out as unique—special. He looked like any other kid trying to survive in a town full of overachieving kids trying to outsmart the next one. When he rambled about Theology, he sounded quite intelligent—almost snooty, but when we talked about everyday shit—stupid stuff, really, he sounded like a normal kid. He sounded like any of the other kids I spoke with back at the orphanage, which made sense since he was a kid. He told me he had just turned 17 and was excited about committing his life to God.

I recall a small debate about religion and homosexuality, but it was not an argument I cared to win or lose, mainly because neither topic interested me that much. Jacob had labelled himself at a young age, he told me. He knew in grade school that he liked boys, and he spent most of his teen years grappling with his sexuality and his belief in God. For me, it wasn't that complicated. I never labelled myself—still don't. Some will call me gay. Some might say bisexual. Others will call me manipulative. Still, others will only ever label me as a serial killer. I don't care. Call me what you want. I have lived my life the way I wanted to, as best as I could. Sometimes it was with a girl and sometimes it was with a guy. Sometimes I did the manipulating, and only a few times was I ever manipulated — blindsided.

Jacob flirted. He was looking for a quick hook-up — he said so, in plain English. There was no miscommunication. He said what was on his mind, however abrasive or direct it might sound. I liked that about the kid. I did not hook up — not for the sake of hooking up. That always seemed unproductive to me, but then I was not looking for sex, or love, or companionship. I was looking for my next victim.

Without leading Jacob on too much, I suggested that we go for a walk — get out of the loud pub. He was only too eager to agree. We walked through Cambridge, he leading the way, meandering along the quaint streets and parks. At some point in the conversation, I diverted our path towards a cemetery — the cemetery on my list. I remember thinking that he had to question our path at some point, but he did not. He followed, like a good disciple, into the depths of the cemetery.

It was not the most private of cemeteries. I felt like someone was watching us at all times. They weren't — watching us, but it felt like it. That is the sort of thing I do not like — being watched. I kill for me — for my own pleasure. I do not kill for an audience — to be recognized.

We wandered the paths, and Jacob stopped frequently. He spoke about the saints and the sinners. He spoke about God and the holy place we were parading in. He was back to talking about his passion — Theology. I honestly believed he forgot that he was trying to seduce me — to hook up, and was back to wanting to educate me about God — his God. I was okay with this distraction. It made it easier for me to lure him into a darker corner of the cemetery — to show him an older tombstone or crypt. When isolated as we became, it was easy for me to strike.

We stopped in front of a large crypt. It was pretty beautiful — old. The date on it was hard to read, but it appeared to be old. I stopped Jacob, grabbed his hand for the first time, and pulled him closer to me. I remember telling him he looked cute in the dusk light as we knelt to try and read the carved lettering of the crypt. Mother Nature had taken her toll — had softened the once-deep, sharp carvings.

As we knelt, our legs touching, our breath getting tangled together in the cooling night air, I raised my arm as if I were going to put it over his shoulder, and instead I grabbed the back of Jacob's head — a large entanglement of his hair, and pulled back, then pushed his head forward, slamming it against the crypt. He struggled, tried to fight free from my grip. I let go of his hair and grabbed his neck as he felt the blood drip down his forehead. Holding his neck tightly, I too could feel the warm blood as I pushed his head into the concrete crypt again and again.

Each time his head hit the concrete, the tear in his forehead got bigger. More blood gushed out. I broke his nose, letting out even more blood. By the time I stopped slamming his head against the concrete, his face was covered in blood with some pieces of loose concrete stuck in the gashes of skin. We were kneeling already, so his fall to the ground was short and silent. His head rested against the crypt, and I watched him try to move, to talk. He could do neither. He looked into my eyes, and I into his, as if that moment should have been romantic. Then I leaned in close to him. Our skin was touching — I could feel his warmth on my cheek as I whispered into his ear.

I don't recall what I said to him. I am sure it was something snarky—something that pointed out to him that he should not follow strangers into a cemetery. What I said was not relevant. Even though they were the last words he ever heard.

I sat next to him, holding him gently, wiping the blood from his face, tasting his blood, and letting it linger in my mouth like a fine wine. I got drunk off his mistake. By the time I stood up to leave, dusk had passed. It was dark—almost black. I could not see anything around us. It was not clear from which direction we had come. I stood and spun around. On the perimeter of the cemetery, I could see light—life, but within the four walls, it was dark—void of life. I bent back down towards Jacob and licked his face, taking in one more big gulp of his blood.

I went through his rucksack and grabbed what little cash he had and then walked into the darkness, vanishing into the night. I walked through the town all night, never sleeping. I was high on blood—energized from another kill. By the time the sun shed light on the sleepy town the next morning, I was back at the train station, cleaned up and waiting for the next train back to London.

I can only assume that someone eventually found Jacob. I did not watch the news or read any newspapers to find out. I did not care, really. I got what I needed and wanted, and that was all that mattered to me.

32

Killing Jacob was fun. Luring him into the cemetery — having to play that flirty game was not as much fun as smashing his head into the concrete crypt. The sound that echoed with his scream as his skull kissed the faded letters was choral. I love it when my victims cry out for help — cry out at all. That acknowledgement of their suffering is part of the excitement. It is those sounds, mixed with any amount of blood, that get me so aroused. Every time I kill, I think back to that day when I watched the little girl get attacked by Chester.

On the train ride back to London, I slept the best I had slept in a long time, since sleeping in Murray's very comfortable bed. I cannot recall what I dreamt about, but I remember being rudely woken by the ticket collector. He was an older guy — not very friendly at all. He took his job way too seriously, in my opinion.

After showing my ticket to him, he moved on to share his lack of friendliness with the next passenger, and as he did, I looked across the aisle to see a young couple. The girl was asleep, her head gently resting on the boy's shoulder. They looked to be around my age. He smiled at me, so I smiled back. As I did, I thought about Didier and Corinne. They lured me in with a smile, too.

The boy followed his smile with a wave, as if our smiles had not already connected us. I waved back. Then he started to talk silently. Maybe he was mouthing words, or perhaps he was whispering. Either way, I remember shaking my head at him to indicate that I had no idea what he was saying. His response was to smile again.

Eventually, the girl woke up, wiped some drool from her lips, and then headed to the toilet. It was then that the boy leaned closer and said he thought I was cute, asking where I was headed. It turns out that we were both returning to London, and the girl traveling with him was his sister — half sister, really, but that detail was not necessary to me then, or now.

They had been visiting their nan somewhere up north — a town I had not heard of before. I cannot recall the sister's name, but his name was Caspian. I remember thinking that was a pretty cool name. He was cute — handsome, even. He was the whitest person I had ever seen. He had flawless skin. No lines. No blemishes. Nothing but a sea of smooth white. They both had blonde hair, bleached to the point of almost being white, yet still vibrant like the sun. She wore sunglasses the whole time in the train, but I can only assume that she had eyes like Caspian — a blue so bright I got lost swimming in them as we stared at each other.

Caspian had a rather thick Irish accent, making it hard for me to understand every word he spoke, but I got the gist of most of what he said to me. The most direct was when he asked me to get off the train with him and his sister. His plan, I would learn as the day went on, was to drop his sister off at home and then go out and explore the city with me. I think the 'explore' part was just a ploy. He knew the city quite well. That was evident as we paraded through the streets and passages, popping into different pubs and shops. We were being silly — something I missed out on as a kid.

Caspian told me all about his life — where he grew up, what he liked, and what he didn't like. He hated haggis, but loved

American burgers. He did not drink alcohol or soda. He told me that he had maintained a healthy lifestyle since he was 12 and worked out regularly to keep himself lean and in shape. He was not obsessed with muscles or looking perfect, but he did look perfect.

As he pulled me through the city, grabbing my hand now and again to make sure I did not fall behind or leave, I felt a tingle. It was not the tingle I got when I had been with Murray, or the one I had as a child when Morris was around. This tingle felt more like how I felt when I killed. I knew almost from the moment I looked into his eyes on the train that I wanted to kill Caspian. I had it in my head that seeing his blood run down his snow white skin would be so beautiful—erotic.

Each time I thought I would be able to pull him in my direction—take him where I wanted to go, he would ramble on about something or some place I had to see, and he would pull me, walk-running in his direction.

When he smiled, I smiled. When he told a joke, I laughed. When we finally stopped in a passage off a busy high street and tried to kiss, I pushed back. In fact, I almost punched him. I had been having a wonderful day with Caspian. I had enjoyed, for the first time since Murray, just being me. I had not thought about kissing or touching or fucking. I thought about slicing, puncturing, and pulverizing. I had hoped to skip the flirting and romantic part of the ritual and jump right into the killing part, but Caspian made that problematic.

We were alone in that passage, and he was trying to comprehend why I pushed back. I could see the look in his eyes. He was straining to understand what sign he had missed, or what he had done or not done to provoke me in such a way. I cannot recall our entire dialogue that day, but I remember that he started to cry, which was so out of character for the person I had only known for a few hours. The whole day, on the train and up to that point, he had been strong, confident—almost arrogant about everything. Then, he was not any of those things. He was practically inconsolable for what seemed like a really long time.

He did stop crying eventually. He rambled on about how embarrassed he was and how he was 'falling' for me faster than he had for anyone ever before. I remember thinking that he knew nothing about me, not really anything substantial, so I was pretty confused, but I played along for a little while.

I wanted to kill him so badly. I could feel the urge surging through my body, but I still had not worked out how I was going to do it, or where. We never stood still long enough for me to think about it all that much. But, as we stood in that passage and he cried, I knew that if I did not kill him right then and there, I would never have the opportunity. I figured that he would run away from me, and that would be the last time I would ever see him; I could not have that. His smooth white skin was so beautiful, and I could not think of anything other than covering it with his blood.

I grabbed him by his shoulders and turned him towards me. He reluctantly looked into my eyes, his still swimming in tears. I could tell he was about to say something to me, but I was not interested in hearing it. By then, I was only interested in killing him, and I almost did—almost killed him right there, but as I was about to slam him into the wall, a door opened, letting out steam and a stench of old fried food. A woman stepped out carrying two large rubbish bags. She looked at the two of us, and before I knew it, I had released Caspian, and we ran out of the passage. I doubt the woman paid any attention to us, and I doubt Caspian ever thought his life was in danger. In fact, I am pretty confident that he was unaware of anything other than being embarrassed because I would not kiss him back.

We must have run three or four blocks before stopping, almost trampling passers-by along the footpath. When we stopped, we were hunched over, hands on our knees, panting as if we had just run a marathon. We looked at each other, and I could tell he was still struggling with my rejection, so I gave in. I knew that my window to kill him was closing, and I knew that the only way I was going to win at that point was to give him what he wanted. So I kissed him. Ironically, it was he who pushed back that time. After all, we were no longer in the privacy of the passage. We were out in the open, and it turned out that he wasn't. No one was paying any attention to us, but that did not change the reality of the moment.

Caspian pushed me to the ground and ran back in the direction we came. I sat on the footpath and watched him dash through the crowd. No one stopped to help me, mainly because no one was watching us. No one cared. I sat for longer than I probably should have, just letting people walk by me. Some accidentally hit me — most did not see me. I am sure some thought I was a vagrant.

Then, just as I was about to stand up, I felt a hand on my shoulder and saw another reach down for my hand. I grabbed the free hand and looked up. I expected it to be Caspian. I had assumed he would have realized what a fool he had been, and that he had come back to reconcile. Instead, I found myself standing face-to-face with Bernard. I recognized him right away, but I wasn't sure if he recognized me, the thief who had beaten him up just days earlier. I did not look different. Maybe a little more frazzled — less focused, but he should have recognized me — remembered me. He did not, or at least he played along as if he did not.

I remember thanking him. I remember his clammy hands — sweaty and sticky. I remember thinking that there was no way he did not recognize me. I friggin robbed the guy just a few days earlier. Then, as soon as I was upright, standing face to face with Bernard, he punched me in the chest and called me a prick.

"You fuckin' stole all my money," he said in a yelling whisper. "I should've just let these people trample you to death."

I laughed at the idea of me being trampled. He saw no humor in the conversation at all.

"Sorry, dude. I needed money. You had money. It was really that simple," I said back as transactionally as I could. "Do you want to go back to your place so I can earn the money and then we can call it a day?" I smiled.

He laughed as if I had been joking, but once he realized that I was not kidding, he blushed.

"It was a lot of money," he responded, as if he suddenly calculated how many sexual favors he could cash in.

I convinced Bernard to take me back to his flat. I still had the urge to kill, and if Caspian was not going to be my victim, I was going to let Bernard fill in.

What I did not know was how far we were from Bernard's flat. We walked for more than an hour before he led me into Brompton Cemetery — a shortcut to his flat. But by that time, I was on the verge of exploding. I had worked myself up about killing Caspian, so every minute that passed had me more anxious. I had to kill.

As we walked through the cemetery, we passed a secluded, overgrown part, so I grabbed Bernard's hand and pulled him that way. Within minutes, we were completely isolated from the other foot traffic. I pulled him close to me—our noses almost touched. I kissed him to put him at ease, and surprisingly, he kissed back. He grabbed my back and pulled my whole body closer as if her were going to swallow all of me. He started to unbutton his trousers, but I pushed him away. He tripped on the concrete steps of the mausoleum we stood in front of and hit his head on the metal door. I heard a crack, but was not sure which of his bones had been broken. He did not move.

As I looked at the young man strung out along the old concrete steps, his trousers fallen, exposing his genitals, I watched a pool of red engulf his head. I wanted to scream.

My hands started to shake. I needed to kill. I did not consider this a kill. I mean, sure, it was a kill, but not one enough to curb my craving. The dead body before me then was an accident—a setup gone wrong. Don't get me wrong. I was happy that Bernard was dead, but I was not pleased at how he died. That moment felt like the time Rob shot himself in front of me. I was cheated.

In that moment, furious that I could not manage to kill someone, I walked out of the cemetery and then ran to the cougar's house. I knew that if I could not kill, then at least I could get high. That was the only other thing that would calm me down—getting totally stoned out of my mind and sleeping it off.

33

Each time Adam got high, he got so stoned that he could not move his body for days. He was with the cougar boys, passed out, living in his dreams—his nightmares. After seeing Bernard die, Adam raced to the cougar boys. He needed to get high—needed to forget about the real world for an hour, or 48. He found himself hanging out with the cougar brothers even more, despite having told himself he was done with them, and he stole their book. No sooner had he stolen it than he was right back with the boys, but he was always too stoned to know if he hung out with them because he was depressed, he missed Murray, or he really liked the free drugs. Well, the drugs were not entirely free. Adam often had to go down on one or both of them, and sometimes their mother, too, depending on how high he needed to get and where he wanted to be.

He needed to be high to forget about Murray. When he was sober, everywhere Adam looked, he thought he saw Murray. Every distant voice sounded like Murray. He hoped that being high would help him forget Murray, if even for a short while, but while he was in a deep slumber, he dreamt of Murray—dreamt of the perfect relationship with Murray. The one that did not exist—might never exist.

*   *   *   *   *

Murray went on living his life. He decided that dating men was not good for him. He needed to be single. It was the only way he thought he could keep from being depressed over and over—from reliving a pattern of relationships he fell too hard, too fast, and where he always got hurt. Murray thought he had gone slow enough with Adam, and he had, but the distance, lies, and vagueness of their relationship took a toll on him. So, he swore off dating guys.

He resumed his flirty bartender behavior, but never went beyond the tease. He stopped feeling sorry for himself and focused on himself, for a change. He started eating healthier and resumed his gym routine. He began learning Mandarin and planned to take a trip to China. He would take three steps forward in his new life, and then he would hear someone who sounded like Adam or see someone who looked like Adam, and he would find himself curled up on his settee, crying.

Eventually, that stopped—the crying, the self-pity, he did not have time for it. The new language, travel plans, and outlook on life finally helped him break out of his rut. But that did not mean that he stopped holding his breath each time the door at The Drunken Unicorn opened. Murray convinced himself that he was moving on, but deep inside, he still missed Adam—still hoped he would walk into the pub ready to commit finally.

*   *   *   *   *

When Adam was not high, he was sleeping, and when he was not sleeping, he was having sex with strangers who were also spending more and more time with the cougar brothers. If he had the willpower to step out of his body and look inward, he could see that he was spiraling into a world he had sworn he would never enter again. When he sold drugs and his body in Vermont, he kept clean, primarily, and focused on getting out of Vermont, on having a better life. He would scold those he sold to in Vermont as he watched their lives fall apart—spiral downward as if they had no control. They didn't; not in that moment. No one has control. Not when you are strung out on some drug cocktail and are convinced that the only way out is with another drug combination.

He was never going to be like those people—lost. As that teenager on the cusp of manhood, he thought he knew everything—he could solve all the world's problems. All teens feel like that, or at least many do. But, in his early 20s, Adam was no different than the people he swore he would not be.

He could hear himself thinking this as he lay on his back in a beanbag chair that was slowly leaking beads. His eyes had rolled back in his head hours earlier, and he was living in a world of his own, oblivious to the real one—the one where Murray lived, where he was real, and where he secretly hoped Adam would come home —come back.

When Adam would finally wake from his self-induced coma, he would be starving, but not for food. He wanted more drugs. His first few weeks with the cougar brothers, Adam would wake up and want to kill, after all, that was his first passion—his favorite thing to do. But, as the drugs spread through his system, filling him with new feelings of joy and ecstasy, the idea of killing started to take a back seat, yet again. It was not that he did not want to kill, but that he thought getting high was more fun than killing. That was, until the cougar brothers cut off Adam's supply.

34

I did not mean to do it. I mean, I did—mean it, but not initially. I never thought they would cut me off, or at least not as abruptly as they did. All good things come to an end. Even I know that. I watched Liam's good life end when he let his jealousy get the better of him. I watched countless people run out of luck as their blood drained away. But I did not plan to kill the cougar brothers, at least not both of them. They were my only connection to the drug underworld. Well, my easy connection. I am sure that if they really did kick me out of their flat and force me to fend for myself, then I would have found a way to get drugs. The brothers were not the only source.

I did not expect them both to turn on me, and so quickly. I had just finished fucking the older one while I got fucked by the younger one. We all exploded at the same time. I remember thinking that it was—the timing. Then, as we sat on their nasty settee, the three of us still naked and sticky—sweaty, smelling a little rank, the older one just came out with it.

"You gotta go, dude," he said just as calmly as he could with his deep, raspy voice. His sexy voice, really. "You suck too much of our blow, man."

I could listen to him talk all day. He had one of those radio voices—you know the ones—that are just perfect for announcements. He could have made a good life for himself as an announcer, that is, if he were not a drug dealer. Anyway, I looked at him and then turned to his brother, who was playing with the hair — peach fuzz, really- that surrounded my nipple.

"Don't look at me, man," he said in a guilty tone. "I don't make the fucking rules."

"No, you just do the fucking," I snapped back at him as I pushed his hand away from my chest. "One more for the road, then," I said as I leaned forward towards the table in front of us. It was covered with drugs — all sorts — pills, powders, liquids. It was like a pharmacy counter.

I did not know what I was going to do. I couldn't go cold turkey all at once, and I was already craving another fix. As I looked at the table, I noticed a box knife and a single razor blade. I leaned forward and grabbed them both, and as I sat back, I jammed the box knife into the throat of the older brother and sliced the neck of the little brother. They both screamed. Lucky for me, anyone who might have been in the house was so stoned that they were clueless about what was going on. I had no idea where their mother was at that moment, and did not really care.

I kept jabbing the box knife into the older brother — his neck, his chest, anything that was soft enough to accept the sharp blade. With each contact, I opened the flesh, and blood spilled out. It was glorious. The little brother grabbed his neck and tried so hard to stop the bleeding, as if he was going to be able to save himself. His bloody hands moved from his neck to my body and back again as if I was going to help. I appreciated the blood he was wiping all over me, but I was not going to help him. I rolled over onto the lap of the older brother and stabbed him some more, and then slit his neck with the box knife, and went in and kissed him so I could feel the gushing of his warm blood on my body. I licked his chest and kissed him some more as the life and blood drained from him. Then I jumped up and over onto his brother's lap and kissed him—taking in his final few breaths. There was so much blood. Without thinking, I stood up and fell back onto the table, smashing bottles and covering everything with blood. I had tarred and powdered myself real good.

I ran my hands over my body, trying to collect the bloody powder, and licked my fingers, hoping to get high. I stood up and then lost my balance and fell back onto the table again, this time smashing it into two pieces. A sharp piece of broken wood sliced my side, adding my blood to the mix. I managed to stand up without cutting myself more, and as I stood between the settee and what was left of the table, I smiled, even though my side and ass still hurt. It felt so good—not the pain, but the satisfaction of killing again—really killing. I felt alive, like I could suddenly conquer the world. I admired my work—the pile of blood-soaked flesh on the settee for longer than I probably should have, but it just felt good to be back in the game—to be back to my old self, however fleeting it would be. I had been bouncing back and forth between wanting to kill and wanting to get high for too long. It felt good to be focused.

I heard noise above me. Someone on the second floor was moving around, and I knew it would only be a matter of time before someone walked in on the bloody mess, so I ran out of the room, leaving clearly defined red footprints like breadcrumbs behind me as I made my way to the toilet. I stood over the sink and looked at myself in the mirror. I was covered in blood, and it felt so good. I licked my fingers and tasted the brothers. I wanted to run back into the parlor and lick them both, but I knew better. I knew that I needed to get cleaned up and out of the house before I got caught.

I washed the blood off my hands, and then grabbed a towel and tried to wash off as much of the blood from my body. The sink was small, and the water pressure was low, making the process time-consuming, but I managed to get it done. I left the blood-soaked towel on the floor and walked back towards the parlor to collect my clothes. I was very aware of my surroundings — my sensory glands were working overtime or something. I was feeling a little paranoid, too. Whatever drugs I ingested when I fell into the table were hitting me — I was tripping.

In the parlor, I struggled to find my clothes and began to wonder if I had never put them on in the first place, but then I couldn't recall where I might have last worn them. Instead of fretting, I meandered around the house until I ended up in one of the brothers' bedrooms, where I grabbed some of his clothes and got dressed. I found a few rolls of money in his sock drawer, so I stuck those in my backpack, which was on his floor — of course, I couldn't remember how it got there. I could not recall ever being in his room before, so naturally I started panicking, thinking that the brothers had been going through my things — everyone's things — when we were passed out in our drug-induced comas. As I returned to the main floor, I made sure to avoid being seen by two girls who had arrived and were standing in the parlor, crying and screaming at each other to call 999.

I tiptoed to the back of the house and out the kitchen door, across their small garden, scaled a low stone wall, and found myself standing on a sidewalk one block from their home. I let out a sigh. It felt good to be out of the house, to be away from the brothers, but most of all, it felt good to have killed again. I could still feel the drugs swirling around in my head, and I knew that I needed to either find someplace to lie low and come down off my high or keep going and find someone else to kill.

*　　*　　*　　*　　*

Sitting on an old wooden park bench, somewhat isolated from the foot traffic of the high street, I could feel the tightness of the stolen clothes. They were snug in a few places that made it uncomfortable to sit. For as chaotic as it was as I slipped out of the cougar brothers' flat, I did remember to grab my backpack, and as I sat uncomfortably on the bench, I examined the rolls of fifty pound notes I stole. I counted almost two thousand pounds. I felt a massive sense of relief—like this was the sign I needed to get my life back on track; to get back to Murray and be the perfect boyfriend. As I continued to rummage through my bag, I noticed a slightly torn card. I pulled it out and read it. It took me a moment to remember who Callum was and why I had a card with his name and contact information, but as that day flashed through my mind, I remembered him. I remembered his cute smile and his thick accent.

I wanted to get back to Murray, and I would eventually, but I knew in that moment that I needed to reach out to Callum. I needed to continue to feed my desire—my need for blood. I convinced myself, like any good junkie does, that Callum would be my last kill. I told myself that I needed Murray, that I should be with Murray, and to do that I would need to change—and I would. But first, I needed one more hit.

When I sobered up, I called the number on the card. It rang for a long time before someone finally answered it—a girl's voice. I almost hung up, but instead I deepened my already deep voice and asked to speak with Callum. The woman politely told me to hold. I could hear her walking — scuffling really, opening and closing doors. It took much longer than I anticipated, but eventually I heard her muffled voice speaking to someone, followed by a man's voice speaking directly into the phone.

*   *   *   *   *

"This is Callum," he said in that thick Scottish accent. It was still difficult to make out every word, but his voice was hypnotic.

"Hi. I am not sure if you remember me, but…" I started to say before being interrupted.

"The cute American boy from the train," he said, his words railroading my own. "I am so glad you called."

"Yeah, well, I found your card — not that I lost it, I mean, but I, um, anyway, I just thought I would call to say hello."

"Yes, well, that is wonderful," he replied with such upper-class elegance. He spoke like a man with money. Callum spoke like he was raised with money — raised without a worry in the world, unlike me.

"Yeah, so, anyway…" I started before being cut off again.

"Why don't you come for tea this afternoon. Shall we say 4 o'clock? Right, it is settled then. See you then. Bye."

*   *   *   *   *

He hung up on me. I was not prepared for such an abrupt ending to our call. He did not give me a location, so I was forced to assume that the address on his card was where I was supposed to be at 4 o'clock that afternoon. I looked like shit. I felt like shit. I stunk and I was jittery—coming off the high of my kills as well as the drugs. I needed to clean myself up if I was really going to see Callum—kill him.

I walked a few blocks into a shop and bought some new clothes with my newfound money, then spent an hour walking until I found a hostel where I could take a long, hot shower. I walked into that smelly, depressing building looking like I belonged in it, but emerged clean, fresh, and ready to kill—um, I mean, to take on the world.

The three-story building was almost empty. All of the travelers were out touring the city, getting lost, or into trouble. Those still inside were asleep or having sex. Hostels are good for that kind of shit. The man at the front desk seemed unfazed by my appearance or my need for a bed in the late morning.

35

I jumped into a black cab and gave the driver the address on Callum's card. The driver was older, probably in his 60s. He was balding, but had a full beard and mustache, which looked silly on his small head. The facial hair was a mix of salt and pepper in color. His accent was easier to understand than Callum's. He told me it would take some time to get to that address. I did not care.

We weaved all around London, turning left then right and the left again. The driver had no patience when it came to traffic, which is probably not they best attitude to have when driving is your profession, but what did I know. I was not going to micromanage his driving. I had no idea where we were going. I mean I knew the address, but I had no idea how to get there — how to get to Callum's house. Every now and then the driver would yell out a profanity, then apologize to me, but I did not care if he cussed or not. Thankfully he paid very little attention to me. The last thing I wanted was this driver remembering what I looked like — where he dropped me off. When news of Callum's death made it to the news I did not want anyone calling me out as a suspect; least of all this driver.

When we finally arrived, I was ten minutes late. The driver sped off as soon as I closed the door behind me, leaving me on the sidewalk alone. I looked at a wide set of steps that led to a door. Above that door were the numbers from Callum's card so I walked up and pushed the doorbell button.

After what felt like forever a woman opened the door, I assume she was the same one who answered the phone. I was beginning to think this dude was pretty wealthy if he has someone taking care of him like it was looking like he did. Maybe it was his wife or girlfriend — maybe his daughter. I did not know — not right away.

*   *   *   *   *

"Hello ma'am, I am here to see Callum," I said in a deep, polite voice. I could not believe my eyes — it was Imogen, the girl from the sperm bank. Of course she did not recognize me. There was no reason for her to remember me.

"Yes, yes. Do come in," she responded, stepping back from the door. "He has been expecting you."

*   *   *   *   *

He clearly did not get unexpected visitors if she knew I was the one from the phone. Once I was in the front hall, Imogen closed and locked the door behind me, then walked passed me and asked me to follow her. Her steps were like that of a ninja. She was silent — almost walking on air. I could hear my own shoes squeaking now and again as we walked through the house, eventually stopping at a set of large, wooden doors. She opened one of them and waved me in, then closed the door behind me. I was waiting for her to lock that one, too.

"There he is," Callum said to me from across the room. "I hope Imogen was kind to you. She does not like me having gentleman callers, especially when they are as young and as handsome as you."

"She was" is all I could say back to him. I was shocked, stunned — oddly excited that Imogen was in the house.

"Imogen is my niece. She checks in on me once a week like I am some old man in need of elder care, or something. She will not be bothering us. She will be leaving soon." He felt compelled to explain.

* * * * *

I was not excited to hear that Imogen would be leaving. The moment she opened the door and I recognized her I got excited at the idea of killing two people. Of course, Imogen or not, I was going to have to kill two people. She heard my voice on the phone — she could probably trace the call's origin. She saw my face. If she were to leave only to return to find her uncle dead, I would be the first person she would report to the police.

Callum pointed to a settee, and we both sat. But as soon as we did, Imogen knocked on the door and then walked in to tell Callum he had a phone call. It was weird because I never heard a phone ring, yet I could see a phone sitting on his desk. I noticed a light blinking. He told me that he had to take the call and that I should follow Imogen out and to the kitchen so she could give me something to eat or drink.

That was my moment. It was how it would all unfold. The kitchen is a great place to kill someone — so many sharp objects to pierce the skin.

I followed her silently. Neither of us said a word until we walked into the large white room. The white walls were lined with white cabinets with white handles. The floor was white. The room almost felt sterile. I looked around for anything sharp, but there were no knives on the counter. In fact, there was nothing on the counters. Imogen pointed to a stool as if silently instructing me to sit. I obeyed.

She walked around, pulling things out of drawers and cabinets, finally bringing color to the room. She placed a bottle of red wine on the counter and put a bottle opener next to it before walking to another corner of the kitchen to open what turned out to be the fridge. It blended right in with all the other cabinets — hidden in plain sight.

I noticed a white phone hanging on the wall with one of its lights glowing. Callum was still on the phone. I stood up and walked over to where the wine was, grabbed the opener, and then walked towards Imogen. Before she could turn around, I grabbed her face, covering her mouth with one hand while I stabbed her — jamming the corkscrew into her side. I pushed it in, twisted it, and pulled it out, then repeated the process again and again. I held her tightly. She was smaller than me so it was easy. I kept stabbing her stomach and her sides for what seemed like a full minute. I lost count of how many holes I had put into her. She had blood oozing out of all of them, and it all felt so warm and wonderful.

As she went limp I let her go and she collapsed to the floor. The white kitchen turned quite red. The cabinets where she tried to grab hold of something, the floor, the counter were all painted in a lovely hue. I, too was covered, just as I liked it. But, as I stood over her, watching the blood drain out of Imogen I realized that I had not thought any of that afternoon through very well. I was covered in blood. There was no way I could walk back into see Callum covered in blood and have enough time to kill him, too.

Rather than panic, I took off all of my clothes, leaving the bloody rags on the floor with Imogen. I licked some of her blood off my fingers before washing up in the sink, sadly ridding me of her color. Every few seconds I looked back over at the phone. The light still glowed.

Washed clean and naked, I walked out of the kitchen and back towards Callum's office. As I got closer I could hear the mumbling of his voice. I stood on the other side of the door for just a moment — long enough to calm myself from the exciting high I just experienced with Imogen, then I opened the door wide.

"I will have to call you back," were the last words Callum said before hanging up the phone. I knew this is why he called me over to his house. I knew the dirty old man wanted some naked twink fun so I did what I do best — took control of the situation.

He stood behind his desk as if her were afraid to move towards me, as if he knew what I had just done to Imogen. But the truth was, he was taking in the sights — my fully naked, muscled frame walking towards him, relaxed and ready for fun. I made it to his desk before Callum moved. He tried to touch me — to touch down there, but I grabbed his wrists and pushed him up against the bookshelves that lined the wall behind his desk.

"This is what you want? Isn't it?" I asked, not really looking for an answer.

He only nodded 'yes,' still speechless.

I got close to him. Our noses were almost touching — we could both smell the other. His breath was surprisingly fresh. Mine smelled of blood — iron, but he would not know that. He probably just thought I had nasty teen breath or something. I did not care. He tried to kiss me but I pulled back and kneed him in the balls.

"I did not say you could kiss me," I said as if I were the master and he the slave in this unrehearsed performance. He said nothing in response. I held him there — his arms raised, his body pressed against what looked like ancient books, for a few moments while I contemplated how I was going to kill him.

"Sit in your chair," I said as I let go of his wrists and stepped back so he could follow my order. He was quite obedient. While he sat in the chair I bent down and untied his shoes, then pulled the laces out of each. Then I tied his wrists to the arms of the chair. I knew the laces were not strong enough to hold Callum down, but were long enough and the knots I made were tight enough that it would be a struggle for him to free himself.

I stepped back and then walked along the wall of books, reading but not really reading the titles to myself, dragging my finger across them as if I were studying them — looking for a specific title. Callum remained silent.

I was a few feet away from him when I turned around and asked him to kick off his shoes. He gently pushed one off with the other. I stood still for a moment so he could take in the sight of my body again — see all that he could have, but never actually would. I walked back towards him, bent over and pulled off both of his socks. It took some work since they were clipped to garters. I had never seen anything like these before and was, honestly, pretty pissed that I had to work that much harder to remove his fucking socks.

When I finally got the socks unclipped and removed from Callum's feet I balled one of them up and shoved it in his mouth. He took the smelly cloth willingly. Then I took the other one and stretched it around his head, covering his mouth and tied it in the back. My bare chest was pressed against his face as I did.

I took a step back and could see that Callum was excited. I was still amazed that he remained silent—calm, as if this was all very familiar to him. I was making it up as I went along. He was tied to the chair and he was gagged. Callum was not going anywhere and yet I still had not figured out how I was going to kill him. He stretched out his legs and placed his bare feet on mine and rubbed. I was not sure if he was trying to get me aroused or if that was his way of thanking me for whatever he thought was going to happen. Whatever he thought was going to happen certainly was not going to happen. I am pretty sure that of all the possible scenarios that were running through his head, me killing him was not one of them.

I let him play footsie with me for a moment while I scanned the room. The best I could find was a letter opener on his desk so I grabbed it and jabbed it into his thigh. He tried to scream, but the gag was on pretty tight. I pulled the letter opener out and put the now red tip in my mouth, savoring the flavor. I was probably a little too erotic with the opener in my mouth, but I was doing everything I could to keep Callum focused on my body and not his pain.

With the tip cleaned I jabbed it into his other thigh and repeated my behavior. Surprisingly Callum remained excited — maybe even more excited. He even continued to play footsie, which I found most interesting. Clearing I was not abusing him enough. He enjoyed pain and bondage, so I upped my game by jabbing the opener into his stomach a few times, each time licking it clean before piercing his skin another time. By the fifth stab I could see that Callum was no longer excited. I think the reality of what was happening was setting in for him, so I sat on his lap, straddling him. I held the back of the chair with my free hand while the the other held the opener.

I dragged it across his face, his chest, around his ear. His body flinched each time I brought the opener closer to him, but relaxed when I did not penetrate him with it. I pushed it into his cheek and dragged hard, slightly piercing the skin. Very little blood slipped out, but I still licked his cheek, taking in whatever he was reluctantly offering.

What I did not notice the entire time I was teasing Callum was that he had been busy trying to wiggle his wrists free. Just as I went in to lick his cheek again I felt his hand on my back. Before he could do anything more I reacted by jabbing the opener into his neck. It went in at an odd angle under his ear and poked out in the back. In that moment his hand fell off my back so I jumped up, away from him, taking the opener with me. Blood shot out of his neck. Before he could use his free hand to try and stop the bleeding, I grabbed that hand and put it on his thigh, then jammed the opener through his hand until I knew the opener had gone clear through his hand and into his thigh, binding his free hand once again.

Callum drowned in his own blood. His body twitched for a few minutes before going completely limp—lifeless. I got closer to him and dragged my hands all over him, drenching them in his blood before rubbing them all over my naked body. I wanted to wrap myself in his blood.

As I sat on his lap, once again, painting my body red I noticed the light on his desk phone start blinking. I assumed that meant a phone was ringing somewhere else in the house. Then after a few seconds the light stopped blinking, but stayed lit. I did not know much about these kinds of phones, but I thought that it meant that someone else was in the house, and had answered the call.

I jumped off Callum, grabbed my bag that I had left on the settee, and slowly opened the office door. I stretched my head out and looked around before tip-toeing into the hall. I needed to find his bedroom—to find some clothes. I could not walk out of his house wearing nothing but a backpack. As I moved through the house I did not hear anyone talking or making any sound at all. I wandered up a flight of steps and eventually found Callum's bedroom. I cleaned myself up and rummaged through his things. I found some clothes that fit enough to get out of the house without drawing attention to myself. I found some money in a drawer and a really nice watch, so I took those and walked back through the house and out the front door.

At the base of the stairs I turned left and started walking—not running, until I was a couple of blocks away, then I ran—jogged for a couple more blocks. I stopped to catch my breath and noticed that I was in front of a cafe, so I went to grab something to eat and that is when I saw Eve for the first time.

36

She was not beautiful—I mean, not in the way that all the girls in the magazine adverts are beautiful. She was not even pretty —like the girls who are just naturally pretty, ya know—the ones who never wear make-up, but always look perfect. She was just plain—kind of just there, hovering somewhere between good-looking and not good-looking. I imagined that she went through life unnoticed, but I noticed her. I noticed her because she looked out of place. Everyone in the cafe was with someone else. Eve was alone. She did not look like she was waiting for someone, or upset that she might have been stood up. She was just there, sitting peacefully, quietly staring at a cup of tea. I wondered if it was too hot and she was letting it cool down, or maybe she was still letting the leaves steep. Perhaps it was already cold. Whatever the case, she sat there silently studying the small cup.

*   *   *   *   *

"Mind if I sit here with you?" I asked her as I slipped into the bench across from her. The cafe was full—this was the only place I could sit. She grunted without looking up, so I asked again once I was comfortably seated. This second time, she jumped, almost frightened, startled that someone was suddenly sitting at the table with her.

"I'm Adam," I said next, still waiting for a more verbal response.

"Eve," she said without looking up. I noticed that her hands were in her lap or on her bench—out of sight.

"What's good to eat here?" I asked, determined to get some words out of her.

"She doesn't say much," the waitress chimed in as she approached the table. "Do ya love?" She asked into the air as she looked in Eve's direction.

"Poor girl is high as a kite right now," the waitress continued. "I let her sit here so she does not get into trouble, and so those lads don't abuse her anymore." She pointed out towards the street as if a group of boys were waiting to pounce on Eve once she walked out of the cafe. I looked, but I did not see anyone.

*   *   *   *   *

I sat with Eve for hours. Eventually, she started talking. At first, she didn't make a lot of sense, but as the night progressed and she came down from her high, our conversation took shape and made sense. It turned out that we had a lot in common—well, a lot more than most people I encountered. We were both down on our luck and had been for most of our lives. We both struggled through life—nothing ever handed to us, and no path cleared.

By the time Eve was fully aware of her surroundings, she realized that she needed to leave. She told me that her father would be waiting up for her and she needed to get home to him. I offered to walk her home, but she refused to let me. She wanted to be alone, or so I thought.

I went out on a limb and asked Eve if she wanted to hang out again—meet up and talk. I had enjoyed our conversation, which was something I hadn't done since being with Murray, yet it was all easier with Eve. She agreed to meet me at the cafe every few days, and that began a friendship that she took to the grave.

37

Like Adam, Eve came from a broken home. Unlike Adam, whose parents mostly ignored him, Eve got a lot of attention, especially from her father, a low-life drug dealer who was known for solving problems with violence. He had been in and out of jail for most of his adult life, and until she got the courage to run away, he had been the only guardian for Eve. Her mother died from a drug overdose when Eve was seven. That was around the same time that her father started sexually abusing Eve.

Eve knew nothing about intimacy. From a young age, she was conditioned — almost trained to perform sexual acts on older men. At first, only her father enjoyed her pre-teen and teenage body, but by the time Eve was a teenager, her father had been renting her out to all of his friends. Those deadbeat criminals would stop by the house for a wet blow from Eve and some white blow from her dad. Unfortunately for Eve, by the time she was 18, she had been raped, beaten, drugged, and abused so much that she just assumed that was how women were supposed to be treated. No one ever noticed her pain. No one ever noticed she was hurting. No one ever cared to see her for anything other than sex.

When Eve turned 18, her father did not throw her a big party. Instead, he tried to rape her again. Unlike every time before when Eve would lay helpless and frightened, she fought back. Eve sat on her bed and her father walked in naked. His large, hairy stomach hung lower than it should, like most of the fat on his out-of-shape body. He opened her door and invited himself in and marched towards her bed, just as he had so many times before. Unfortunately for her dad, Eve was prepared for him that evening. She was tired of being abused by him—by everyone, so she did what she assumed her father would do to an intruder. As her father leaned on the edge of the bed, trying to wiggle himself into her, Eve grabbed the large knife she had stolen from the kitchen earlier that night, and she swung it at her father's penis like a novice fencer. Her eyes were closed and she was crying, but she kept swinging. She heard her father scream, and she felt the sting of his palm. She knew that would leave a mark.

Moments later, Eve heard a loud thud. She opened her eyes, and even though the room was dark, she could tell that her father was no longer on top of her. She quickly turned on her bedside lamp and noticed her father lying on the floor of the bedroom. His naked flesh was splattered red, and in addition to a few cuts on his arms and his stomach, Eve had managed to slice open a vein on her father's penis.

As she looked over the edge of the bed and down at her father, who lay on the floor crying like a baby, Eve contemplated killing her father. She convinced herself that he deserved to die— that he should pay for all of the abuse he put her through, and should be stopped from abusing anyone else. She still had the knife in her hand.

She could have killed him. She should have killed him. Instead, she laid the knife on her father's chest and told him that if he ever touched another child, she would come back and kill him. Then she grabbed the bag she had already packed and ran out of the flat. Eve never returned. She never checked in to see if her father had died on her bedroom floor or if he survived and stopped touching young girls. She never followed up because once she was out of the house, she fell back into the same routine she had when she lived with her father: selling her body for money and for drugs.

Eve lived a sad life. She never traveled outside of London. She had never been shopping or sat on Santa's lap to tell what she wanted for Christmas. She barely even celebrated Christmas. Eve was one of those kids who managed to slip through the cracks of society. She never brought attention to herself, so her teachers never knew anything was wrong at home — that her father beat and raped her. In her later teen years, Eve prayed that she would get pregnant so someone would notice and do something about the abuse, but her prayers about that, like about everything else, went unheard.

Eve had been living on the streets for almost a year before she met Adam. Every man she encountered wanted to sell her drugs or buy her body. Every man was just like her father, so she was taken aback when Adam was kind to her, and he was kind to her, until he was not. Adam never abused Eve the way her father had. Their relationship — his abuse was consensual. Adam protected Eve, and in exchange for that protection, Eve did anything and everything Adam asked of her.

38

I found myself hanging out with Eve a lot. I was not necessarily attracted to her—not romantically and certainly not sexually, but there was something about her. It was as if she had become my new drug of choice. Her life sucked more than mine, so maybe I liked being the one better off for a change. The bar was really low. Maybe it was her access to drugs. Since killing the cougar brothers, access to anything remotely psychedelic had proven to be a challenge. Maybe it was her access to people willing to spend money for meaningless sex. I had become good at that over the years.

After a few weeks of being around each other almost every day, Eve finally felt, I guess, that I was ready to meet her pimp. I knew that Eve worked the streets—in our short time together I hung out with her while she worked. If she got picked up I found something else to do, or I got picked up, too. All through this I did not realize that she was working for someone else. I assumed she was like me—working for myself. I tricked because I needed cash for something specific. I did not trick for the sake of tricking, as if it were my regular job. Eve did.

One evening, while we were sitting in the same cafe we always sat in—met up at, I walked in to see Eve sitting with two girls. They looked older—tougher, but not too much older. The two girls were sitting across from one another. Eve was trapped, sitting on the inside of the booth. As I walked in I could see the two girls scolding Eve—not yelling at her, but verbally punishing her for something. They all went silent as I approached the booth.

Eve introduced me to Matilda and Eleanor. They did not invite me to sit down. Instead, the two looked at me, scanned my body from head to foot, most likely trying to determine how much of a threat I was going to be to them. I think they thought I was a pimp looking to take Eve away from them. I was polite; friendly as I spoke. I smiled and laughed trying to lighten the dark mood of the booth. Eve never looked up. Neither of the girls ever smiled.

The girls fired a few questions my way about who I was and where I was from and what my intensions were with 'their' Eve. I remember laughing at them as I answered. The more we talked the less of a threat I believed them to be to me, and the more I wanted to kill them both for the way they talked to Eve.

Eventually Matilda and Eleanor stood to leave. I stepped back so they could pass me and then I slid into the booth, sitting across from Eve. I watched Matilda and Eleanor leave the cafe before I started rapid firing questions at Eve about them.

It turned out that Matilda was Eleanor's girlfriend—someone along for the ride. Eleanor was the meaner one, according to Eve, and was the pimp who demanded so much time, effort and money from Eve. There was a flood of stories about Eleanor and her many girlfriends—Matilda being the latest one, that Eve shared with me. She held nothing back in telling me what she really thought about Eleanor and Matilda—where they live, what their schedule was like, and where they hung out. Eve had no idea that she was giving me everything I needed to kill the two girls so I sat back and let her vent. She really needed to let it all out. I could see how much better she felt after she was drained of words—of anger.

In turn, I filled Eve's ears with thoughts of freedom, of self-reliance. I told her that she could easily break free from Eleanor and Matilda, if she really wanted to be free — to make her own decisions. I could see in her eye in that moment that she was scared — afraid of being alone. For as fucked up as her life had been, Eve had never been alone. She always had someone looking over her — crushing her spirit. I was not there to change that for her, hell I turned out to be a bad friend, too, in the long run, but we will get there. For now let me just say that I got Eve thinking about other possibilities, at least for a brief moment.

Later that same night, long after we swapped stories, Eve and I were back out on the street corner. We had each taken a few hits of the blow that Eleanor gave to Eve to help her through the night. It was good stuff — really fucked with your head. At least it did with mine. I could not imagine being Eve or anyone else under Eleanor's thumb — that high and having to sell my body.

I must have fallen asleep or passed out from the intensity of the drugs because when I woke up the next morning I was still sitting on the same stoop from the night before. The sun was revealing all of the flaws that go unseen at night. Trash was everywhere on the street. My head was pounding and Eve was no where to be seen. I wanted to believe that she would not have just left me there, so I assumed she went home with a trick and we would catch up later.

I stumbled back to the hostel that I was calling home to sleep off an awful headache. I remember being woken up by a scrawny boy pretending to be a thug. His arms were covered in tattoos and his pants hung low off his waist. He was tiny — skinny. He kept talking to me as if I were hearing him clearly —

understanding his words, but my head was still foggy. I was still trying to wake up. I finally sat up and that is when I saw Matilda behind this kid, who sat down beside me with his hand on my leg as if I might try to run.

Matilda sat down on the bed across from mine and began to lecture me about ownership—about boundaries. She lectured me like I was supposed to obey every word that fell out of her mouth. She even smiled when she spoke, but it was not one of those nice smiles you see on nice people. It was one of those 'don't fuck with me if you know what is good for you' kind of smiles. You know the ones. She went on and on for way too long about how I was going to stay away from Eve; how I was going to stop putting ideas in Eve's head about freedom. That is when I realized that Eve was trying to do what I told her she should do, but because she really did not have the strength to do it, she was fucking it all up, and it all backfired on her. Eleanor, and Matilda, were clearly coming down hard on Eve. If they weren't then Matilda would not have been in my hostel room threatening me with her twig-sized body guard.

I let Matilda yammer on for as long as she wanted. I wanted to be sure she got every word out that she intended because I was going to make sure those were her last words.

"Do you understand?" she asked—her final words to me before I lifted my leg and kicked her in the face. My bare foot smashed into her nose so hard that all three of us heard it crack. The room we were in was so small that I had kicked her into the other wall, which was brick. She had blood oozing out of her nose and down the back of her neck.

Before her thug had a chance to react, I lifted my left arm and elbowed him in the throat, leaving him speechless. As the two

237

lay across the two beds I stood, got dressed, collected my belongings and headed for the door. Before I opened it I turned around and looked at them both. They were still alive, but they were in pain. I told them that if they ever laid another hand on me, or on Eve, then the pain I just inflicted on them would feel like a walk in the park compared to what I would to them.

I promised them both that I would not only kill them, but I would hunt down every one of their relatives and kill each and every one of them until the whole town was flooded in their blood. I know it was dramatic. That was what I was going for. I wanted to scare the shit out of them, and I wanted them to think that I was done with them, so long as they left me and Eve alone.

They had no idea that I had every intension of taking their lives. I just could not do it there in the hostel—not where I sleep. I slammed the door behind me and headed down the hall and out of the hostel. I knew I would never be back to that one again. Instead of heading off to find Eve, I crossed the street and sat down on a bench in the park, facing the hostel and I waited.

I did not sit for long before Matilda and her thug stumbled out of the hostel. They looked around, almost confused about what direction to go before they stepped onto the sidewalk and began walking. They did not see me across the street. I feel like they would have come running over to me if they had. So I watched them walk away and when I thought they were far enough ahead, I stood and went after them.

We walked for an hour. At one point I was sure they knew I was behind them and they were weaving in and out of streets just to annoy or lose me. Eventually I saw them turn into Brompton

Cemetery. I could not believe my luck. They were walking right into my favorite place so I followed them in.

As I turned into the cemetery I could not see them. The main path that runs through the center was sparsely filled with people, none of whom were Matilda or her thug. I walked a little further into the cemetery before I felt an arm pull me off the path—something right out of my own playbook.

I was pulled hard enough that I felt to the ground in this umbrella of brush—bushes and trees creating an isolated bubble for mischief. I looked up and saw Matilda and her thug looking down at me. They were not smiling. The thug pulled out a knife and as he leaned in towards me I kicked him with my foot, much like I had done to Matilda back at the hostel, only this time my foot went into his stomach, knocking him to the ground. He dropped his knife. Matilda dove to grab it, but I had already managed to stand up and grab the knife. We looked like two skinny sumo wrestlers ready to rumble, leaning in towards one another while her thug lay on the ground holding his stomach.

I remember telling them both that they had just made the mistake that would cost them their lives. That made Matilda smile and as she did I swung and dragged the knife across her face putting a huge gash through both cheeks and tearing her lips. I think I even nicked her tongue. Blood started flowing out of her face faster and with more venom than her words earlier back in the hostel. She grabbed her face as if to keep it from falling off and that is when I started stabbing her arms and stomach and any part of her body that I could. Her tug tried to stand up a couple of times to help her—protect her, but each time I kicked him back down. I was determined to take them on one at a time.

After about 15 stabs Matilda fell to the ground. She was a beautiful sight—torn flesh and blood mixed with loose dirt. She could not scream because of all the tears in her face. While she was on the ground I sliced booth of her ankles to make sure she could not run, or at least not run far.

With Matilda laying on the ground I turned my attention to the thug. I was so angry at him, or I was pushing all my anger towards him—I am not sure which, but I tore into him a lot worse than I did with Matilda. I put the knife through both of his eyes. I jammed it into his throat. I rammed it into his left ear. At one point I stepped back to catch my balance only to realize that I had put more than 20 stab wounds into his head alone. The blood that he produced—that his body fired back at me was almost overwhelming, even for me. I was covered in his blood, and Matilda's, too.

I took my attention away from the thug for a moment to realize that Matilda had stopped breathing. She bled to death rather quickly. I turned back to the thug and he was the same—lifeless. The two of them lost so much blood so quickly. I sat down on the ground between where they both lay and tried to swim in the pool of blood, but like the police officer all those years ago, Mother Nature was taking the blood away from me, soaking it up.

I smiled.

39

I had to wait in the cemetery until almost closing time before I was able to leave after I killed Matilda and her thug. I knew that if I stepped out, everyone would see me covered in blood, as if I showered in blood, and they would call the police or an ambulance. Something would not go the way I would want it to go, and I would be in a heap of trouble. So I waited. I took all my clothes off and, as best as I could, I used them to wipe as much blood off me as possible. By that time, I had already licked a lot of it off my arms and hands.

My backpack had blood on it, a lot of blood, but thankfully, inside I had a change of clothes. My days of being stranded, naked, were over. I left my blood-stained clothes with Matilda and her thug, stepped out on the walking path when I was sure no one was looking, and I walked out of the cemetery. I felt the rush of the kill. I felt unstoppable. I felt like I was ready to go and talk with Murray — to ask him to take me back. But, as I started walking, heading in the direction of The Drunken Unicorn, I walked right through a crowd of people, one of whom was Archie. I had not seen him in so long. I almost did not recognize him. His hair was longer. His build was a little bigger. He recognized me immediately, and as I walked through his crowd with my head down, he grabbed my arm, pulling me back into his group.

I remember looking at him confusedly. He seemed a little annoyed that I did not recognize him right away. "Dude, it's me. It's Archie."

I played along and said, "oh yeah, how's it going?" to make small talk, but that was a mistake.

*   *   *   *   *

"How the fuck do you think it's going?" he yelled back at me, defensively.

"I, uh, well, I am not really sure," I replied, still not aware of how I was supposed to know him.

"You ready to kill me now, bitch," Archie sang as his crowd all cheered him on. "You are not so tough when there are a bunch of us, are you, punk?"

*   *   *   *   *

It was in that moment that I remembered. It was then that I could see that memory as clear as day. I did tell him I would kill him the next time I saw him. I was honestly surprised that, knowing that statement, he would have stopped me at all. I mean, if my threat meant anything, it meant I was going to kill him. Maybe he felt stronger, more confident, because of the bunch of steroid-taking assholes who surrounded him, and he felt sure that they, together, would be able to kick my ass. He wasn't wrong. I would never try to take on a group of guys. But then I never start a fight I know I am not going to win. If only Archie followed the same philosophy.

I talked a little trash to him in front of his buddies to get him agitated. It worked. He started throwing all sorts of words at me as if those were going to hurt me somehow. I kept telling him to settle down before he went too far—reached a point where he would not be able to turn back. My philosophical view only agitated him more.

He was worked up about seeing me, about the last time he saw me, and he was on something, or smoked something. Maybe he and his buddies were already drunk. Perhaps they had come from a pub where they watched a football match all afternoon. Whatever state of mind Archie was in at that moment was not a good one, and before I knew it, his friends had fanned out and formed a circle around Archie and me. They were preparing for a cockfight.

The crowd got louder. Their rants and shouts were more vulgar, more violent, but all were designed to fuel Archie—to make him feel like he was invincible. They had all convinced Archie that he could easily overtake the skinny, weak kid—me. I played into that notion—let them all think they were right. Archie took off his shirt as if he needed to show his feathers—his newly formed muscle, as a form of intimidation. It did not work.

When Archie thought I was distracted by all the noise and motion around us, he lunged forward and took a swing at me. I weaved and he completely missed me. He stumbled. I stood silent. He got his footing again and repeated his last move. So did I. This time Archie fell to the ground. His buddies were yelling at him more than they were screaming at me. They were teasing him—ridiculing him for missing two punches on what they all said was an easy target.

To prove this to Archie, one of the guys jumped out of the crowd and into the circle, running towards me with the speed of a leopard. He swung, I ducked. I swung, and he fell to the ground. As he slid across the pavement, both of his knees and an elbow were torn open. I could almost smell the fresh blood joining the party.

The crowd was yelling and laughing and hurling insults at me, at Archie, and now at the fallen soldier. I turned to walk out of the circle—to leave, but the circle stopped me. Another guy pushed me back towards the center—back towards Archie, who was ready to punch. I pulled a knife out of my pant pocket—the same one that had just killed Matilda and her thug and as Archie ran towards me and swung, I ducked again and ran the knife across his stomach. He never saw the knife—no one did. It all happened too fast.

Archie fell to the ground, clutching his stomach and screaming. Almost immediately, some of the guys noticed all the blood on Archie's arm and hand. Many of the guys ran off—a few stuck around—his closest friends. A couple of them pushed me or kicked me as they ran to their friend, to Archie. Some were yelling at me, still.

I remember looking down at Archie in that moment and telling him about my last words to him the last time. He looked up at me, suddenly aware that I remembered who he was. I lied to him and told him I always remembered. I hadn't. I figured it out—remembered by the time he took off his shirt and got ready to throw his punch.

I let him know that I was not kidding. I let him know that the blood he was losing was not going to be the last blood I take from him if he does not back down. Then I waved my hand around, holding the knife, swinging it around like a lunatic. His friends backed away, letting me through the crowd. I licked the blade of the knife and then put it back in my pocket as I walked away. I thought that was going to be the last time I would ever see Archie, but I was wrong.

*   *   *   *   *

A week later, as I was consoling Eve at the cafe about the loss of Matilda, Archie walked in. Eve was not upset that Matilda was dead. She was more worried about how Eleanor would take the loss of her girlfriend out on Eve and the other girls. Eve told me that Eleanor was kinder when she had a girlfriend, when she was getting laid. Single Eleanor was a bitch, apparently.

Eleanor was sitting at the booth across from us and looked up when Archie walked in and started yelling at me. I remember thinking to myself that he had to be the biggest idiot around. He never knew when to let something go. I know the type—I am the same way. I am not sure if he came into the cafe because he saw me from outside or if he was there to see someone else, but he came straight over to me. Instinctively, I pulled out the knife from my pocket again in an attempt to stop him. He stopped in his tracks and held his stomach. He lifted his shirt to show his stitches to me— probably to everyone. He was bandaged, but he told me, the whole room, that he had 25 stitches. He kept yelling that I did that to him. It was hard to argue that case when I was holding a knife—the very knife that carved through his stomach.

I remember hearing Eleanor yell at me—ask me where I got the knife. It was in that moment that I realized that she probably recognized the knife. Eve had told me earlier that the kid who was found with Matilda—the little thug—was Eleanor's little brother. Their father had given Landon—that was his name—the knife as a birthday present a few years back.

Archie accused me of slicing him with the knife. Eleanor accused me of stealing the knife, possibly of killing her brother and girlfriend. Eve looked at me, frightened. Instinctively, I jumped up and ran out of the cafe. I remember yelling to Eve that I would find her later. I had to find her—save her from Eleanor. I knew that if Eleanor believed that I killed her girlfriend and her brother, and I believed she thought that, then she would take her rage out on Eve.

I did not run far. I crossed the street and entered the building directly across from the cafe. I ran up the stairs until I reached the roof, then hid at the edge, looking down at the café below—at the chaos forming. The police arrived. Lights were flashing, lighting up the whole block in blue. I watched Archie give a statement and then be released. I watched Eleanor provide a statement. She held onto Eve tightly as she did, making sure not to lose sight of Eve.

I am not sure what Eleanor said to Eve or the police, but I knew that my luck was starting to run out. I contemplated running to Murray and apologizing, hoping to start over, but I knew that the only solution was to get out of town—I knew I was never going to get out of the country, at least not legally.

I watched Archie walk away from the cafe. I knew I would never make it back down to the street before he would turn onto one and be lost to me for who knows how long, so I just sat and watched him until I could no longer see him. Fortunately for me, three blocks down the road, Archie turned into a pub. My luck had turned around, so I sped down the stairs and slipped out into a passage and eventually made my way to the pub without being seen by the cafe crowd.

I stood in front of the pub looking in. It was hard to see everything, but I could see Archie. He was talking to a guy who handed him a small bag. At that moment, I banged the pub window with my fist to get Archie's attention. I got everyone's attention.

Archie did not react as if I had banged the window at him. He appeared to play it cool and finish his transaction, then he finished his pint and walked towards the door. To tease him, I started walking away. Once he was back on the street, Archie yelled out to me—demanding that I stop. I did, then a moment later, I turned around. By that time, he was just a few feet away from me. His left arm was wrapped around his stomach, and his right hand held a bag filled with white powder. He was waving it as if he were inviting me to get high with him. He was.

* * * * *

As I sat on the settee, about to snort my fourth white line, I wondered which one of us was more pathetic. Archie was leaning back on the settee, shirtless. The large bandage across his stomach was stained red—I am sure it needed to be replaced. I was sitting next to Archie, our bodies touching, and I wanted to burst out laughing. I snorted and fell back and rested my head on Archie's shoulder.

He could have trapped me—led me back to his new flat, where a group of guys were waiting to pounce on me. He could have laced the powder. If Archie really wanted to hurt me, he had plenty of opportunities, but he did nothing. He sat on the settee, high as a kite, and let me rest my head on his shoulder. He mumbled a bunch of incoherent words and, at one point, turned his head toward mine and kissed the top of my head. At that moment, I was unsure if he knew what he was doing. Maybe he thought he was with his girlfriend, or boyfriend. He was so high—we both were—that anything could have happened. Eventually, we both passed out.

I woke up sometime later—I had no idea what day or time it was or where I was. Archie was still next to me—still sound asleep. He looked so cute—so young and innocent as he lay there, mouth open, drool coming out slowly. I noticed that we were holding hands. I had no idea if that was because of me or him. I just woke up hand in hand. I looked at his bandage, and it was more blood-stained. I felt pretty sure that Archie probably shouldn't have been running around or getting high with that serious of an injury, but I wasn't a doctor. I peeled the bandage off Archie's stomach, expecting him to move or wake up. He did neither.

I rubbed my fingers in the oozing blood that had been escaping around the staples holding his stomach together. I licked my fingers a few times. It tasted too much like metal. Without letting go of Archie's hand, I bent forward and snorted a few more lines, then with my free hand, I started removing the staples in Archie's stomach. They were surprisingly easy to pull out. With each one removed, his stomach opened more, letting out more fresh blood. He still did not move.

By the time I took five staples out, Archie's body wiggled. His grip on my hand tightened. I knew he had to be feeling some pain—maybe not. We were pretty high, or at least I knew I was still very high. I leaned towards Archie's stomach and licked his skin, tasting his blood. It was warm. He was warm.

With my face covered in Archie's blood, I sat back on the settee and enjoyed the moment. I was drunk on blood. I was in heaven. But I also knew that I had to kill Archie. I could not let him go—at least not without risking him ratting me out.

I leaned forward and grabbed the baggie of powder from the table. We had only snorted about half of it. I poured what remained in the bag into Archie's open wound. Then I bent over and licked him. The rush was more than I was prepared for. I only stopped because Archie's body started shaking. I pulled back and saw white foam coming out of his mouth.

I let go of his hand, stood up, leaned in, and kissed Archie on the forehead. I am not sure why I kissed him at all. I walked into his bathroom to clean myself up, but instead I sat down on the toilet and fell asleep sitting up.

Eventually, I heard someone screaming—yelling, really. It was a deep, accented voice. I jumped up and grabbed the shower curtain, pulling it down to the floor. I made a lot of noise. I stumbled back into the living room to see a tall, thin Indian kid standing over Archie. He had blood on his hands. We matched.

I remember the kid yelling; asking who I was, why I was there, and if I knew what had happened. He could tell that I was probably still a little high. He rattled on about how Archie promised to stop doing drugs—blah blah blah. As I looked around the room, I noticed a few framed photos of Archie and this kid, and I realized that I was in their flat—that they were dating.

I ran over to the kid, arms stretched out as if I were going to hug him—console him. I did. I gave him a big, tight hug. I said something about Archie being a nice guy or some shit like that—the stuff you say when you are trying to console someone. Then I pulled the knife out of my pocket again and stabbed the Indian kid 20 times. He screamed. I covered his mouth. He bit my finger. It was a total shit show—a comedy of errors. I just kept stabbing him. Eventually, he went limp and fell onto the settee, almost on top of Archie.

I went into their kitchen and cleaned myself up as best I could, ransacked the place, pocketed a wad of cash—probably from Archie's drug dealing, then walked out their front door.

40

When I left Archie's flat, I contemplated running back to the cafe in hopes of seeing Eve, but then I realized that I would also see Eleanor, and I was not ready to deal with her just yet. I was riding a high, that was for sure. Between the drugs and the adrenaline, I was on cloud nine. I could still taste Archie—his blood still lingered. Then I thought about going back to Murray again—something I think I will do all the time, but never do. I am not sure he would recognize me—see the monster that I had become; always was.

Instead, I walked the streets looking for Eve—visiting all of her regular pick up spots. I figured I had a better chance of seeing her without Eleanor if I caught her at work, and I was right. I turned a corner and noticed a group of girls, gays, and trannies lingering— all hoping to get lucky; to get paid. I recognized some of them. A few of the guys were regulars at The Drunken Unicorn.

Eve turned and saw me. I could tell she was scared and confused. She started to walk away as I called her to stop. I almost begged her to listen to me. I caught up to her and grabbed her arm. She yelled, nearly screamed for help, but I convinced her to listen. I bribed her with drugs. I think I really wanted to explain myself to Eve; maybe even tell her the truth—tell her what I could not tell Murray. I wondered if telling Eve I killed people—a lot of people, would be a good thing, or a terrible idea.

*　　*　　*　　*　　*

"There is something I want to tell you," I said, still holding her arm tightly. "I mean, I need to tell you."

"I don't know if I want to hear it, Adam."

"What? Why not?" I asked. I could hear the frustration in my voice. "You need to understand something about me."

"No, I don't," she yelled back at me. "I saw that knife. I know what you did."

"I did it for you," I lied.

"What?"

"That is right," I continued my lie. "I know you want to be free of Eleanor and Matilda. I did not mean to kill her and that little twig. It just happened. You know? They attacked me. I just defended myself."

"No one has ever done anything nice for me," Eve said as she started to cry, like I was some friggin' hero, or something.

"Let's go get high!" I said as I hugged her.

*　　*　　*　　*　　*

Eve and I got high—so high that when I woke up two days later, I had no idea where I was. She took me to a slum of a flat all the way in Essex. We drank. We snorted lines. We popped pills. We were having the best time. I saw Eve walk out of the room with some guy. I assumed he owned the flat, or maybe he was the one who supplied us with all the drugs, and she was going to repay him with sex. I did not know, or really care. I was nestled into an old settee. Some girl was next to me, rubbing my arm, and it felt so

252

good—the sensation was orgasmic. I remember leaning over and kissing her. That was two days ago. I cannot recall if I slept for two whole days or was in and out of drug comas during that time. I was still sitting on the settee. The girl was gone—probably had been for a while. No one was in the room, and I could not hear any noise coming from anywhere in the flat. It was eerily quiet for a few minutes before I finally heard Eve's giggle. It got louder as she walked down a hall towards the room I was in. When she came into sight, she was still holding the hand of the same guy I saw her leave the room with, and I wondered if they, too, had been passed out for days. I didn't ask.

"This is the guy who killed Matilda." I heard Eve say to the tweaker she was clinging to. "He is one tough mutha-fucka." She exaggerated those words as if trying to emphasize them—emphasize me.

I could not believe Eve was telling my secret. I was still dazed but focused enough to know that I had to start a new list of people who had to die because they knew my secret. As I looked up, I realized that Eve was trying to tell me that the guy she was holding on to was the killer, not telling him I was the killer. That is when I knew she was still so high that she had no idea what was going on or where she was, for that matter.

I stood and grabbed Eve from the guy. He did not resist. He was almost thankful that I took her off his hands as he wandered back in the direction they had just come. I sat Eve down while I put on my shoes, then we stood and walked out of the flat.

A couple of days later, I went to meet Eve at the cafe again. She was my new drug connection, and as hard as I tried to stay clean, or as much as I told myself that I was going to keep clean, I always wound up snorting, shooting, or swallowing something I should not. She had the same problem. When we were together, we proclaimed that we would stop—get clean —but the more I thought about it, the more I realized that we were bad for each other. I encouraged Eve to get high. She encouraged me.

I expected to see Eve sitting in her usual booth, but when I opened the cafe door, Eleanor was seated where Eve should have been sitting. I remember yelling at Eleanor as if my tone would make her quiver and tell me what I wanted to know. Instead, when I yelled at Eleanor, a handful of guys who were sitting at various other booths all stood up and surrounded me. Just one of the guys was big enough to beat the shit out of me—to put me in the hospital for a long time, so I am not sure why Eleanor thought she needed so many of them, at least not for me.

Two of the guys grabbed me, one on each arm, and dragged me through the cafe and out the back door. A van was waiting. The two thugs threw me in the back of the truck and slammed the door. The driver of the van sped off, and I tumbled around the back of the van before I could sit or get a grip on anything. I slammed into the back door and cut my arm. I could feel the blood, but I was not amused. I was never interested in my own blood. I yelled at the driver, but he ignored me. The passenger, however, turned around and yelled back at me, and I was surprised to see that it was Eleanor. She slipped into the van quickly before it took off.

Eleanor and I exchanged a lot of obscenities with each other. It was clear that she was still angry. I was convinced she knew that I killed her little brother and her girlfriend. It did not really matter anymore. I was getting sloppier with my kills—well, not the killing part, but the walking away part. I think that by then, I was so tired of hiding who I was, and so thirsty for blood that I was taking lives more quickly, and not caring how I did it or who saw me do it.

I knew then, just as I know now, that it is only a matter of time before the police caught up to me. But at the moment, in the back of that van, I was less worried about getting caught by the police and more focused on getting out of the van. I was high, so I was not making the most rational decisions. When I saw the crowbar sitting on the floor behind the driver's seat, rattling as he sped, I did not think of the consequences as I picked it up and slammed his back a few times before missing and smacking the back of his head. The force threw him forward, and his face kissed the windshield. It was in that moment that I realized that he was not wearing a seatbelt. His nose was broken, and blood splattered all over the windshield. Blood was oozing out of the back of his head, too. For a split second, it was glorious, and then I realized that I had just killed the driver of the van that was speeding down a busy road. Before I had time to think or grab onto something, the van swerved and hit a car before rolling over a few times.

When I woke, I was lying on the street, and a uniformed woman was trying to resuscitate me. I could hear a lot of commotion, but it was muffled. My head was pounding and my vision was blurry. It took me several minutes to realize what was going on, and once I did, I sat straight up as if I had just risen from the dead. Then I stood up. The EMT kept talking to me, mumbling words. I am sure she wanted me to sit back down and to take it slow, but I had realized what had happened. I could see Eleanor's body hanging upside down, still trapped in the van by her seatbelt. Her arms hung down, almost touching the ceiling of the van. I could see a good-sized metal pole sticking out of her chest. It extended out through the broken windshield. There were many other poles — pipes all over the road. Some were still rolling off the lorry that had been jack-knifed during our accident. I was stunned that I was alive — that I was the one who was going to walk away from death. I knew I should have been the one to die. I know many people; if they knew I was the one who had been killing all of those people across the country, would have loved it if I were the one to die that day.

I ignored the EMT and hobbled away through the crowd. I knew that I could not get caught — could not be stopped and questioned by the police. Too many drugs were swimming through my veins, and too much blood was on my hands. I knew, or at least I felt, that I would say the wrong thing or do the wrong thing and find myself locked up. I knew I had to find Eve. I wanted to find Murray.

41

I am not going to make any excuses for my behavior. I will say that when I walked away from the crashed van, instead of taking that as a sign to really clean up my act, go back to Murray and have a normal life, I went looking for Eve. I needed to get totally fucked up. I needed every drug I could find to run through my veins and help me forget—maybe help me die.

It took me hours to find Eve, and then it took hours for her to clean me up. I did not stick around to let the EMT bandage up every cut I had. She was too busy trying to bring me back to life. I fought Eve, too. I did not care about the cuts and scrapes. I just wanted to get high. I remember giving Eve a black eye that day as we fought—me for drugs and her to help me heal. I guess we know who was the better person, inside.

Her dealer showed up to Eve's flat with quite the party platter of narcotics. I remember that he started spewing words like he was a waiter telling us the specials of the evening. I did not care. I wanted everything he had. The three of us were sitting on the settee. He was saying words and numbers. Eve understood, but I did not so I got up and started pacing the room. The two of them continued to lobe words and numbers back and forth, but no product or money exchanged hands. Impatient, I grabbed a lone candlestick from the mantle, turned around and swung it at the dealer. His head hit Eve's. She got a headache as he sat there with his head split open. Blood oozed out. I leaned over him and grabbed the bag that was still in his hand. As I did, I tasted the blood—licked his right ear. I wanted more, but I wanted the drugs even more.

I remember yelling at Eve to come or stay—I did not care. She jumped up and ran after me and the two of us fled towards Brompton Cemetery. I knew we could hide out in the bushes and get high without anymore interruptions.

*   *   *   *   *

I don't remember how long we hung out—hid out in Brompton Cemetery. We got high, passed out, woke up and repeated. We were both filthy—dried blood, dirt—we were a mess, but I did not care. I remember jumping out of the bushes now and again to steal food from picnickers who were too busy being in love to notice. I remember leaving Eve for hours at a time, always telling her to stay in the bushes as if her life depended on her staying hidden. I remember we argued. I remember hitting her.

I did not remember pulling Catherine into the bushes. Not at first. Later I did—remember. It was not until days later. That is when I knew I needed to kill Eve. I had to be sure there were no lose ends—always making a list of those who needed to die to protect my secret.

*   *   *   *   *

But I guess it does not matter now, does it. Here I am, standing, shouting to you all as if I needed you to hear my story—to hear how I got here. I knew I would be caught one day. It had to happen eventually. I was trapped on an island—there was only so far I could run and only so many places I could hide. But now I am tired of running and I am tired of being tired. My life has sucked from the very beginning—been fucked from the start. I guess I could have changed it, at least tried to change it for the better. I feel like I tried, but maybe that was the drugs.

It does not matter anymore. I don't matter anymore.

'Bang.'

42

Murray was working when he heard the news. Sam, a regular at The Drunken Unicorn, walked in and almost screamed that the serial killer had been caught. People cheered. Many did not know why they were cheering, but they cheered. Those who knew cheered louder. They felt safer.

For almost a year, the police had been looking for the killer. There were too many killings for them all to be random. Some were similar — a lot of dead bodies were found in cemeteries. None of the murders involved guns. Well, there were some gun murders, but the police did not lump those into the hundreds of other deaths that seemed loosely connected, somehow. They could not solve the case, any of the cases. Dead people were everywhere — in plain sight — and yet no murderer could be found. No one could point a finger at any real lead. Without knowing, Adam managed to keep the police stumped.

The wake of Adam's kills were nightly news stories, but he did not know. He never watched television or listened to the radio. Adam believed that he was getting away with murder, which he was. All the while, the police were finding bodies and building a case that a single person, or a group of people, was ravaging through the country, killing innocent people.

It took awhile before Adam caught on to the fact that the police were looking for him. For many months they were looking for someone — anyone. It was not until the final months that they were able to put together a better profile. Police stations all across the country fielded calls — leads — in hopes of solving the murders. A few times, they thought they were close, but they never were — close. Adam killed randomly enough, at first, making it hard for the police to connect any dots, but as Adam got sloppy, as he killed more often, the police started to build a profile. If it weren't for Catherine, Adam might never have been found. If it weren't for Eve, Catherine might never have been raped and left for dead. If it weren't for the cougar boys, Adam might never have met Eve.

If Mrs. Fastiggi had not been driving her boys on errands all those years ago, she might not have been in that horrific accident that left she and her two other boys dead. Finn would never have been forced to move to Vermont, and in a moment of rebellion, he might not have met and gotten Lori pregnant.

The authorities would spend years trying to determine what made Adam tick — what made him kill so many innocent people. They would trace Adam's life all the way back to the trailer park where Adam first saw blood, and still, they would never understand what happened to fill Adam with so much hatred. And therein lies the problem. Everyone would continue to think that Adam hated people, or life, or even himself. People could only feel good about the situation if they could label it and neatly categorize it — categorize Adam as a bad person: a broken person.

Adam did not hate. Adam loved, sometimes, and some people, but from a young age, Adam loved blood so much more. And because everyone — the media, the authorities; everyone was so focused on trying to figure out why Adam killed, no one paid any attention to his spawn, until it was too late.

Be sure to check out more adventures

by John Paul

The Garden of Death

Published 2022

For the Love of Death

Published 2023

The Shadow of Death

Published 2024

www.ingramcontent.com/pod-product-compliance
Lightning Source LLC
Chambersburg PA
CBHW061519020726
47502CB00006B/2146